BEAUTY'S CURSE

BEAUTY'S CURSE

Copyright © 2020 Brantwijn Serrah.
ISBN: 9798697957585

Written by Brantwijn Serrah
Edited by Celia Breslin
Cover design by Christian Bentulan
and Brantwijn Serrah

USA TODAY BESTSELLING AUTHOR

BRANTWIJN SERRAH

DARK EROTIC ROMANCE

ALSO BY BRANTWIJN SERRAH

Join Brantwijn's newsletter for a free book!
Get updates and special offers from Brantwijn and other indie authors.
https://www.brantwijn.com/newsletter

AUTHOR'S NOTE

Hello, my Wayfarer,

Welcome to the first book in my new series, *Beast and Beauty*. If you, like me, absolutely devour the tales of *Xena, The Witcher, Game of Thrones,* and *Shannara Chronicles,* I think you'll find *Beauty's Curse* to be a sexy and exciting adventure.

I wrote this story with a desire to explore several different kinds of characters and their ideas of themselves. First and foremost, of course, is the character of Sadira, my leading lady. In her, I wanted to look at what can shape the mind and desires of a submissive. Yes: *that* kind of submissive. Sadira represents a woman with a unique—and complicated—initiation to the world of power exchange.

This story is about navigating the shadows of a questionable past, and the potential of a better future. It's also about finding the beauty within the beast inside. And along the way there might be a few supernatural twists and wicked magic turns, and maybe a monster or two.

If there's one thing I hope you will take away from this adventure, it is the complexity of desire, and the intimacies of trust, and belief. That while one experience can go terribly wrong, it can lead us to one magnificently right. And that can have a surprising amount of meaning to who we essentially are.

Though I hope all romance readers can enjoy my work, if you are uncomfortable with graphic descriptions of bondage and (sometimes questionable) Master/slave dynamics, this book may not be for you. Though I do have many other titles you may find to your liking, on my website at www.brantwijn.com.

Come once again into my world, Wayfarers,

Brantwijn

DEDICATION

For Ken, as always, who never fails to support and celebrate this little dream of mine.

For Teri, who cheered for me every day.

For Jo, who is absolutely the best ever at resolving plot holes and ending hooks.

For Rebecca, who mentored me expertly through the process of writing and publishing this book.

And for Schala, my muse, my cat, my boss.

PROLOGUE

Nobody has known the clutches of a viper as well as I. I bear the mark of the sacred serpent, and I have lived my life snared within his scales. His venom never destroyed me. It *shaped* me. Turned me to poison too. Deviant. Dangerous. A creature only a snake could love.

He molded me into his chimera. His *beast*. He wound himself around me, knots and ropes and chains made of scales, binding me to him.

Twisting my love into a curse.

BEAUTY'S CURSE

BEAST AND BEAUTY, BOOK ONE

by Brantwijn Serrah

CHAPTER ONE

THE WAR OF the Sands is over. My king... is dead.

I knelt alone in the castle's master chambers. The enemy had bound my ankles and tied my hands behind my back, and hempen rope chafed my wrists as I tested it, twisting one way and then the other, looking for give. Dull, seething frustration made me sick to my stomach as the knots held tight.

The king is dead. So why do I feel nothing?

I'd watched Master's head cleaved from his body. It fell to the sands right in front of me, and the whole while he wore a look of laughter on his pallid white face. Cackling like a crazy man, even in death. And my only thought?

Good riddance.

"I loved you, Alaric," I hissed in the hot, murky darkness. "In a broken and twisted way. And I hated you just as much."

Outside, the roar of the enemy's victory rose into the night. Hundreds feasting and dancing on Master's grave. Lord Khan: the tyrant king of Vashtaren. The serpent sorcerer. At last, his power lay broken, his clan in chains.

His woman, their prisoner.

How could you let yourself be captured, Sadira?

I shifted, grumbling as the cotton smock clung to my sweat-dampened skin. My captors had stripped me of my armor along with my weapons and left me nearly naked on Alaric's opulent bed, except for the one pitiful scrap of cloth.

And my collar. No one had removed my collar.

But that's nothing new. I hung my head, straight black hair falling like a hood around my face. *I've lived my whole life in this collar. Why should tonight be any different?*

A fresh chorus of cheers rose from the courtyard. The voices of the barbarian invaders from across the northern sea, and with them, the cries of freed slaves. Children of the oppressed. Mercenary warlords from the desert clans Alaric betrayed.

Alaric's death didn't upset me. It didn't even surprise me. He'd had no shortage of enemies. More than once, I'd wished *I* could sink a blade into his heart.

I tugged again at the knots binding my hands. Still no give.

The bedchamber's cloying incense of cinnamon and bergamot made my head pound. The chalky white body paint covering my skin now ran in sticky tracks and rivulets, smeared by sweat and tears. The soldiers who'd brought me here left me only one torch, and it flickered by the door, just enough to see my reflection in the mirror over the hearth and know how laughable I'd become.

How? How could you let them take you alive? *The lord of leash and whip is gone, and you could have run. Yet here you are, trussed up as a prize for a* new *tyrant to claim.*

The captain of the enemy horde. Bannon Sha'kurukh, Red Bear of the Highlands.

In the Ruined Sands, people lived like lion prides. As a new male staked his claim by murdering the cubs and taking the mates of his rivals, so Bannon must take his inheritance by claiming everything that had once been Alaric's. He would occupy the castle Alaric had ruled; he would kill the soldiers who fought Alaric's war.

He would bed the woman Alaric left behind.

I tugged harder, still to no avail. Scrapes and bruises from the battle stung with sweat. My spine ached.

And the enemy's raucous victory carried on below.

THE HOUR GREW late, and at last, the celebrations died down. The Red Bear had not come.

Maybe he's forgotten me. I shifted, groaning. The soldiers who tied me knew nothing about proper rope technique. *Thank the sacred serpent I can still feel my fingers and toes.*

But what if no one came for me until morning?

Just then, footsteps approached outside the great iron doors. I winced as I straightened, putting my shoulders back and holding my head high.

The doors swung open. It was the great Red Bear at last—but shadows shielded him from view.

There he lingered, a waiting silhouette. Though his eyes were hidden, the gravity of his gaze weighed on me.

Why hesitate? The tingle of gooseflesh swept down my arms as I tried to match his glare. He couldn't be afraid of a helpless, fallen soldier. Could he?

No. It's not that.

I knew what I looked like. Smeared makeup and scarlet tattoos circled and spiraled over my body, augmented by brands and scars. Rings and studs of desert gold pierced my ears, nose, and lower lip. What would this foreign invader see? A living fetish. A wild freak. Bannon's clan didn't mark themselves this way. Neither did most tribes of the Ruined Sands. Not even the slaves.

I was special.

After a long, pregnant silence, Bannon Sha'kurukh stepped into the room.

Up close, he stood much taller than I'd expected. Bannon resembled the gladiators of old colosseums: men who wrestled boars and tigers and toppled great fortresses. A solid, wooden round shield was slung on his back, and a decorated broad axe hung from his belt.

A diadem of braided leather held his long, brick-red hair away from his face, and he bore a tattoo of his own—an ursine pawprint—on the left side of his bare chest. Blue warpaint made a band across his eyes and three short lines down his left cheek. His skin shone, the color of dust at sunset.

He considered me a long time, wearing a grim frown, before removing his axe from his belt and laying it across the wooden table by the hearth. He slid the shield from his back and leaned it against the table leg.

Two guards followed him in. One retrieved the torch from its bracket and lit a blaze in the fireplace, while the other placed a clay pitcher and two rough cups beside the axe. Then they disappeared, pulling the doors shut behind them.

The Red Bear crossed his arms over his chest.

"Infamous Sadira." He stroked his neat, short beard. "Lord Khan's personal concubine. They said you never left his side. Yet I saw you on the field these last days, fighting alongside his infantry. You're more than just his kept woman, aren't you?"

When I offered no reply, he relaxed, spreading his hands before him.

"You were magnificent in battle. I wish we could have met under different circumstances."

Picking up the pitcher and one of the cups, he poured a measure of water. He crossed to the bed and offered it to me.

"Are you thirsty?"

I lunged forward and struck him with my shoulder, sending the cup splashing to the floor.

"We both know what you're here for," I snapped. "You've allied yourself with the warlords of Vashtaren. You've killed the king and taken his castle, but now they demand a *true* act of proving. You have to claim *me* to seal your victory."

A dark frown creased his face. "The practice has been explained to me. I have no desire to take you by force."

"*Ha!*" I fell into a slump and blew a stray lock of dank hair from my face. "Welcome to the Ruined Sands. I am your reward. Your *property*. But I am also a fighter, and Lord Khan taught me to kill even as he forced me to kneel. Untie me, and I will do to you what I *wish* I had done to him."

Scrubbing a hand over his mouth, Bannon seemed to reconsider. He circled the great bed to the other side, laying one hand on the bedstand and lifting the implements on it one by one. Chains, whips, black candles—tools of dominance and discipline. Alaric's toys.

"The mercenaries warned me Lord Khan's woman lusted for pain."

He gripped both ends of a leather strop in his hands, then gave it a hard, sharp snap. The crack of the leather brought me instantly to attention, and I sat straight up. I couldn't help the enticing image it conjured: the Red Bear, my *foe,* bending me over to whip that strop across my behind.

The firelight gleamed red-gold in his hair. Darker crimson curls dusted his broad chest and descended in a trail from his navel down his abdomen, disappearing under his leather breeches.

How curious, that fine track of curls. Here in the Ruined Sands, the worshippers of the seven-headed serpent had grown pale as alabaster and bleached as bones, and all kept their body hair stripped clean. Alaric's people were like living sculpture: elfin-featured and all with the same straight, shockingly white hair. More than once, I'd wondered if they were also cold-blooded, like their serpent god.

Other Vashtarens were nearly the opposite, ranging from a deep mahogany to a rich, smooth olive complexion, with dark hair coiled in braids and locks or thick, cloudy curls. But I'd never seen a people like Bannon's before. Tawny and glowing, with hair in colors of burnt crimson like rich river clay, or shocking lengths of gold, or feathery brown like sparrow wings. On the battlefield they stood out like a stampede of painted stallions.

And here in the dark... gilded by firelight...

The barbarian rested a knee on the bed and bent toward me, tucking a lank sheaf of my dark tresses behind my ear. I caught a whiff of him: no pretty perfumes or scented soaps. He smelled of rough exercise, of smoke and steel and oiled leather. He'd bathed off the blood and dirt of battle, but the scent of war lingered on him still.

Would it be so bad to yield, Sadira? What is there to fight for? Alaric's honor?

Bannon took my chin in his hand.

"I would have you willingly, Sadira. The ways of these men are not my ways. I concede only because I must, to end this war for good. I can't avoid the act of claiming you... but I can make it peaceable. Will you submit?"

He is magnificent. A great bear indeed. Why stand between him and his victory?

I searched his face. The man who murdered my king. He held me bound—but hadn't he also set me free?

No. I will not be given to this man, just trussed up and handed over. If he wants me, let him earn me.

I spat in his face.

"*Not your ways,*" I mocked him. "But they are *my* ways. Do you think because you call me concubine, I'll fuck whatever prick presents itself? I won't yield to a man who isn't strong enough to *make* me. Alaric would have me on my back already and gagged against this useless chatter. Do as he would, Red Bear, or go back to your people in disgrace. *Half* a man, who can murder an insane oppressor but cannot pacify his woman."

Bannon straightened, wiping the saliva from his cheek.

"What did he do to you?" he marveled.

"Ropes were not the worst of it." I shot him a scathing look of challenge. "Come, barbarian. Here is your desert treasure. *Take* it."

His eyes flashed. His spine stiffened, and a muscle ticked in his jaw.

"If that's the way you want it."

Then he planted his hand on my chest and shoved me onto my back.

I twisted to one side, but Bannon climbed onto the bed and seized me by the heels. White body powder smeared his fingers, and I kicked at him with both feet, catching him under the ribs. His gave out a harsh, startled huff of air, face twisted with shock and fury, and rebounded, pouncing on me.

"They warned me you would be vicious!" His skin pressed hot against mine; my heart kicked into a gallop. "Will you really make me sink to the level of your ruthless king?"

"We have our parts to play," I choked out. "If you can't take me... you can't *have* me."

He thrust me down face-first into the thick animal pelts covering the bed, and his voice came out a low growl. "You should have yielded."

I threw all my force against his hold, wrestling him like a cornered feline, hissing and spitting until he brought one callused palm down with bright, stinging hurt on the vulnerable flesh of my behind.

"*Ah!*"

Another salacious image sprang to mind: Bannon lashing me, punishing my hot, pinkened flesh with sweet strokes of his leather belt. The first tears sprang to my lashes—tears of sudden, wicked exhilaration.

"You had the choice," he reminded me. "I could have untied you, laid you back on these pillows, brought you such delicious pleasure. *You* wanted brute force."

So different from Alaric! So forceful and hungry, so strong. *I don't wish to harm you,* he'd said, and so he hadn't... but he'd woken the beast in me, all the same.

He pressed me down into the furs. The heat of his touch stoked a tingling pleasure over my skin. Smears of ivory body paint marked his flesh like scars of war, and Bannon rolled me onto my back, closing one big hand over my throat.

Sacred serpent!

His fierce, dark gaze sent a shock straight to my core.

He really is *a warlord. He is the great Red Bear!*

No more cinnamon and bergamot. Now I reveled in the scents of sweat and iron, of slick skin and bitter pheromones as Bannon leaned in close.

"I fought on the battlefield against hundreds today. I killed scores of your warriors. I *beheaded* your king. Do you think I can't handle his whore?"

A shiver slid down the back of my neck. I licked my lips, frozen in the hard, brutal darkness in his eyes.

"Untie me and see," I dared him.

"I thought you liked being bound."

His voice rumbled like desert thunder; his coarse beard rasped the sensitive skin of my neck. I sucked in a ragged breath.

Bannon seized the neck of my shift and ripped it away, uncovering my breasts.

The exposure—the raw pleasure rushing to my skin, bare to his scrutiny—brought a breathless cry to my lips. I thrashed back and forth as he ran callused knuckles over the hard, gold barbells piercing each pink nipple.

"Look at this." He gave one a tentative tweak, sending a sweet shock through my chest. "Pretty decorations for a fighter, Sadira. Is this the fashion among your armies? Or your brothels?"

"Get *off* me!" I strained, writhing away from his touch.

He removed his hand from my throat, letting me breathe in deep, awash in bittersweet euphoria and beautiful outrage. Tears ran down my face; fury and yearning had become a heated ache at my core.

"Don't you—"

Bannon grabbed the warm globes of my breasts in greedy hands and rolled his thumbs over the cold metal studs. I arched my back and gave out a startled gasp: naked helplessness flared at his touch like bright light across my skin. Without warning, he lowered his face, nuzzling, squeezing, tasting.

I screamed and kicked my bound feet—a helpless tantrum. Too soon, though, it devolved into a straining, needful writhing.

When Alaric bound me, when he loomed over me and whipped me, he'd painted his pleasure in pain, yes—but also in ugly terror. I feared him when he did these things, feared his vicious torture even as I loved it, lust and heat and need welling up from the poisoned heart inside me.

Now, at Bannon's hands, each harsh grip, each smart slap, brought only indignant, petulant *desire*.

"Sadira. One last time. Will you submit to me in peace?"

My skin prickled under the heat of his breath. Violent streaks of white and red marked my breasts: welts, makeup, and my own natural, rose-honey complexion, flush with desire. It made a bright contrast pressed to his warm, beautiful, dusky body.

I swallowed the thick lump in my throat. *What is he* doing *to me?*

After everything—after the end of the war, the death of my king and tormentor—could I really be finding selfish pleasure in this?

"I am a soldier and a slave of a conquered nation," I panted. "And I am not yet ready to yield."

I lifted my head, staring down at him between my breasts. "So *prove* you are strong enough to master this monster."

Bannon's erection strained beneath the leather of his breeches, unmistakably ready. As he shoved his leggings from his hips, it jutted up from a nest of dark curls, salaciously hooded—not like the men of the desert at all. He stroked it in one fist as his other hand grabbed my chin and forced me to look him in the eye.

"Ready, whore?"

The poisonous thing inside me raged, brought to full life with that hard word, that beautifully cruel word. I squeezed my thighs together, knowing now I *needed* him. Not only to cast away the stain of Alaric's possession, but to *feed* my own gluttonous, deviant desire.

"Down."

He pushed me to the bed and moved to climb up behind me. Holding me by the shoulders with one hand, he struck me on the haunches with the other. It stung, and I groaned, writhing under my ropes. Bannon gave me no warning as he tore away the last of the flimsy fabric covering me, then spread my aching thighs.

"More gold?" He fingered the dual rings piercing my labia. Next, he found the smooth jewel studding my clitoral hood. I tried to stifle a sound of pleasure but the sweet indignity, the cold exposure, drew it from deep within. Bannon ran two fingertips over the adornment, gently pressing, teasing, tugging.

"Lord Khan likes his whores bejeweled," he mused. He didn't wait for an answer as he moved into place behind me, grasping my hips.

He entered me in one bold, smooth, unexpected stroke.

"*Fuck!*" I cried. Fresh tears of joy sprang to my eyes, and I clenched my teeth. *Oh*, it ached, and it was satisfying and good, but so raw. So *animal!*

"Is this how your barbarian women like it?" Electricity raced through me, tempting and teasing, making me giddy. "Spread like a bitch on hands and knees?"

"I wouldn't reduce a woman of my clan to *this*."

I'd never been so poignantly *aware* of a man inside me, so attentive to the newness and lovely strangeness of him, the way he moved as he claimed me. Deep, sweet titillation threatened to break my last, lingering resistance as Bannon found his rhythm.

"How's this for a man who can't tame a woman?" he demanded. "Do you think your people will accept my conquest, now I have Khan's favorite slut beneath me?"

"Oh—" I couldn't fight him anymore. All I could think of was how much I *wanted* him to play this out to the end. "Yes, please, Bannon! You win—"

"Oh, *I win*? Is this all it takes, Sadira? Are you so easy to subdue?"

I arched beneath him, groaning, burning up with wicked delight.

"How do you like the feel of barbarian steel?" He hissed in my ear, breath hot on my skin. "Does it measure up to the sorcerer's cock? Is your lust for punishment sated?"

"Yes!" I cried. "I submit! I am yours!"

"I told you I wanted you willing. *You* made me fight you. Perhaps now I'll take my pleasure and leave you disappointed."

"No, please! Don't... don't make me beg... "

"Oh, suddenly you're all sweet concession and flattering appeals." He startled me with another sharp slap on the ass. "I don't think so, Sadira. Coo and plead all you like, but I've seen the perverse little bitch beneath."

I could only manage a half-mad grin.

"*Beast,* barbarian. I am a *beast,* as he made me."

He twisted his knuckles tighter in my hair. "Moan. Let everyone hear how the *barbarian* fulfills your sick ritual."

I obeyed, raising my voice in pleasure. I didn't care who heard me—I hoped the whole castle heard. I'd just caught my breath when he renewed his forceful pace, fucking with nearly primal compulsion.

Yes—like that, Bannon—show me the beast in you, *too.*

With a final, delicious plunge, he reached his peak. His climax spilled forth, hot semen flooding my sex, heavy cock throbbing. I cried out, exhilarated, salaciously satisfied by each deep, thrumming motion, until the wicked pleasure called up my own resounding orgasm. It rolled to life and struck like a cymbal crash, uniting agony and ecstasy in a violent, beautiful completion.

Bannon held me there, face-down in the furs, until his last tremor faded. Then, finally, he relaxed, letting me go. I rolled onto my side, aching, relishing the hum of bliss still resonating through my body.

He climbed up from the bed. "I hope the bitch is tamed, then?"

"You did what you had to," I breathed. Our confrontation, pain and pleasure alike, left me pleasantly, fantastically weak.

Bannon adjusted his trews, then pulled a knife from his belt to cut my bindings. I uttered another long, lovely moan as the ropes slid free, and I stretched my arms out before me, working out soreness and stiffness from hours of restraint.

"Still intend to put a sword through my heart?" he asked.

I shook my head, staring at my hands. "You... are not like him."

"No," he said. "Never."

"What will you do with me now?"

Sitting up straight, I wrapped my arms around myself. The air of the desert night swept cool upon my sweat-drenched skin as my heart rate slowed, and the surge of numbing euphoria swallowed me down.

Bannon returned to the table before the hearth and took a seat. He picked up his axe and drew a whetstone from a pouch on his belt.

The heartless sound of him sharpening the blade was his only answer.

CHAPTER TWO

YOU WERE SUPPOSED to die for me.

In the night, Alaric came. A naked body draped with serpents. The largest of them was the seven-headed Akolet, sacred serpent of the Ruined Sands. The apparition drove me to my knees, and the rattling of snake tails filled my ears.

Slave, you were meant to die. Your life belongs to me.

Alaric's people pulled me out into the street. They who had called him king and prospered under his reign. I recoiled under their cold, smooth hands, pleading as white fingers like bones locked on my limbs. They lifted me from my feet and carried me through the capital streets while others stood aside, jeering and cursing.

"Whore! Sorceress! Queen of snakes!"

Native and slave alike condemned me, and I belonged to none of them. No clan would claim the king's personal pet. All despised me.

"Stop!" I cried out. The slaves threw garbage at me as I lifted my arms in defense. "Please, don't you know I hated him, just like you? I *hated* him! Please, I am *not* his queen... "

So they called me slut and serpent witch instead, and ridiculed my desperation. My skin bore his marks, a list of sins: foul hungers for the king's punishment; drunken lust that so often silenced my loathing. The people read the words on me and saw the poisoned heart within.

They carried me to a stone cairn in the desert. Before it yawned a great pit: the grave of Alaric Khan. The rattle of snakes rose above the shouts of the crowd, then drowned them out as his followers brought me to the edge.

Come to me now, Sadira. Your life is still mine.

I screamed.

The cultists cast me down into the grave, though I fought their hands like a fish fighting the current. It was useless. The blackness of the sacred serpent's maw broke open to swallow me.

As long as you live... you will carry me with you.

I fell, down and down—

—and crashed in a heap to the cold stone floor.

I bolted upright, wrestling with the blankets twisted around my body. Clean, white sunlight filled the chamber. Outside, the sounds of activity rose from the courtyard. Sawing, scraping, axes and picks striking stone. A voice called out, indistinct, and others called back in reply.

My heart sped up to a gallop. I'd fallen asleep on the bed. Alaric *never* allowed me to sleep on the bed. The bed was for fucking only, and only when he decided. I belonged on a cushion at the foot of it, like a dog, and if he caught me lounging upon his pillows and furs—

Except Alaric is dead.

Blinking, I clutched one of the blankets to my chest. Could it be true?

I did not dream it. The invasion. The battles. The...

"Barbarian," I breathed.

I brushed my fingers to my lips. *Yes... I remember now.*

The marks of our contest still ached on my skin. Bruises, dark purple under the smears of makeup and the tan curves beneath. His hard grip... his rough hands.

Oh... I gave a long, pleasurable sigh. *But it was...* good. *How could it have been so good?*

A warm breeze drifted through the open window. Probably no one cared now if their prisoner, untied, threw herself from the casement. I'd served my purpose, after all.

They never exactly outlined what comes next. I rubbed at one ankle, finding the braided impression of the ropes still hadn't quite faded. *No provisions for the woman they sacrifice in their* traditions.

My *traditions,* I amended. I hadn't been born a native of the Sands, but I lived by their rules.

Closing my eyes, I took stock of my body. Welts stung my arms and hips; my nipples smarted, still tender from last night's torment. My thighs throbbed, weak and sore. Between them...

A soft groan escaped me as my fingers slipped down to my aching sex. Aching thanks to the wild, brutal barbarian. Aching *for* him?

But he is the enemy. Master's murderer. How could I possibly...

"Bannon?" I murmured, eyes fluttering open. When had he left?

Wrapping myself in one of the furs, I climbed to my feet. The doors to the chambers stood closed. When I opened them, two soldiers waited outside.

"Where is the captain?" I asked.

They ran their gazes over me, taking in the sight of the blanket, my disheveled hair, the streaks of kohl and powder. As they traded a glance between them, their expressions turned venomous. It was on the tip of my tongue to ask why, when all at once, it came to me.

I was still their prisoner. And a prisoner should probably not look so well-ravished on the morning after her king's defeat.

Should I feign guilt? Chagrin?

All at once, my doubt melted into fury.

"I will speak with him," I demanded. "Go and get him."

"Just who do you think *you* are?" asked the younger of the two guards. He had dark black hair in a shaggy mane and the sour smell of beer lingered on his breath. "You're not queen of this castle anymore, and the Red Bear isn't keeping you here as a guest."

His nose wrinkled. "Get back into your pretty rooms, or we'll find you a more fitting place in the prisons. *Witch.*"

A twinge hit my chest, and I reflexively brought up a hand to touch the ring on my leather collar. I shouldn't have expected them to take an order from me, but *queen? Witch?* Did Bannon's people honestly believe I'd been either of those things?

I bit my tongue on a harsh retort and tried a softer tone. "I... would like to speak to my captor."

"Back in your rooms," repeated the other guard, a woman with broad shoulders and short-cut, summery blonde hair. "He'll see you when it suits him."

"Will you at least tell him I have asked for him?"

The young man brandished his axe at me like a shepherd's crook, shooing me into the chamber. "Whatever you like, *your highness.*"

"*Don't* call me that!" I snapped.

"Fine. Then let it be *whore.*"

He pushed me and I stumbled, tripping over the fur to land on my ass. The soldier snorted laughter, and pulled the doors shut before I could regain my feet.

I stared, wide-eyed. After several moments, a cold trembling seized my limbs, and with an angry scream I hugged my knees to my chest.

Bannon did not come. I waited for him for hours, pacing from the bed to the window casement, then to the dog pillow where I usually slept. Soon an awful tension throbbed to life in my temples; I quit pacing to close the shutters and curl up on the bed, hiding my face from the light.

These sheets still reek of Alaric. That awful ritual oil on his skin. Did they smell like this when I woke? Or is it the headache? Eye of Akolet, I can't stand it!

He was gone from this place. He was *dead.* So why did I cringe with the certainty he would burst in at any moment?

The way he looked in the end... those last moments on the battlefield...

The War of the Sands—the battle between King Alaric Khan and the barbarian captain whose people he'd enslaved—had stretched a little longer than a year. When the enemy armies came for the capital city, though, it had fallen in only three days. The serpent worshippers crumbled under the boots of their foe. Akolet hadn't saved them.

Neither had Alaric. Alaric emerged from his castle a gaunt skeleton, unarmed, with nothing but hissing, rattling reptiles for his armor. The king marched to his death wild-eyed and cackling.

They said you never left his side. Yet I saw you on the field these last days, fighting alongside his infantry soldiers. You're more than just his kept woman, aren't you?

In fact, I had been. Alaric trained me in more than one role, and I'd served him also as his personal guard. Within his bedroom, I was his bitch to breed; beyond it, I was his attack hound, practiced with blades and with barehanded brawling. And I never *had* left his side, either serving him or shielding him, no matter where he went.

Except those final days. When the enemies had come to Vashtaren. Alaric sent me away. He sent *everyone* away and locked himself in the innermost chamber of the castle—the Shrine of the Sacred Serpent—alone.

Why?

So, I hadn't been by his side when he arrived on the field at last. I'd already been captive, and I watched Master's lunacy unfold before me along with all his other soldiers.

And when the Red Bear struck him down, even the snakes scattered. The great Alaric Khan—Akolet's chosen son—fell naked and abandoned on a field of blood.

I felt no remorse. Fear, perhaps. Dread and futility. But no remorse.

I rolled onto my back, covering my face with one arm.

The morning lagged on. The heat of the day and the rattle and bellow of work outside soon filled the room, even with the window shut. As the headache grew too deep and too constant to bear, stabbing like a pick into my temples, I rose again, letting out a soft groan.

My stomach gave an obstinate rumble: I hadn't eaten since yesterday before the final battle.

I won't speak to the guards, though. Not to be humiliated and tossed back in here like a mangy dog.

The ones I'd met this morning had probably been relieved of duty by another pair, but I doubted I'd get any better reception than before.

Alaric had kept a personal shrine to Akolet in a tall, heavy cabinet against one wall. Within, it held a marble sculpture of the seven-headed serpent, and an altar of many hands lifted before it in offering. He'd have sealed jars in there, too, with dried fruit and wine.

My stomach growled louder.

The only person who can object is dead, I reminded myself, and opened the cabinet.

Seven pairs of glittering, gemstone eyes stared back at me. A rush of goosebumps ran up my arms, and the skin on the back of my neck crawled. Casting my gaze down from the serpent effigy, I reached for the first of the offering jars.

As soon as my fingers brushed the lid, my head gave a nauseating throb. I ignored it. After eating just two dried dates and a sprig of grapes, though, I lurched for the chamber pot and threw up. So, I settled on nibbling from a stale hunk of bread and took two drops of a cannabis tincture to soothe my frayed nerves. I shut the doors to the shrine and put my back to it, shuddering.

Is it over? Is it, really?

Alaric had ruled Vashtaren since before I could remember. He intended to carry on his family's twisted legacy forever.

A legacy built on the backs of slaves.

Reaching for the clay pitcher left from the night before, I managed a few swallows of warm water. For a hundred years, the Khan dynasty led a nation in worship of the serpent god, and they thrived on cruelty. Akolet smiled on their greed, and their armies—along with their sorcerers and ancient, secret arts—were unmatched. They stole from neighboring nations, abducting their children to use for human livestock. Forced laborers. Concubines and rent boys.

Not anymore. From across the northern sea, Bannon Sha'kurukh had come, and finally struck the snake's head from its body.

Alaric, his forefathers... the whole flock of Akolet's followers... they reaped what they sowed.

No true grave existed for Alaric. Not like in my dream. The Red Bear had consigned Lord Khan's body to the desert, sundered and scattered for the scavengers to find.

But...

As long as you live... you will carry me with you.

I brought my fingers up to the ring on my collar again, running them along its cool, smooth surface, sliding it around and around through its shackle in the leather.

The cannabis started wearing away the edges of the sickening headache. I slipped into a doze on the bed, and drifted in and out of heavy, sweltering dreams, pitching back and forth atop the blankets. Hot, damp, sheened in sweat, when I woke, I found myself in a shocking darkness.

Eye of Akolet! Raising my head from the pillows, I shot an accusatory glance toward the window. *What time is it? Could it be evening already?*

Outside, the dry winds of approaching night groaned. Bannon had not come.

I slid from the bed and crossed to the casement, sliding open the shutters once more. The whole day had gone by.

He doesn't want to see me. I touched the base of my throat, thinking of gallows. *Maybe he's decided my fate after all. Consigned to the prisons... or maybe...*

Would he sentence me to die as Alaric did, and bind me to that psychopath forever?

Catching sight of myself in a polished glass, I shuddered. I *looked* like Alaric. At least, I looked like one of his people. Almost. He'd never found a way to change my hair to white, so he'd dyed it jet black and commanded me to keep it combed to a perfect, geometric straightness, and rendered me hairless everywhere else. Daily, he'd required me to darken my eyes and lips with kohl and powder my skin to a glimmering ivory.

Now I seemed a patchwork golem of light and dark smears, bruises, oily scuds of sweat and paint, and bold tattoos like blood.

This made me think back to Bannon, and his hot, tawny skin on mine. Ruddy, dusky, lined with marks of battle, pressed to my exposed, rose-honey curves. Warm. Yearning. *Wild.*

I touched my face. The woman in the mirror did the same. I searched the reflection, considering the work of the king.

My tattoos wound around me in changing patterns, intertwining with scars and brands. Tight knots of thick designs in some places; light, flowing calligraphy in others. They cavorted over my left eye, ringed my hips, and climbed my limbs. A flaming sun spiral circled one studded nipple.

These were the work of Alaric and his most loyal followers: the alchemists and magicians making up the Order of Akolet. Each mark, by its very existence, proclaimed me the property of Akolet's chosen son, and vessel of his will. The piercings advertised my various initiations: the consecration of my body; the taking of my virgin blood; my training in rituals of domination and dark, fleshly delight.

A map of my sexual identity, written on my skin. Even the makeup did little to hide it. What would a northern barbarian make of it?

I cared little for the greasy dye in my hair and the arching kohl. The rest could not be helped. I'd learned the futility of shame or embarrassment for the sake of modesty. Whatever else Alaric did to me, he'd taught me primal pleasure and desire. Intimate self-awareness and a lawless, unapologetic hunger. The *monster* I'd promised Bannon.

These things spoke to me, sang down to my blood and bones, to a part of me Alaric maybe hadn't created at all, but merely understood.

I hated the sorcerer, yes. I didn't hate the passions he'd cultivated in me.

"Still... " I strode past the mirror, heading for the inner chambers. "I am not the person he's painted. It's time to wash *her* away."

At least this was a problem I could solve.

The baths were divided into two rooms, the smaller of which contained a narrow stone bathtub for me to wash. The king himself kept great heated pools further within, in the larger section, but I never set foot in his opulent marble grotto unless Master ordered it. He'd ruled over every miniscule aspect of my life, from the times I could eat my meals to the times I could relieve myself. Bathing had been no different, and for my regular washings, I used the tub.

The dark ink Alaric used to hide my natural hair held stubborn against washing out. Repeated rough scrubbings with soaps and oils, even the application of lemon juices, wouldn't rinse away the dark grease. When my scalp began to sting, I alternated my attempts between working out the dye and coating lank tresses with creams to soothe the damage.

In between rinses, I scrubbed the powders and kohl from my body and face, leaving the water of my tub like a pool of swirling, coruscating oils. I'd emptied and refilled it twice before I saw any significant improvement. Finally, my persistence paid off: blackened strands washed out to gold, and the last of the makeup rinsed away.

I savored the crisp shiver of the air on my dripping skin as I circled the bedchamber lighting torches. Once the room was lit, I stood before the mirror once more, naked and pinkened from excessive washing.

I look... like a wonderful stranger.

The woman Alaric had hidden for years gazed back at me. I'd never had the right proportions for a girl from the Sands, and I had gray eyes instead of black or green or blue. Now, with the dyes and powders discarded, I wore the look of another people. I couldn't say *which* people, but I fit my own frame at last.

The fresh air from the open window had cleared out the sickening incense. *How does the smell linger so long anyway, with no one burning the damn stuff?*

Instead, as I sat on the edge of the bed smoothing lotions over my skin and brushing out my hair, the warm, clean scent of the furs welcomed me. Warm, clean fur, and sweet soaps, and lemon in my damp blonde locks.

I'd just teased out the last of the tangles when the scrape of the iron doors made me jump.

Bannon had come. At last.

CHAPTER THREE

THE BARBARIAN FROWNED and cocked his head to the side. He stepped into the room, closing the doors behind him.

"My soldiers say you've been quiet for a long time. They thought you might have taken your own life but were afraid to enter."

He peered at me, one corner of his mouth quirked in confusion. I hadn't dressed after the bath, enjoying the hot desert night on my wet, naked skin.

"Afraid?" I asked. "Of me?"

"Who can guess what dark curses Lord Khan's witch will cast, now she is unbound?"

I snorted. "Oh, yes. *Witch.* Your men are suspicious fools."

"Are you saying you wouldn't wield your black arts on your enemies?"

"I couldn't if I wanted to." I set aside my hairbrush and spread my hands before me. "I am no sorceress. No member of the Order. I have no magic."

I expected some sign of spite or disdain. A bitter bark of a laugh. Instead he only stared, as if trying to make up his mind about something. My nakedness seemed to leave him absurdly confused.

When he spoke again, his voice had dropped an octave. "You... are not Vashtaren."

Running one hand through my clean tresses, I cocked an eyebrow. "Didn't you know?"

"I didn't."

"Ah. Well then, surprise, barbarian. Even Lord Khan's *witch* is one of the slaves you came to free."

He took a step toward me, then hesitated. One hand came up to his brow, and he kneaded his temple.

"You... a slave? But then... why did you fight me when you knew I came to break your chains? Why demand—why *partake* in his sick rituals? Why ask me to... to *claim* you?"

"Because I am of his world, even as I am not." I touched the scrolled leather collar around my neck. "I was neither born of the Sands, nor of Alaric's own tribe. But of all slaves, I am the one most deeply possessed. I don't remember the land I came from. Nobody does. Alaric is all I have ever known. Whatever nation bore me, I am part of his wild desert now."

"All you have known?" He clenched one fist. "You mean he took you as a *child*?"

"Not as you are thinking. Whatever else Alaric was, he was not that."

"A small comfort." He pivoted away from me and began to pace.

I watched him for several moments, curious. How amusing: I had done the same only hours before, stalking back and forth in restless unease.

"It changes nothing, you know," I offered.

"But it does." Moving to the table by the hearth, he poured himself a drink from the water jug and downed it in one anxious gulp. "I should have refused. I should have tried harder to talk you out of it."

"If I'd wanted to surrender, I would have."

"Perhaps you believe you are like him," he said, "and deserve pain. But *I* believe no such thing. Last night, I took no pleasure in—"

"Didn't you?" I asked.

He threw down his cup, shattering it on the stone. "Of course not!"

A flicker of red lust slipped through me like a finger down my spine. I shifted position, tucking my legs underneath me and running my fingers through the soft animal furs. "I think there is too much fighter inside you, too much of the bear, to not have felt the thrill in dominating."

"I can *see* how I bruised you!"

I lifted one shoulder in a casual shrug. "What are a few bruises, when primal creatures indulge their desires?"

When he didn't answer, I rose from the bed. I crossed to Alaric's bedtable, considering the crops and shackles, all the tools he'd used on me in moments of fearful delight. Oh, he had worse punishments than these, and when he'd wanted to, he'd abandon all restraint and go far beyond even my tolerance.

If I offered one of these riding crops to Bannon, or gave him one of the silk scarves to bind my wrists, would *he* take such mad risks with me? Would he push me to my breaking point?

Or past it?

Bannon wasn't Alaric. Bannon wouldn't feed the beast in me, cool its heat with indulgent punishment. If he knew the poisoned heart of my passions, he would crush it under his heel.

As men do with all serpents.

But I closed my eyes and thought of his harsh fingers twisting in my hair. His rough grip on my hips and the bright stinging slap of his palm on my backside.

I should hate him. I should loathe *him, he who killed Master and took me as his prize. It's what a loyal slave would do: strike him down in vengeance for my king.*

So why did I only want his touch upon my skin once more?

I selected the leather leash which matched my collar and moved to Bannon's side.

"You never answered me last night. What will you do with me, now you have claimed me as your own?"

"I haven't decided." Stepping away, Bannon rested one arm on the fireplace mantle and tapped his fingers on it in an agitated rhythm. "If you're really one of the slaves, and not his lover, it... changes things."

"What I was to him was a plaything," I explained. "A pet. He had my loyalty, but only because he held my leash."

"A... pet," Bannon repeated.

"Yes. His personal servant, guard dog, and submissive."

31

His jaw tightened. When he looked at himself in the mirror over the hearth, his hazel eyes burned, dark and disturbed.

I lowered my gaze to the floor. "Will you make me a prisoner?"

"I don't know."

My voice dropped to barely a whisper. "Will you execute me?"

"I don't want to," he said. "But there are those who believe you'll curse me and my people, if you're allowed to live."

"I've told you I have no magic."

"Which is exactly what I'd expect you to say if you did."

Stepping forward, I held out the leash, offering it to him. "Do you think me so insincere? Don't you remember what I told you last night? How I hated him? And when you proved your strength over me, didn't I yield? Didn't I give you what you needed for your victory?"

His frown returned as he took the leash and set it aside on the table. "What we shared last night was a battle. Yes, you yielded. It's nothing more than I would have expected from Khan's personal whore."

If he meant to hurt me, he failed. I'd been called worse. I fidgeted with the bronze ring, biting my lip.

To Bannon, I wore the mantle of the enemy, *and* of refugee. Both, and neither. He'd conquered me and won a heavy burden of regret in the offing. We'd lain together, but only by necessity. A necessity he might forever resent.

Now—by the laws of the Ruined Sands, at least— I belonged to him. His woman, to do with as he pleased. To most, that meant his to fuck at his leisure.

Perhaps I *should* have balked at the prospect of sharing a bed with him. Still, I didn't.

We were the same, in a way. Strangers, not of this land but forced to bear its cruelty. I'd learned to assimilate over the years, but he was new to it all. He believed in another way.

"Will you sleep in here tonight?" I asked. "It is your right, as victor. Or will you simply use it as my prison until you decide my fate?"

"Sleep here?" he repeated. "With you?"

I gestured at the dog pillow. "When Alaric ruled this chamber, I slept on the floor. I can do so now if you wish. I am yours. You may do what you like with me, even if it means you cast me aside. All I can do is obey."

The corners of his mouth twitched. "No, no. That's not necessary. But you will remain in these rooms until I decide if you're prisoner or... "

"Or prize?" I suggested.

As if I'd somehow stung him, the great Red Bear cringed. He seized the second cup from the table and poured another drink of water, avoiding the question.

"Have you considered perhaps I enjoyed being the prize?" I asked. "The *sick ritual* we played out last night began in war, but it ended in bliss. I didn't expect it either, but then, I had no idea what sort of man you'd be."

Hugging myself, I admitted, "I suppose you can't understand what it means for a woman chained to a man she hates, to find real pleasure in the man she beds."

33

Bannon set aside the cup and gripped the back of the chair, leaning his weight upon it. I dared to move closer. I lifted hesitant fingers towards him, and when he didn't pull away, I touched his rough forearm.

"I don't believe you are so troubled by the act of claiming me. You are troubled because I myself demanded it."

He remained still, so I slid my hand up to his bicep and pressed myself to his back.

"You have a soft heart, which tells you to be meek, and merciful, and tame. But you have a *hard* cock, oh great Red Bear, and now a willing woman at your beck and call. You've done what the warlords of the desert require, and so I, like the rest of Alaric's treasures, am yours to take."

And my submission is perhaps the best thanks I know how to give.

Beneath my touch he grew tense, but I pressed my lips to his shoulder blade and exhaled against him.

"I am an *avid* worshipper of carnal nature," I whispered. "Pain, yes, *and* passion. You can't imagine how deeply I want them. How deeply I could want *you,* barbarian. I think you are lost in this desert like me. We can fight one another... or we can find some solace in our shared circumstance."

He shook me off. "Is your loyalty so easy to claim? You serve the man with the biggest cock?"

I tossed my head. "There have been plenty of well-endowed men in this castle and even in this room who would never have the strength to overpower me."

"So, you serve only those who will abuse you?"

"*Master* me," I corrected. "There is a difference."

Why wouldn't he look me in the face? Was he so disgusted?

Shame crept up my shoulders. Shame! I knew what others thought of me and my desires, but I'd never felt *shame* before. I'd never felt *dirty.* The way he acted, after the hot spark in his eye last night, after the harsh and hedonistic struggle—*now* he shrunk away from me as if I carried some plague?

Unruly petulance kicked in my chest and, finally losing my patience, I pushed away from him.

"You are better when you are a beast, like me." I spat on the floor at his feet. "Not this shrinking boy. You were better when you took me, forced me to yield. When you *fucked* me like no man has. When you broke me and made me *beg.*"

Bannon whirled on me. "Would you not *talk* like that?"

"Do barbarian women never talk like this?" I taunted.

"No. They do not."

"Ah."

Before he could stop me, I pressed myself to him. One quick hand slipped up behind his neck while the other ran down the front of his trews, seeking and finding the ready, stiff shape of his cock beneath the leather. I gave him a firm, warm squeeze.

"But you wish they would. Don't you?"

With a rough snarl, Bannon thrust me aside. I cackled, cackled like the witch he took me for, as he stormed out the doors and slammed them shut behind him.

My laughter continued, manic and unpleasant even to my own ears, until I wanted to cry. Sudden alarm overtook me. I rushed to the doors and threw myself at them, pounding my fists. All around me, my own voice wailed like a hollow spirit in a storm.

"Don't leave me here, Bannon!" I called. "Please! It's too much to be here alone, to be trapped with all the things that were his. Please, *please,* do what you will with me, just don't leave me here, with *him* all around me!"

CHAPTER FOUR

HOW DARE HE? How dare *he!*

Him with his talk of whores and sorceresses, his naked disdain, when he knew as well as I did, he'd *wanted* me in the end. Not gently, not as tender lovers, not as equals, nor as brokers of peace between our nations. He'd wanted me with a primitive, haunting hunger, a surging demand beginning and ending at his rigid cock.

He'd liked *fucking* me. I'd been no more than his toy, instrument of his indulgence, and he'd taken as much pleasure from it as I had. It might have destroyed another woman—a woman of *his* nation, maybe—but to me, his primal, greedy passion led directly to mine.

Why pretend otherwise?

He stayed away for days. Only my guards made any appearance, coming in the mornings with a tray of breakfast and at night with an evening fare. When they did, I retreated deeper into the inner rooms to avoid them. I'd give them no satisfaction to look upon me or cast more ugly words at me. As soon as I heard the click of the lock, I prowled away into the darker passages, and waited for them to leave.

Once they'd gone, I emerged to find my meal. I expected no better than thin gruel and gritty water, but to my surprise, they left me real food: hot eggs stirred with bits of beef and bright vegetables, bread, even a glass of wine. A *lady's* breakfast. A *queen's* breakfast.

Served as though I were a queen? It gave me a dull, uncomfortable stomachache. Instead of pleasure, I picked at my food with sullen disinterest.

Why *do they all think me Alaric's queen? Do I look like a queen? In this slave collar?*

After the second such breakfast, anxiety set in. Bannon had left me alone too long, and still with no word of what was to become of me. The bedchamber stewed with an evil silence. I managed to sleep in the bed at first, but soon it swallowed me. Opulent covers twisted and knotted around my limbs as if to strangle me, and I dreamed of Alaric's hands closing on my wrists, my waist, my throat.

Did I hear him in the inner rooms? The tread of his footsteps following me down into sleep?

I moved to my dog pillow and shivered with the memory of Master looming.

On the third morning, the sensation of his nearness would not abate. I dressed, avoiding the mirrors, certain I'd see him glowering back at me. Surely, I'd only dreamed of his death. Any moment Alaric, not Bannon, would throw open the doors of the great chambers, and I would be punished for preening and donning clothing without his permission.

As if to strike home this fear, a sudden tug on my sarong snapped the clasp of my belt clean off. The silken green material pooled at my feet. I stared.

I pulled the belt too tightly. Or I snagged the skirt on something without noticing.

Green. I hated green. Alaric had favored drab designs in brown and putrid olive—like a python's coloring—or else bright, virescent lime, like acid and venom.

What is wrong *with me?* I gathered up the skirt and tied it with a simple knot instead. *Am I so used to being under Alaric's watch, I can't even dress myself without Master to instruct me?*

No. I would not be so pathetic I could not do something so simple as *dress* myself. I was more than a slave, after all. A *soldier* could manage her own needs. I could survive without constant supervision.

I fell back on my physical training to ease my mind. Of course, the guards wouldn't give me my blades—the khopesh sickle-swords taken from me upon my capture—but I'd trained in unarmed combat as well. *Chorremachi*: the way of the snake and scorpion. Its fast and complicated rhythms demanded sharp focus, and for a time, the exercise occupied me.

But I swear I can still feel him here.

Sickly sweet perfumes of ritual and dark, depraved magic. Sex on his pallid white skin; *his* sex clinging to me.

Alaric's heated baths would wash it all away and ease sore muscles after hours of exercise. The kitchens and therefore the ovens were at work, which meant the water from the pipes would be steaming hot.

When I imagined the pleasure of a long, leisurely soak, however, my chest tightened. I'd be pulled under to drown. Somehow, the scalding water would boil me or choke me with long, grasping fingers. Evil, lingering magic. Revenge from a dead tormentor.

Once, I thought I heard his voice: the familiar hiss and murmur of empty, hypnotic sorcery, whispering through the air around me.

Your life still belongs to me.

I shut my eyes tight and clasped my hands around the ring on my collar. Was this what he meant? Was I doomed to madness for failing to die in his name?

As long as you live...

The room, the baths, the bed, the food. Everything still belonged to Alaric. Even as his body lay broken and divided across the empty sands, I couldn't disobey his word. I waited for Bannon alone, but never *truly* alone.

I threw my next tray of breakfast at the morning guard and drove him from the rooms with a shriek. When a second guard came in to give me dinner, I sneered and threw a vase. It smashed upon the iron door just as the barbarian woman slammed it shut.

Think I'm a witch, do you? Fine!

After that, whenever one of the foreigners entered, I snatched Alaric's tomes down from the bookshelves. I flipped through the pages, murmured gibberish, and whispered evil promises. I even waggled my fingers at one fresh-faced boy when he came in looking particularly nervous, and laughed as he scurried back into the hall. The laughter rose to a cackle and shook me to the core, until a cold frisson ran through my shoulders and stole all the humor away.

He is not here, I reminded myself, sinking to my hands and knees, shivering. *He is dead. He is not here.*

ON THE FIFTH morning, when I stirred from my dog's bed and opened my eyes, Bannon sat on the low stool before Alaric's writing desk.

My tray of food rested at his elbow. When he saw I'd woken, he seized the tray in one hand and thrust it at me.

"You," he said, tone even and clipped, "will eat."

I blinked at him. Overcome with relief, my shoulders eased, releasing the tension of long, unstructured hours. Without a word, I gathered my legs beneath me, placing hands on my knees, and bowed my head.

"Are you deaf?" the barbarian asked. His tone never changed, but his steady, unreadable manner brought a tremor up my spine.

"Put it on the floor," I whispered, never looking up. After a moment, I added a barely audible, "Please."

"On the—" He snorted and practically dropped the tray on the stones at his feet. "If you insist."

I crept forward on hands and knees, like an animal, and crouched low to eat. I lapped a thick porridge topped with minced dates and raisins, and nibbled at a thick slice of hearty nut bread. A mug of goat's milk proved a little more challenging, until I took the handle in my teeth and poured it into the porridge bowl.

I'd eaten like this, on all fours, for Alaric's pleasure. I'd adopted the manner without even thinking of it, or how my new Master would take it.

41

Bannon studied me. I sensed his attention roaming over my body, my primly tucked arms, my breasts pressed together by the posture, my long legs, my rounded bottom. On impulse, I glanced up at him and caught him staring back.

Something fierce smoldered in him, and a heated flush rose to my skin. Holding his gaze, I ran my tongue over my lips, tasting fresh, cold goat's milk.

Did your jaw just tighten there, barbarian?

I lowered myself to lap, but snuck peeks up at him between licks. His attention remained locked on me and he said nothing, expression full of stony contemplation.

After a few moments, I used my nose to nudge the tray aside and, still crouched on all fours, I bent to kiss his feet. He must have bathed, because they were clean, not covered with the dirt or grit of the all-pervading desert.

"You don't have to—"

He fell silent when I tilted my face up to him. After a slow, quiet second, I resumed my kissing.

I moved my lips to his ankles, then his calves. Scooting closer, I nuzzled the firm curve of his muscle, closing my eyes to enjoy the warm scent of his skin. Finally, I leaned on his calf, and needed go no further.

As I rested there, the soft touch of his fingers brushed my cheek, then combed through my hair.

Gentle now. Compassionate. Maybe he'd forgiven me.

When I opened my eyes, he stroked me. His caresses came gentle and slow, but his expression burned with lust.

"Thank you," I whispered. "Master."

Bannon looked away. "Don't call me that."

"I'm sorry. You claimed me. I don't know what else to call you."

Taking his hand in both of mine, I rubbed my cheek against it, opening the fingers so I could rest my face in his palm. His scent of steel and leather seemed not so strong now, with the heat of battle days behind him; now he smelled of warm autumn, of bonfires, and a faint hint of sweet liquor. He must have had a touch of wine with his last meal.

"I accept the consequences of being your prisoner, Bannon, if you decide to keep me prisoner. But please don't leave me without some answer. Throw me in a dungeon or make me your pet, but don't make me guess and fret and fear for what will come."

"My... pet," he muttered. "That is what the Vashtarens expect? Like a cat, to mewl at my feet and wind about my ankles?"

"To do those things," I agreed. "And more."

He grimaced, but he didn't move away. His fingertips threaded through my hair again, and I smiled.

"I like this." I pressed closer to him, leaning my whole body on his leg. "You have such wonderful hands, my barbarian."

"Did you tell your esteemed king the same?"

"Alaric didn't care for me to say anything, whether it came to his pleasure or mine. Even if he had, I didn't like his hands. Cold, long-fingered things. Reptilian. Yours are warm, and broad, and kind."

"Why do you behave now?" he asked. "After terrorizing my soldiers? Do you think you'll escape punishment by playing precious and sweet?"

"I am sweet because you are here now." Lifting my head, I kissed his palm, then each rough knuckle as I folded his fingers shut.

"Your soldiers make no secret what they think of me. *You* have been gentle, though, and offered me mercy. You may punish me now if you like. I've acted out, and there are consequences for bad behavior. I will accept it, but at least you are here, and I am not alone."

Bannon raised his eyebrow. "You don't fear what I will do?"

"I don't. I respect it. Part of me needs it."

"He really has made you a deviant."

I released his hand with a sting of defeat. The hurt eased a little, though, as he sighed and traced his fingers along the curve of my ear.

"What will you do if I go?"

"I don't know. I can't stand being in these rooms by myself anymore. I can *feel* him, Bannon, *everywhere*. If you came at night, at least—"

"And share a bed with you?"

I came to a halt, mouth falling open as a thought occurred. "Do you already have a woman? Does this shame you—do *I* shame you—because you are wed?"

"No." He averted his gaze, then after a beat, he added, "My wife died years ago."

"I'm very sorry."

We sat in silence, and I tilted my head to rest upon his knee while he stroked my hair. Neither of us seemed to know what to say next, but I didn't mind. Here was peace. If he punished me, I would at least find order and structure in it, rules to abide by rather than nervous, rolling hours to fill with tension.

If he didn't punish me, at least he was here, and *real,* and I could touch him and smell him and know I was not losing my senses.

"It's the uncertainty which makes me restless, barbarian," I whispered. "If you don't tell me what's to become of me, I'm afraid... I don't know... "

"It isn't so easy." He nudged me aside. "Goddess Sherida, you are troublesome. I don't wish to keep you like this. I have no desire to lock you in these rooms, where one tyrant already imprisoned you. If you were his slave, like the others, then there's no reason, and nothing to be gained by keeping you in fear."

Joy welled up like a spring in my chest. Old rules cautioned me to tame any outward display, until I remembered the rules had all changed.

"Thank you," I whispered.

"But what if you lie?" He cupped my chin in his palms and made me look him in the eye. "Who can say whether this game you play is some mad ruse? How do I know you aren't pretending to be my willing consort, all the while meaning to stab me in my sleep? If I set you free to go as you will, I may expose myself to some dark vengeance from his most twisted follower. I can't decide whether you served him out of perverse, sadistic loyalty... or if you were only his victim."

"You *do* know," I replied softly. "I have told you what I am."

"But I don't understand." Deep in his eyes, something dangerous smoldered. "And... I don't understand why your lust for subjugation... so *intrigues* me."

Ah, my barbarian! A bright thrill sent a shiver down to my core.

I pressed myself closer, hands on his knees, beseeching. "You do feel it, don't you? The bear in you, the wild beast, hungering."

"Is that what it is?" He let go of me. "A hunger? Or is it sick depravity? Transgression a better man would resist? I *will not* become the same kind of monster as Alaric Khan."

"This is not about Alaric," I told him. "Please... will you let me show you?"

Bannon frowned. His throat worked, and his voice came out in a hoarse rasp.

"What exactly would you show me?"

"How a slave—a slave of *my* nature—serves her Master. You may decide for yourself if it pleases you."

He glanced aside, and his fingers tapped the desk. He didn't stop me as I nudged apart his knees and sidled up between his thighs.

"May I suck your cock, Red Bear?" I whispered.

He bit his lip, and then one strong hand rested on my head, guiding me down.

I freed his cock from black leather trews, and it sprung up from its nest of rich, dark curls. How *quickly* he hardened. I beheld it, curious, stroking tentatively. *This* I knew how to manage.

His grip tightened and he pushed me closer. I obeyed the unspoken command and took him into my mouth.

The wild taste of salt and skin delighted me. I groaned and ran my tongue along his rigid length, so hot, so deliciously heavy with need. I offered long, adoring strokes, circling the head, inviting him deeper. He'd gone from hesitant to eager, as though all he'd wanted was a little prompting, and with it he summoned up the most urgent erection.

I, too, hungered, and as it happened, I liked the taste of barbarian. As he held me stiffly in place upon his cock, I savored him, alternating my rhythm.

Releasing him for a second, I glanced up with a smile. "I don't mind if you are harsh. You can order me to do whatever you like. I'm not too soft for sharp words. Say to me what you could never say to one of your women back home."

He pushed me back down. "Just... just shut up and suck."

His voice stoked an impish, wicked vibration throughout my body. A hot flutter in my chest; a warm, welcome melting in my stomach and loins. Greedily, I devoured him, lavishing him with my tongue for an unforgettable finish.

"Fuck... you little... "

He hesitated. Pausing to madden him, I rolled my tongue over his slick, smooth crown and planted a kiss upon it. Sneaking another glance up at him, I found him staring back.

"Yes?" I whispered.

"You little *slut*," he bit out. Then he let his head fall back in a groan. "*Fuck*, you must love sucking cock. You're so *good* at it."

Covetous desire, like a madness climbing higher and higher, filled his voice. The same fever burned in me, a carnal demand.

"Thank you," I said between panting breaths, next time he loosened his grip and allowed me to rise. I punctuated this with a long, luscious stroke from the base of his shaft up to the tip, then ducked down to circle my tongue along the soft, hot flesh of his scrotum.

I wanted more still. I trembled for him to fill me. My needful sex craved him.

And will he?

Bannon moaned, a low, throaty sound. If the guards remained stationed outside my door, they must hear him. I caressed his testicles with a genuine pleasure—I *wanted* the others to know what I did. If they believed me a whore, then let them think me the wildest, most talented, most tantalizing whore in the Sands.

And let them know only he *is worthy of me.*

His hands dug into my hair, knotting blonde strands in his fists. He held me captive, and with soft, panting grunts he thrust deep. I received him in a rush of joy—oh, I recognized these gestures. I knew them wholly on instinct, a private, primitive knowledge shared in our hot flesh and racing heartbeats. Culmination. Completion.

I released him for an instant, letting out a breathless sigh. "Yes... my barbarian... my Master. My only desire is to please you."

His hands dropped to my shoulders and he pushed me away. "*Stop.*"

CHAPTER FIVE

BANNON LUNGED FROM the chair as though I'd burned him. Pivoting away, he fumbled to rearrange his trews.

A pang of terror beat in my chest. *What did I do?*

Alaric had shoved me away like that before. He did it when I'd done something to anger him, something to warrant punishment. Not *discipline,* not *play,* but true punishment.

Or to hurt me. Sometimes he did it for no reason at all but to make me suffer the bite of rejection.

I stared, wide-eyed, at Bannon's back, fighting the tremble in my limbs. "What's wrong?"

Bannon hung his head, seemed to consider his answer, and ran a hand through his hair.

"You said it yourself. You've been a slave all your life. One of the prisoners I came to free."

After a pause, he faced me again. "It isn't right. Making you act as... as he would."

I brushed my fingers to my lips. I had no answer—or maybe I had too many answers. *He did not make me feel the way you do,* I wanted to tell him. And *I yielded to you. That was* my *choice.*

And, *this is who I am.*

"Why do you still wear that collar?" he asked. "All the other prisoners have cast theirs off."

I touched the ring. Of course, Bannon wouldn't know the collar *I* wore was not the same as those displayed by the other slaves. Every one of us had been marked in our servitude with a neckpiece signifying our place: black silk for kitchen, scullery maids, and house servants; black braided cord for stable hands and court pages; black leather for the harem.

But mine was different even from those of the other concubines. A thick, embossed leather band with no end. No buckle, no clasp—just a square bronze lock stamped with a ritual glyph.

A lock with no keyhole. Because of Alaric's most important, most prevalent rule.

Master's pet wears a collar. Always.

"Well?" Bannon prodded.

"I never even considered it." I looped a finger through the ring and nervously twirled it back and forth in its shackle. "I've worn the collar of a slave every day of my life. I might not even know who I am anymore without it."

A look of grief crossed his face. Pity? Revulsion?

And we were having so much fun just a moment ago...

Bannon stepped toward me and reached out a hand. "Come on up from there, girl."

I accepted it, and he helped me to my feet. As I straightened, though, the first burning tears came to my eyes. I hurried to grind them away.

"Sadira?" Bannon's brows knit. "What is it?"

"Please... " I whispered. "Don't feel guilty, Bannon. Not for this. Not for the claiming."

I squeezed his hand in both of mine. "You are not my enemy."

He rubbed the back of his neck, glancing from the door, to the arch leading into the inner chambers, then to the window casement and the courtyard outside. The one place he didn't look was me. My hands dropped to my sides, and my heart gave a low, aching throb.

He pities me. He pities me, and he hates himself for touching me.

Bannon bent to gather up my breakfast tray. "I'll tell the guards you must be allowed to leave these rooms."

I nodded in silent thanks. I didn't know what else to do.

He made an awkward, wordless retreat, wearing the hangdog expression of a man creeping from the bed of a prostitute. It bruised me in a way I didn't expect. I sat on the floor, spinning the ring of my collar in its shackle.

As he stepped out of the room, though, I heard him stop to exchange words with my guards. All at once, I perked up, realizing what he had said to me.

I could leave Alaric's chambers. I could go out into the castle, escape my isolation and the spiraling chaos inside.

The moment Bannon's footsteps faded down the hall, while my guards still muttered audibly between themselves, I rose to dress. Grabbing up a fiery orange sarong and gold breastplate, bothering only

51

long enough to twist my hair into a braid, I rushed to be set free.

The soldiers—two men this time—stared, shocked, when I threw open the doors.

Maybe they hadn't expected me to be ready so quickly. Maybe the sight of my desert attire scandalized them: the breastplate, a purely ornamental piece and not one fit for battle, lifted my breasts but left them bare. A fashion no one in Alaric's retinue would find alarming.

The way these two men searched me, full of stark disapproval, stoked fierce rebellion in my heart. Straightening my shoulders, I planted hands on my hips and regarded them with equal disdain.

"I'm going out. To the courtyard."

"You sure?" one of them—the one at whom I'd thrown my breakfast—sneered. Without bothering to hide it, he eyed my breasts, staring at the spoked tattoo circling my left nipple and the gold barbells piercing each pert tip. I'd linked a delicate set of fine gold chains between them, and the jewelry sparkled in the torchlight.

"Bannon ordered you to let me out," I snapped. "I heard him tell you."

"Aye, he did." He scowled. In one hand he carried a long-handled, one-sided axe scribed with angular northern runes. This he brandished at me as he continued, "I wouldn't advise it, though. Most folk in this castle still harbor nasty feelings toward Khan's witch. Not all of them are from our foreign ranks."

"The loyalists we took prisoner call you a cutthroat whore," his partner said. "While those we freed say you betrayed them from the start. Nobody wants you out and about."

The gossip stung, and I didn't doubt a word of it. Choking back the hurt, though, I lifted my chin.

"I'm going to the courtyard. If you don't wish to escort me, you can stay here. It doesn't matter to *me* if you disobey the Red Bear."

Without waiting for any reply, I strode out into the hall, smooth and lithe as a desert lioness. The men did follow—I'd never questioned they would—but I gave no indication I noticed.

The master chambers took up a large portion of the castle's third floor. Below, on the larger second and ground floors, people moved busily about the corridors, in and out of rooms. There were many new faces, more occupants than before Alaric's demise.

Or maybe it only seemed so because the slaves had emerged from their dark corners and quiet hiding places. They had no reason anymore to be afraid of the king and his soldiers, or the Order of Akolet, his malicious sorcerers. No more cringing and bowing their heads when one of Vashtaren's royalty approached. A weight had been lifted from them all.

Color flooded the halls. None of the stark, stony Vashtarens, leached of life and warmth like living sculpture. Bannon's bronze-skinned soldiers with their wild, rich manes walked alongside former captives and servants: elegant ebony people of the river valley, with their thick, dark hair in locks and braids and coils; warm, round faces of copper complexion and deep, sparkling brown eyes; fair and freckled, sun-kissed folk from faraway fields and hills; ruddy, broad-featured desert natives, the people of Vash who'd never taken up the arts of the serpent-worshipers, and were persecuted for their denial.

One of Bannon's folk crossed my path, working alongside a girl I recognized from the kitchens. She'd wrapped her head, neck, and shoulders with a rich purple shawl, covering her long dark hair—a style forbidden before Alaric's defeat. Along with her barbarian partner, she passed out loaves of bread to soldiers and refugees recovering from injury.

A pair of tall, tanned sisters who'd worn their own slave collars of black silk only days ago now waited at the end of one hall, decked in soldier's armor they'd repainted with symbols of smooth lines and shapes and spirals, depicting soaring birds and galloping horses. They'd gathered their long, steely-blue hair into intricate topknots, held in place with polished bone needles.

I marveled over the drastic transformation all around me. No dark wigs or hair dyed black, as mine had been. No pale, ivory powders lightening the skin, or dramatic kohl to hide the natural faces underneath.

There's no need to hide anymore. The last of their oppressors stand chained in the prisons below. The captives are free at last.

But the sense of their scrutiny weighed me down. People I'd grown up alongside, people who'd taught me how to tend to the household, how to manage kitchen labor or serve noble guests, now they studied me, pausing in their business to fix on me with wary, curious stares.

I am the only unknown. I am the one for whom no one can find a place.

Even to those this castle oppressed, I'd always been different. I'd been *his*.

So, I'd changed my appearance. No longer made myself up. What did it matter? Reptiles shed their skin. They camouflaged. The markings underneath always remained the same, though... just like mine.

Lifting my head, I focused on my destination, and kept moving.

"Wait."

The order intruded on my thoughts so abruptly, I obeyed without thinking. The habit of servitude simply took over. The command came from a stranger, though, and as I whipped to attention and registered the woman's unfamiliar sneer, fury—mixed with shame—flared to life in my gut.

"What?" I snapped. This woman held no right to me, no authority. I silently cursed myself for following the command. My cheeks burned.

She strode toward me with the air of a leader. She must be one of Bannon's lieutenants—tall and broad-shouldered, her brown sable hair braided close to the scalp on one side and left free and wild on the other. Her sharp glower cut into me, full of the same disdain as all the others. She carried a set of manacles in one hand.

"The sorcerer's witch," she declared, "doesn't strut about the place unchained."

I struggled to keep my voice level and cool, as tension tightened my jaw. "Your captain permitted me to leave my rooms."

"Sure, you can leave them," the lieutenant replied. "But you'll be wearing these when you do."

She lunged to slap the restraints on me. In a swift panic, I jerked away, clutching my wrists to my chest.

No, not this woman. Let it be Bannon if it must be anyone but not this woman, this... stranger!

The lieutenant snatched for my arms. I moved to weave into the attack, the natural inclination for a *chorremachi* fighter—sweep into the opponent's balance, then swing away—but my guards seized me by the shoulders. The manacles snapped on my wrists and bright red anger, fueled by anxious fear, exploded in me.

Everyone had witnessed it. The crawling sense of curious eyes surrounded me. My chest tightened; short, harsh breaths fought to escape, and my heart raced.

"Fine." My cheeks and breasts blazed with a furious heat. I wanted out into the courtyard at once. I needed air. Spinning away from the lieutenant and all the staring onlookers, I strode toward my escape.

It's not as if you haven't been publicly bound before.

Tears burned under my lashes as I recognized Alaric's voice—Alaric's snaky, slithering, hateful voice—taunting me from the depths of memory. Making me small. I pushed aside a young desert boy in my way as I stormed through the passage.

"It's not the same!" I hissed under my breath. "It's not. No one gave that bitch permission to touch me. I did not give her permission!"

You're a prisoner, you idiot, that inner voice jeered. *The enemy's whore. No one needs permission to humiliate a whore.*

Bright sunlight startled me to a stop. I'd emerged onto the wide stone courtyard at last.

Oh, thank goodness.

The lazy warm scent of the desert autumn found me. I swallowed back the close, pinched feeling in my throat, and inhaled fresh, sweet air instead. The knot in my chest loosened a little.

The jangle of soldier's gear behind me told me the guards had caught up, but I didn't care. Pulling myself together, I stepped out from under the castle eaves and tilted my face up to the warm glow.

A cluster of Bannon's people and the castle's former slaves gathered nearby. Stacks of debris from many battles had been organized near damaged sections of wall, ready to begin reconstruction, while workers met in huddles discussing their plans.

Beyond damaged ramparts, I could make out the dry white streets of Vashtaren's capital city. Mostly deserted. After the fall of their king, the few locals who remained—probably without the means to flee—must not be keen to mingle with invaders from across the sea. Bannon and his armies had come to liberate the slaves, not those who prospered under the serpent's rule.

The southern side of the courtyard looked mostly empty, with no signs of labor and only a handful of the castle denizens sitting under low, wide palm fronds. The rest area, I surmised. A central fountain bubbled clear, cold water into the air. It stood lonely, though, abandoned for the cool respite of the shade. I took a seat on the hot stone rim and closed my eyes, basking in the light.

I didn't mind the sun, even though it burned my skin so much easier than it did the pallid white Vashtarens, or any of the other people of the desert. The morning's golden-white radiance whispered with the promises of real freedom. I wanted to drink it up, all of it, and hold it glowing inside of me.

Eye of Akolet... how these last few days had exhausted me. How they'd frightened me. For the first time, I wanted nothing more than to run from this place. From Bannon, who couldn't decide what to do with me. From these foreigners, convinced I would continue a legacy of black arts despite Alaric's death. From the servants, slaves, and consorts. My guards were right. None here believed or trusted me.

Shall I go, then? Like the people of Vashtaren? Even if I fled, I could never escape. All of Vash knows about the king's sordid slave girl and what he did to her. And even with him gone, I'll always harbor this strangeness in me. These aberrant hungers. Like asking Bannon to put my tray on the floor, like a dog's dish. I... want this. It gives me clarity.

It is who I am.

Where would a woman of such darkness find welcome, if not the Ruined Sands? Whom could I turn to, and where could I go, where I—and all the ways I'd learned to love—would not be a freak?

He's made you a deviant.

No. I had always been a deviant. Alaric had only recognized it in my soul and called it out.

Ignoring my guards, I sunned myself, working to forget all the rest of the castle, the people around me, everything but the warm light bathing my skin. It would redden and sting before long if I wasn't careful, but for now, I basked in its blessed, unblemished serenity.

"Sadira!"

My heart gave a jump, and I jerked to attention. A slight figure with closely shorn, dark brown hair hurried toward me across the courtyard. Even as I shielded my eyes from the glare of the sun, I didn't recognize them.

"Is it really you, Sadira? The Red Bear let you live?"

CHAPTER SIX

I ROSE TO my feet, covering a gasp with one hand. "Eye of Akolet! Rayya?"

"It *is* you!" The other woman—perhaps the only friend I had ever made in this place—beamed as we came face to face. "We didn't know... we weren't sure if the Red Bear imprisoned you with the Order's sorcerers, or if he... "

Rayya didn't have to finish the sentence. A quick glance at my guards and their shining weapons was enough.

A quiet buzz of interest stirred among the workers around us. A group of bricklayers watched with wary expressions, setting a prickle of discomfort rustling across the back of my neck. Rayya must have been working with them: she carried a load of white clay bricks in her hands, setting them down on the rim of the fountain to wrap me in an embrace.

I took a step back and marveled at the sight of her. Rayya had been another of the castle concubines—a harem shared by the sorcerers in the

Order of Akolet. Not every slave in the harem had served one singular master, but Rayya belonged to one of Alaric's most loyal men, and like me, had served as his exclusive plaything.

The last time I'd seen her, Rayya's luxuriant hair fell in a thick, straight sheet, all the way down to the waist. Her master forbade cutting it, and instead made Rayya brush it for hours, until her natural cloudy curls lay perfectly smooth, and then wind beads and gold spirals into it for his fascination.

He'd ordered her made up as well, with shimmering silver wings of kohl around bright hazel eyes, and lush, carmine pigments darkening her lips. Her long legs and slim hips made her far more athletic than voluptuous, and she had almost no breasts to speak of, but her master had special corsets made to feature and accentuate them regardless. All this, to Rayya's miserable humiliation. The craven old sorcerer's insistence on an overtly feminine mien made her more a caricature than anything else, and no one had been more uncomfortably aware of that than Rayya herself.

Today, my friend wore uncomplicated clothing probably borrowed from the barbarian men: leather trousers and a sleeveless jerkin. Her shorn hair sprung up in beautifully natural, tight, coarse coils. For once, her face was free of paint, and her lovely chestnut skin had taken on a healthy, happy glow. The slave collar she'd worn was nowhere to be seen.

I rested my hand over my heart with a smile. *She looks happy.*

Rayya glanced at the shackles around my wrists. "He hasn't been cruel to you, has he?"

61

"Not cruel, no." Taking her hands, I sat back down on the fountain rim. "He is a conquering leader, Rayya. He can't be too soft."

"But you aren't one of them."

I blinked in surprise. Even if I'd shared their fate, I'd never expected the other slaves to take my side.

I knew there was a reason I always loved you, Rayya.

I cleared my throat of the lump rising in it and glanced down at the water before my friend could mention it.

"Oh, Ry, I'm not anyone." I smiled as I said it. "Have they treated you well enough, though? You and the others?"

"Like kin." Rayya took a seat beside me. Her smooth arms had grown firm, new muscle already; she must have started work with the bricklayers, or some other team, the very day after Alaric's fall. "We don't want coddling, and the Sanraethi are happy for us to work alongside them. Even those of us who are not from their lands."

"The... Sanraethi?"

"Sha'kurukh's people. Their home country is Sanraeth, in the far north. There's a supply caravan coming with new building materials soon, and they're sending a younger brother of their king to take regency here."

"And what will you do, when a barbarian sits on the throne of the Ruined Sands?"

Rayya lifted one shoulder in a shrug. "It can't be any worse than Lord Khan."

"I suppose not," I agreed. "You look wonderful. The work outside suits you."

Glancing at the load of bricks, Rayya nodded. "I enjoy it. Being in the sunshine, working with my hands." She held them out, showing me the pale splotches of dried white clay covering them, a sharp contrast to the rich tone of her skin. "I used to play by the river with my brothers when I was young. We built bricks like this from the clay along the bottom and raised dams and castles and fortresses. It's silly now, perhaps, but it... it's rejuvenating."

I licked my thumb and swiped it over my friend's freckled cheek, scrubbing away a stray smear of the clay. "I could use something to soothe my mind. Maybe the barbarians will let me join you."

"Sanraethi," Rayya corrected. "The Red Bear, was he... hard with you?"

This time, I knew she meant the claiming. Everyone knew what the conqueror had to do in order to cement his victory.

"He asked me to concede defeat." I leaned back, tilting my head toward the sky once more to drink in the afternoon heat. A chuckle escaped me. "He said he would make love to me, or even forego the ritual altogether. I wanted no such mercy. It isn't my nature, and I know these lands and these people. I suppose it's better to say *I* was hard with him."

Rayya pursed her lips with a frown.

"He's a compassionate captor," I added, perhaps as a sort of concession. "He's strong, and I admire strong men."

And he is kind. At his very heart, I know he is kind.

"Why has he shackled you?"

"His soldiers shackled me," I corrected. "They don't trust me. And I'm told the castle population doesn't, either."

Rayya made a face, stealing a quick glance toward the other workers, who'd gone back to their business but still sent scrutinizing looks our way every few moments. All the confirmation I needed.

Rayya stood. "I'd better see to my work."

"Thank you." I reached up and gave Rayya's hand a squeeze. "For coming to speak with me."

"It doesn't matter what others say." Rayya regarded the brands and tattoos winding over my skin. "You suffered as much as any of us. Maybe even more."

I tried to sound cheerful. "I'm alive, though."

Rayya jerked her head in a quick nod, then hesitated a moment before retrieving the bricks and hurrying back toward the construction.

Well. At least I am not a curse *to everyone.*

A shout rose on the far side of the courtyard, jarring me out of my thoughts. I glanced up in time to see a young, wiry man lunge from his work in the rubble and throw aside one of the women standing nearby. The woman—one of Bannon's people, much shorter than her attacker—dropped to the ground under his shove. Then he leapt on her, raising fists to strike her over and over.

I jumped to my feet and sprinted for the fray. "Stop it!"

Some of the workers tried to seize the attacker by the arms, while others reached for the girl to help her to her feet. The young man twisted and whipped about in their grasp, biting at the hands clamped on him, and in one swift move he twisted away to continue his assault.

"The sacred serpent turns his fangs upon you!" he shrieked. "Slayers of the chosen king! Usurpers! The serpent will poison you and all around you! Cursed! *Cursed!*"

Planting my shackled hands together, I vaulted a pile of crumbled stone and darted toward him. As one of the guards reached for the young man's fists, I slid to the ground in a wide sweep, and knocked the boy's legs out from under him. He wasn't heavy, or very strong—he must have gotten the upper hand in the fight purely by surprise.

Swinging my own legs around, I pulled into a crouch and then into a somersault, spinning and landing astride the young man's chest. My knees scraped on the sandy courtyard bricks.

I pinned his elbows with my legs and clasped my bound hands together, pressing them down on his neck.

"*Stop,*" I demanded.

The crowd bubbled into a confusion. Staring down into the face of the boy—and indeed, he *was* only a boy, gaping up at me in wild-eyed confusion— I recognized him right away. The son of one of the chambermaids. One of the Vash folk, though not of Alaric's tribe.

He was in the hall only a few minutes ago. I pushed him aside to get to the door.

His eyes, rimmed with red as bold and bright as blood, gave me a nauseating shock. Eyes full of fear and fading madness. Crimson tears streamed down his cheeks, and he shouted for help, shooting plaintive looks at the spectators around us.

"Get her off me! What is she doing?"

"She's defending an innocent woman, you rat."

Bannon had appeared, flanked by two of his warriors. He put a hand on my shoulder to tug me off

65

the boy, and when I moved, he leaned down to seize the boy by the collar and jerk him up off the ground.

"Just what in the name of Sherida do you mean by attacking one of my people?" he barked.

"I—I don't know! I don't know what happened!" the young man stammered.

He's not lying. I furrowed my brow, watching his lower lip tremble. *He really has no idea what he's done.*

I switched my attention to the woman he'd beaten. Some of the other workers had helped her to her feet, and she shook, her face a mask of fury. Her nose and mouth were a mess of blood, and she'd have a black eye, from the looks of it. She held one arm at a sharp, stiff angle.

"She's very hurt, barbarian," I said to Bannon, tilting my head toward the victim. The lady looked fierce, at least. Sooner to retaliate with a punch than to show fear. "She needs to be seen to."

"Mara." Bannon gestured to one of his soldiers—

the lieutenant who'd slapped the manacles on me earlier. "Take this woman inside and see her patched up. I'll deal with the boy."

"I'm sorry!" the boy begged. "I don't understand—I don't know what I did! I... I..."

I climbed to my feet and stepped closer to Bannon.

"I believe him," I murmured, soft so none of the others would hear. "See his eyes? Something's wrong with him."

Bannon scowled. He still held the boy by the collar, and the boy wriggled and struggled in his grasp.

"Have him tied up and kept in the barracks with the guards for the night," Bannon ordered another soldier standing nearby. "I'll give him the benefit of the doubt this time. It's hot out here. Perhaps the sun robbed him of his senses. But I can't ignore an attack on one of my own, so I'll see to his discipline once we've given him the chance to recuperate."

The soldier inclined his head. "Aye, captain."

Bannon set the boy on his feet, and two of the others stepped in to tie him fast with ropes.

"You're all right?" Bannon asked me.

"Fine." I brushed a bit of grit and sand from my shoulder. My scraped knees and scuffed palms stung, but I'd endured far worse. Mostly by choice.

"I've never seen such a style of combat." He rubbed his chin. "What did you do there?"

"*Chorremachi*," I replied. "The way of snake and scorpion."

"You're fast." He eyed the shackles on my wrists with some suspicion. "And agile. Managing such gymnastics with hands bound... "

"I've had practice." I considered the boy as the soldiers guided him away. "I was Alaric's personal guard dog, remember?"

He was in the hallway. I pushed him aside to get out of the castle. I touched him.

I'd broken one of Alaric's cardinal rules: never to touch another man's body, unless by Alaric's own permission.

Cursed, the boy had said. And *cursed,* the barbarians called me.

Those red eyes...

I looked down at my hands.

What did I do?

CHAPTER SEVEN

I'D SEEN THOSE bloodstained eyes before. I understood what it meant.

Cursed. You're cursed.

The confusion in the courtyard left everyone distracted—including my guards. As soon as their attention shifted to Bannon and his orders, I slipped away, back into the castle. I wanted to search the archives, the stacks of tomes and scrolls Alaric and the Order kept before his death and the subsequent imprisonment of those dark magicians still alive.

Their library stood abandoned now. No one to watch me consulting the black books. No one to interrogate me about the boy and his red-rimmed stare.

"Stupid of me to come here," I mumbled as I perused the shelves. "They already think I'm a witch. All I need now is for one of them to catch me with the Order's grimoires."

I might not have magic of my own, but there had been a time when Alaric obsessed over finding it in me. He'd revealed these writings to me when I'd been only a girl, and he'd tested me for signs of talent. I'd never shown any at all, and eventually he gave up. I remembered the ancient volumes, though. Maybe one of them held the answer to my question now.

Of course, back then, it wasn't the spellbooks that caught my attention.

The library held other knowledge as well. Tomes on the art of fleshly desires; pages full of etched illustrations, beautiful bodies on full display; erotic tales of sexual domination, punishment, reward. As a young woman I'd discovered them, between fruitless studies on magic, and they woke my first needful, deliciously sinful curiosities. I came to look forward to my study time, and the stolen moments when I could feed my wicked, illicit fascination.

In my earliest years as a slave—after Alaric had begun my training but before he demanded my sexual servitude—I resisted him. I balked at humiliating orders, petulantly defied his authority. I flipped the platters he instructed me to hold and shoved away the feet he tried to rest on my back. He'd publicly flogged me three times before I'd reached seventeen. The third time, he explained my next insubordination would be my last. He would cast me away and send me to live as a common prostitute in some hard desert city.

"At least I might profit from a perfectly good body," he'd said, "if not a willing spirit."

It didn't upset me in the heat of the moment, with my back, buttocks, and thighs burning from the bright welts of my punishment. He'd summoned a whoremonger some days later, though, to appraise my value and offer a price. *That* frightened me.

An old Vash medicine woman came with the brothel keeper. She'd stripped me and prodded me, tested my virginity, scrutinized the weight of my breasts and the health of my complexion. Alaric had not yet marked my body, nor bejeweled me with anything beside a simple gold stud in one nostril.

The examination filled me with uncomfortable, alien guilt. I had no fear of sex, not at all. But if Alaric exiled me to a whorehouse, *this* would be my fate: perused and appraised by strangers, grasped by unknown hands, stripped and sampled like a cheap ware in the marketplace. A gourd. A cask of nuts. A skinny goat.

He knew even then how to scare me. How to make me feel totally alone.

Afterwards, I knelt for my king in contrition. I did not willfully disobey him again.

Alaric's power over me always came down to this. Threat. Fear. Indignity. Disgrace. He allowed me to feel safe if it suited him. When it didn't, he dangled the unspoken threat of dismissal, just to see me shake. In time, he lured me too with drunken, decadent pleasures and shameful, secret needs. As I grew older, I realized he'd probably always known about my *real* studies in the library. Perhaps he'd even counted on them all along.

When I was eighteen—or rather, when Alaric declared me eighteen, since no one knew my true date of birth—he collared me. I'd already worn the standard slave's choker made of black silk and buckled with a clasp bearing his family sigil. That night, though, he replaced it with something more personal: ornate black leather, stamped with the images of lotus flowers, and fit with a metal ring.

"Locked forever," he informed me, tugging at the back of the collar as if to test the heavy bronze buckle, stamped with his own crest, symbol of his royal rule. "My claim on you. Eternal as it is beautiful."

The strangest part was the *tenderness* in his tone. The pride in his face when he hooked a finger through the ring of the collar and drew me into my first, unexpected kiss. He tasted of desert spice, deep, hard liquor, and stark, hot metal.

I hated him. And I loved him.

I flipped a page in the text I'd picked out, reading over the words without absorbing them. *Or I loved his assurance. The security of his ownership. I was a vessel to him, but not a common gourd.*

The rules of our relationship evolved with my new collar. Alaric no longer permitted me to wear clothing in the upper rooms or in the ceremonial spaces of the Order. I could not speak until spoken to. I could touch no other person, nor allow myself to be touched.

As I touched the boy today. But that couldn't really be the reason he lost his senses, could it?

The guard outside my room. He pushed me, that first morning. And I took Rayya's hand today. And Bannon... Bannon and I have done a lot *of touching.*

None of them had gone mad. So, might it have only been coincidence I'd crossed paths with the boy right before the fight?

Alaric had determined me useless, magically. Still, he brought me into the chambers of ritual, where I bore witness to him and his Order in their worship of the serpent god. They prayed for wealth and power, and made offerings of flesh, decadence, and debauchery. Often, the women of their harem played a part, symbolic prey upon the altars, their spiritual and sexual energies consecrated to the seven-headed Akolet as their lords claimed them.

Not me, though. Not at first. Alaric would never relinquish me to the sorcerers, not until he himself had taken first blood. Instead, I became a focus object—the maiden counterpart to their concubines; a living convergence point for their invocation.

My fingers followed the lines of a diagram in the book: one of the summoning circles the sorcerers often used. I'd never feared the Order's magic. Never minded being made party to their strange acts of sacrament. I surrendered, as much as anyone, to the surge and sway of bodies, the intoxications of wine and the bitter smoke of lotus and poppies.

But...

Those red-rimmed eyes.

I'd seen the sorcerers grow rigid with tension and tremble with power. Some said the spirit of Akolet himself came upon them, guiding them in his will with visions, and their eyes bled from the power of the divine. Always, afterward, the fiery glow of their eyes turned to raw, scarlet marks, as though they'd been stung by scorching desert sands, and rivulets of blood trickled down like tears.

Possession. Conjuration. Corrosion.

Sometimes, even I had been taken by the magic. The occasions blurred in my memory, a vague and unsettling series of images and deeds in a swirling blackness. Always, afterwards, came the migraines, lasting two or three days, making me physically ill.

Then came the day of my true initiation. The day Alaric consummated his ownership in full and took my virgin blood as tithe.

I have no trouble remembering that *ceremony.* My fingers came to my lips, and I waited for the chill to fade from my shoulders and the fluttering in my stomach to ease. As though that ritual—and it *had* been a ritual—could somehow drag me back to him, even now.

He'd ordered me to his chambers on a sweltering, stormy day. He'd worn only a pair of black suede breeches, and the shape of his hardness strained under the tight fabric. Before we began, he had me don long sleeves of soft, supple calfskin, and long, smooth stockings of the same. From an oaken jewelry box, he selected two small gold weights in the shape of teardrops; they hung from delicate loops of wire, which he tightened around each of my nipples.

Naked but for these adornments and of course, my collar, I knelt before him at attention, hands resting upon my thighs.

Alaric came to stand in front of me, looking down on me to admire his work. He opened his trews to release his beautiful ivory cock and began to knead it before me.

"Look upon it, girl," he commanded, and I did.

Perhaps I should have been afraid. Perhaps ashamed or humiliated. Yet I found it captivating. My body woke to him, slowly at first and in ways I didn't yet fully understand, but I recognized one thing clearly. *This* did not frighten me. Far from it. This *excited* me.

"Have you seen a man's nakedness before?"

I'd seen plenty of men with women in darkened
alcoves of the castle and sometimes even the shrines,
embroiled in orgiastic worship. I'd witnessed Alaric's
own ritual orgies, and wild bacchanals in the great hall
commemorated with wine, women, feasting, and
fucking. In these walls, nakedness could hardly be
avoided.

"I have, Lord Khan."

"Have you touched one?"

Physical contact was a different story. "Touching
is forbidden."

But I had certainly wanted *to touch. Even then. Before
then. I remained chaste because he'd have cast me out or killed
me if I hadn't, but I knew lust. I'd coveted the soldiers who
trained with me. I'd longed for hard, needful hands on my body.*

Even his interrogation, prying and critical,
sparked a nervous arousal in me. The gold weights
dangling from my breasts pulled at my nipples, and
they stiffened with a sweet, sore flutter of guilty
desire. Between my thighs, my pussy ached. An empty
hunger I'd nursed for years trembled on the verge of
wicked fulfilment.

Alaric seized me by the hair—a gesture of
ownership rather than torment or violence—and
tilted my face up toward his.

"Do not *lie* to me."

"No, my lord," I insisted. "I have touched no
one."

"I think you *lie*. You've always been a disobedient
slut, haven't you?"

Such harsh words. But I liked them. They carried
a hot, forbidden sting, and I understood perfectly
what he meant to do with me. Though his tone
chilled me, it was only another sort of ritual. Not

accusation. *Play.* He hadn't given any instructions, but I thought he must expect me to play, as well.

I wanted him. At least, I wanted his body. The fierce organ he stroked in such lazy familiarity was a key made to unlock me. Perhaps in later years I would grow to loathe him, but on that hot, dark day, with the looming promise of passion and pleasure making my breasts tingle and my virgin sex deliciously wet, my hunger outweighed any fear. When he called me *slut*, I wanted to be sluttish. I wanted to be an object, a bearer of his indulgence.

Indulgence which would feed directly into my own.

"I haven't!" I said. "My king, I swear I haven't."

"Open your mouth."

He gave me his long, rigid shaft, sliding it all the way to the back of my throat until I choked and squirmed, reflexively pulling away.

"*No*," he ordered.

The urge to gag overcame me, but his grip on my hair tightened and he held me fast. I squeezed my eyes shut and calmed my reaction.

"That's right," Alaric murmured. With his free hand, he stroked the straight, dark tresses of my hair. "Very good, slave."

He tasted of salt and the savory heat of desire. As I relaxed, he teased me with steady motions of his hips, and I received him, silent but eager, moving with him in instinctive, supplicant yearning.

After several moments he withdrew, seizing me under the chin and forcing me to meet his gaze.

"What a good little cocksucker. *Too* good. Tell me, how many men have you pleasured before, little slut?"

"None!" I replied in an urgent whisper. "I have followed your rules!"

He ran his thumb over my bottom lip. Under his fierce scrutiny I shivered, and a delicious flush warmed my breasts. He let me take him into my mouth once more, this time more deliberately, cradling the back of my head until he nearly choked me. There he held me, testing my resolve.

"How many have you *fucked?*"

He didn't release me, so I could only give a slight shake of my head, offering muffled sounds of denial.

"If I fuck you," he warned, drawing me into a rhythm. "If I fuck you and find out you're lying, you will be a very sorry little girl. So, you had better admit it now. How many men have you had behind my back?"

"None!" I gasped as he finally released me. Tears streaked down my cheeks—tears not of anguish but of strain and delight—and I stared up at him, hot with desire.

"A woman bleeds her first time. If there is no blood, I will know you are a whore."

"My king," I'd begged in a hoarse voice. "I have no desire but to please you!"

This was what I'd been trained to say when he was unhappy with me. Sometimes he would relent and offer me gentle praise as reward, or else he would put me on all fours and spank me for my transgressions. This time he said nothing, kneading and kneading his shaft as he stared down at me.

His eyes were red then, weren't they? In the library, in the bright, quiet heat of the afternoon, I flipped another page in my tome and frowned as I struggled to recall. *The same blood-rimmed eyes of the sorcerers in their conjurations?*

He'd been in the throes of some spell. *What* spell? I'd neither known then, nor cared, because he'd brought me to the verge of something momentous and magnificent. Years of celibacy, ready to be ended; a frustrating restraint I'd gladly cast aside.

For some women, chasteness might be a virtue. For some, a welcome freedom or inner comfort. Not for me. As womanhood bloomed in me, so too did the curious hungers of heat and passion. They prowled within, like a restless beast in a cage. I was no pure or righteous virgin. No, I was just what he called me: a slut. A wanton, needful, glorious slut.

And I embraced it.

"On your hands and knees," he'd ordered, and I'd obeyed.

"Show me what I want."

Revolving in a slow circle, I bared myself to him. An electric thrill shot through my body.

Alaric knelt behind me, probing the slick folds of my sex with two long fingers. "Already wet for me, when I haven't even touched you."

I didn't know how to answer, so I repeated my litany. "I have no desire but to please you."

He seized my hair again, pulling my head back and leaning close to whisper in my ear.

"Do you understand what I mean to do to you, my desert flower? This has been your destiny ever since you came into this castle. Poor girl from a forgotten people. Tonight, I erase that legacy. With this stroke, I make you *my* creature. My pet. My toy. Nothing—and nobody—else."

"Yes, my king."

"No. Not king. Now I am *Master*. Not your lover. Not your protector. Not your salvation. I *own* you."

He grasped my hip, and entered me with one fierce, mean thrust.

"You. Are. *Mine*."

I clenched my teeth, fighting back a cry. I'd been so ready, so eager, it shouldn't have hurt. He *made* it hurt, claiming me not in pleasure but in pain. And yet, still, the sting faded to a delicious ache in moments, and I gave a rough, low moan of delight.

"Yes." Alaric tested my resistance with a series of slow, careful strokes, gripping me by the hair with one clenched fist. "Say it, little whore. Whose are you?"

"I—"

I broke off, my voice cracking. More tears came, spilling down my cheeks, and I grit my teeth.

"I am yours—Lord Khan—"

"*Master*."

His fingers twisted in my hair and pulled, while the other hand grasped me by the hip, pulling me to him. Each thrust sent the weighted jewelry swinging in tiny arcs, sending sweet twinges of pain through my breasts. I balled my hands into fists on the floor before me.

He fucked me hard, grunting with effort, but also in a restrained, almost perfunctory way. My body throbbed, burning, aching from the violent invasion; at the same time, sheened with sweat, wet and needful, I teemed with decadent pleasure. How could I have gone so long without such addictive, mounting intoxication before? What yearning emptiness I'd known before his cock filled me, claiming every deep inch of me.

At last he drove himself to the limit, until I thought he'd split me open. His cock throbbed, pouring pulse after pulse of his seed deep inside me. I bit my lip not to cry out, shamelessly gratified as he filled me, flooding me, then withdrew to release the last sweet, hot spurts across my buttocks.

I held myself there, on all fours, panting with drunken delight. There'd been no rushing orgasm of my own, but I hardly cared—gluttonous pleasure suffused me, my body weak and wet.

My toy, he'd called me. And that's what I'd been. Nothing but a toy for his use.

Dizzy, I somehow found the strength to peek over my shoulder. *Have I pleased you,* I wanted to ask, but Alaric's attention was fixed on the place of my sex.

"Telling the truth after all." He continued kneading his shaft, though it grew soft in his grasp. "What a good little slut you are."

And so, he had claimed me. So, he'd begun his slow poison, feeding the lustful beast within me in forceful passion and punishment.

I ran a hand through my hair and wondered. The arcanists of the serpent god retained physical echoes of their spiritual machinations throughout their sacraments and rituals, and for some time thereafter.

Those red eyes—the burning, fearsome heat in him. He did more than claim me. He chose the occasion for some sort of spellwork. Why didn't I see it then?

Why would a mere boy show the same stigmata now?

It couldn't have been my touch that brought on the Vash boy's fit. As deeply as Alaric's rules were ingrained in my mind, a simple *touch* couldn't trigger such a reaction. I'd said it enough times already, I *had no magic.*

So what brought it on?

I'd thought the boy was only a scullery servant, son of one of the kitchen workers. Could he have learned something—something powerful and malevolent—from someone in the Order of Akolet?

If any of the sorcerers had taken an apprentice so young, surely I'd have known it. I'd been privy to the Order's innermost workings, even if only as a slave.

But he took on their stigmata somehow.

I rubbed my chin and tapped my fingers on the yellowed pages of the book.

What was the color of the boy's real eyes? The eyes behind the red-rimmed glare and the bloody tears? Had they been the clear, shining topaz color possessed by most Vash natives? Or the rare but lovely indigo black?

Or had they been the bold, virulent green of a viper?

I'd jumped into the fray so quickly. Disengaged the boy and startled him into confusion so fast. Now, I couldn't remember.

Except for one second—perhaps no more than a *fraction* of a second—they'd been the eyes of my Master.

This is his power over you, I scolded myself. *The power to frighten you. That is all it is.*

"But he is dead," I said out loud, a ward in the face of old ghosts. "He is *gone.*"

Is he?

Then why did I still sense him—hear him, *smell* him—everywhere within these walls?

.

CHAPTER EIGHT

BANNON FOUND ME, still in the castle's library, late in the afternoon. I recognized his arrival without looking up. The instant he entered, he sent an odd frisson through my skin—a sense of *chasing away* my echoing seclusion.

I snuck a glance in his direction as he approached. My guards hovered behind him, scowling, but at his instruction they retreated into the hall.

"Reading?" he asked.

I shot him an oblique look, then dropped a pointed glance at the parchment on the table in front of me.

"Well... " He ran a hand through his hair. "Of course. You *would* be reading. In a library."

I let the scroll roll back in on itself and watched him as he took a seat across from me. Silence stretched between us. Bannon sighed, tapping his fingers on the winding, metal serpent on one of the book covers before him.

"The god Akolet," I told him, dipping a nod toward the book. "The deity Alaric and his forefathers worshipped. The Vashtarens believed they even carried the soul of Akolet within them."

I pondered the cover, then shrugged. "Now that you've taken Alaric's head and claimed his castle, maybe they'll call *you* the serpent's chosen son."

Bannon wrinkled his nose. "Is that what you believe?"

I gave a snort.

"*I* saw Alaric at all hours, in all seasons. I watched him lose his temper and throw fits over meaningless slights. I had the pleasure of cleaning up after him when he took sick, so no one else would discover he caught the sweats and the shits like any commoner."

I pushed the tome aside. "I never saw anything godlike in him at all."

"You loathe him so deeply. Yet he somehow kept a hold on you."

I held up my wrists, reminding him of the manacles his own lieutenant clapped on me. "I told you ropes were not the worst of it."

Bannon fingered the chains with a weary sigh. "What am I going to do with you?"

"I am the enemy's soldier and his pet. I know what *he* would do, were he you."

"*Never* believe I will do the things he's done."

I cocked an eyebrow.

"Oh, *don't* give me such a sardonic look." Bannon gathered up three of the books I'd carelessly set aside and stacked them up, clearing the table between him and me. "You said yourself I'm not like him."

"No," I agreed. "But you *are* a warlord. And until you decide otherwise, I am your prisoner."

He stared at me with a mixture of anger and puzzlement.

"Are you always so conflicted when you win a war?" I asked.

His lips twitched. He stared at his hands for a long, silent beat. Then, reaching across the table, he cupped my cheek.

"I just wish I hadn't done it to you. Hadn't... *claimed* you."

I straightened. "Barbarian, had you not claimed me, we both know Alaric's people would still be fighting you, and you'd have lost the support of the mercenary tribes. The Vashtarens fear you now, and their fear is their loyalty. At your command, the prisoners of *decades* have been released! Not just those of your own nation but countless others subjugated by his family!"

Rankled, I gathered up my own books and rose to return them to the stacks, thrusting them back into their places. "If you had not *acted* like their master— and mine—you would have no victory. More than likely another one of his followers would take what you did not, and the war would continue. And *I* would've been bound and fucked either way."

"How can you be so blithe about such a thing?"

I spun back to him and threw up my hands. "You *did not* rape me, Bannon! I told you my conditions to yield. You satisfied them. Your prize was my body and everything it symbolized in conquest."

He said nothing. I uttered a long, slow sigh, and pinched the bridge of my nose.

"You made it very clear I could deny you if I cared to. I wanted to see exactly how determined you really were, underneath all your tender manners."

Bannon scowled down at the table. "When I accepted my king's order to travel across the sea and reclaim the people stolen from our clans, I had no intention of finding myself entangled with my enemy's woman. Even when the *customs* of the desert were explained to me, I did not think it would lead to this."

After a moment, I sauntered back to the table and leaned over it, taking his hand in mine.

"Are you not *hungry* inside, as I am? I do not doubt you are an honorable man, and I have seen the kindness in your heart. But bears are primal creatures, barbarian. Certainly, there is a reason your people named you for one."

His gaze flicked up to mine and amber eyes flashed with heat.

"I *felt* it in you." I climbed onto the smooth wooden surface and crept closer to him, voice low, fingers closing on his wrist. "The way you touched me, held me beneath you... the iron heat of your cock inside me... "

"Goddess Sherida, the *mouth* on you!"

"You melted this morning when I asked permission to pleasure you. Not so tender then, were you? You were needful, and ravenous, and it stiffened your beautiful tawny shaft to have a soft, willing servant to receive you."

Sitting upright, I smiled. "I *like* the way my new Master fucks me."

"Why do you still call me Master?" he demanded. "I don't have any intention of keeping you enslaved."

I pondered him, bringing up a finger to tap my lips.

"Barbarian, may I show you something?"

Bannon's brow knit, but after a brief consideration, he nodded. With a knowing smile, I slid off the table and moved back to the bookshelves.

It didn't take long to locate the one I wanted: a leather-bound tome of mottled black and scandalous ruby red. There were no markings on the cover but when I laid it open in front of Bannon, his lips twitched, as though he could guess what he would see within. I opened it to the first page, which simply read *The Mastery of Pets and Consorts.*

"I discovered this years ago," I explained. "Alaric's training didn't always align with these customs, but the intention was the same."

I flipped to the first section—*The Practice of Sensual Mastery*—and showed him the elaborate plate accompanying the title. A man, perhaps one of the ancient desert nobility, towered over a naked girl, who lay at his feet gazing up at him. Rather than fear or awe, however, her expression glowed with languid, almost feline satisfaction. The expression, perhaps, of a woman recently well-fucked.

The man held a chain in one hand, connected to a collar at the woman's throat. Though he wore a short *shendyt* wrap around his waist, the artist had used shade and highlight to give suggestion of a massive, rigid erection straining beneath the cloth.

"There." I whispered into Bannon's ear as I moved my finger from one figure to the other. "You, barbarian, are this man. I would happily be the woman."

Bannon still said nothing, but his eyes roamed over the image with interest.

"This," he finally murmured. "You... *want* this?"

I recognized the husky tone in his voice, the same one he'd had this morning.

"It is who I am," I told him as together we turned pages.

"You wish to be bound. Yet my lieutenant told me how you recoiled from her today, resisting the shackles she put on you. You fight my guards. You *hate* being confined."

"I never said I wanted to be chained by your lieutenant, or to be kept imprisoned by your guards," I scoffed. "*Those* circumstances were thrust on me. It isn't the same as yielding to a Master I welcome and want."

The book contained mostly illustrations and diagrams. The second set of images depicted a lady Mistress taking a whip to her pet, a male. Opposite, two women shared a third whose arms were bound behind her.

"And you?" he asked. "Does it mean you, also, would take me as your pet?"

He tapped a picture of a dark-haired Mistress straddling her blindfolded slave. The woman threw her head back in ecstasy, arching her spine, breasts jutting. She peered through heavily kohled eyes half lidded in lust, and the beads of a golden headdress bounced around her shoulders with the force of her fucking.

Like me, the woman bore tattoos and paint, and piercings through her nose, nipples, eyebrows. Besides her dark features where mine were fair, we did look similar.

I shook my head. "No. I am no Mistress. I delight in feeding *your* hungers, my barbarian. My pleasure comes from satisfying you."

Setting aside the book for a moment, he drew me nearer so he could take my chin in his hand. Almost obliged to, I slid down onto his lap, never breaking our eye contact.

"You are hard." I ran my tongue across my upper lip. "I can feel it."

"A condition I find myself in more and more often lately," he rumbled.

I pulled closer, spreading my legs to straddle him so he could feel the heat of my yearning for him. "Something you ought to understand, *Master...*"

Lightly, I ground against him, and my lips brushed the cup of his ear. "I am a wanton slut at heart. For a brute like you, a man who can conquer me so utterly, and fuck me with such savage demand... *oh*, I will come for you. The feel of your cock... the *taste* of it... My mind is full of fantasies, and in them you use me night after night, feasting your desires, and make me come so ferociously I lose my mind."

Bannon licked his lips. For a second, I expected he would brush me off, maybe even storm out of the room as he had before.

Instead, he whispered, "Show me."

I grinned. Without another word, I looped my shackled wrists around his neck and pressed my hot sex—naked, under the sarong—to the rigid swell of his cock. Even such simple contact electrified me and made my nipples tingle. Falling into a leisurely, gyrating motion, I let out a moan.

"You *smell* like sex to me, and—*ah!*—oh, I could come for you for *days...* "

His hands crept up my thighs to cup my rear, and he dug his fingers deep into my flesh, clutching me tighter against the heft of his erection.

"*Yes*," I breathed. "I like that."

As if to test me, he squeezed harder. "*This?*" he growled. "The little deviant likes pain so much. Why?"

Because I am a beast at heart, I almost said. *Because the sacred serpent has envenomed me to the very core.*

"I always have," was what I told him, riding, rocking, pressing my naked breasts with their winking gold studs and fine gold chain to his broad, bare chest. "Pain is beauty. Deep, dark, black beauty, gilding lovely pleasure."

I panted, arching close. "It brings such delightful awareness... aching tension and a rush of release. It heightens *everything*."

"Are you so close to your climax, Sadira?" His voice came out hushed and full of heat. Through his trews, his cock gave an eager throb.

"If you desire."

"I do," he commanded. "If you really are such a wanton, let me see it. Show me how hungry *you* are."

My thighs tightened around him as I reached the tipping point, and, shuddering, I clung to him, coming, gasping as my body seized. He tilted my head up so he could look me in the face as I trembled and made a soft, sweet sound of pleasure.

"See?" I asked him, breathless. "I am such an easy slut to please. And you, such a forceful, powerful stud. You claimed me, barbarian, and now I long to satisfy you."

His grip on me eased; warm palms caressed tender flesh, gently soothing away the sting his grasping fingers left behind.

"This... practice," he murmured. "I want to understand."

Unlooping my arms from him, I brought up one hand to touch his face.

"You have given me freedom. Do you see that, barbarian?"

"Yes," he replied. "But—"

"How I choose to use my freedom is up to me, isn't it?"

"Of course."

"And if I choose to will it to you? If I *want* to be with you, to be yours? To give you all of me, at least as long as these circumstances hold us together. Is it unworthy?"

He frowned.

"I will not have you assume I am damaged," I said evenly. "Or that my desires are evidence of that damage, something to be doctored and restrained. Whether Alaric Khan harmed me in some way, it doesn't matter now. Not when I submit myself to you. When you claimed me, you treated me to a passion which undid every link in the chain he forged to leash me."

"I left marks on you. Bruises," he retorted.

"Which thrill me." I shivered and cupped his face in my hands. "Each time I feel the ghost of agony from a mark you made on my body in the heat of your passion, I only yearn to be captive to you once more."

Taking a chance—something I never would have done with Alaric—I kissed his lips.

"Subjugation is liberating," I whispered. "It frees me from the chaos in my own mind. I can lay down my strength, my responsibility, and become only an object of indulgence and pleasure."

"But how can you desire such violence, after what Khan did to you? You told me yourself you hated the man and would have put the sword through him with your own hands. Am I to victimize you until you feel the same of me?"

I stroked his coarse beard. "Violence did not make me hate Alaric. I would be lying if I told you there'd been no passion between us. There was. A *lot*. Perhaps because in the depths of my hatred, there existed some wonderful addictive bliss in indulging his—"

Poison.

"Depravity. Like a drunk who guzzles down wine to the brink of death. Alaric satisfied my gluttony to excess. The transgression, the taboo, excited me. So, no. Violence is not what made me hate him."

"Then what?" Bannon laced his fingers together behind my back, firming his hold of me in an easy, comfortable way he might not have even been aware of. "What made his personal consort into his enemy?"

I mulled over it, dropping my hands to my lap.

"Alaric didn't want me tamed," I finally said. "He didn't seek to master me through the promise of fulfillment, an exchange of my power for the reward of pleasure. Alaric... "

A weary sigh escaped me. "Alaric *liked* to hurt me. He derived joy from terrorizing me. From making me fear him. Sometimes it ended in my pleasure as well as his, and so, in a sense I was satisfied. Other times—

especially as I grew older—it ended in threats and horror."

My heart gave an earnest throb, and I tilted forward, pressing one palm lightly to his chest.

"I submit to you because I *wish* to, Bannon Sha'kurukh. I never had a choice with Alaric, whether I liked it or not. *You* are my first choice. I trade my strength for the enticement of yours. Surrender is a relief in light of the pleasure you give me... and that which you take."

I paused, closing my eyes, and fidgeted with the gleaming ring on the front of my collar.

"I want to know the touch of a man whose desire drives him to the limits. One whose stamina for primal passion matches my appetite for the same. If you do want me, I want to know how insatiable it makes you, so you *would* be like a bear fighting to mate, to demand me, possess me. If you can give me that, I will wear your marks with pride. Can you understand my lust for such *violence* now, barbarian?"

I thought perhaps he did: a warm flush colored his throat and cheeks, and if I wasn't mistaken his erection, having briefly subsided, grew rigid and adamant again.

"I want a lover who will bind me and hold me down," I said in an insistent little growl. "For I fear I will shatter to pieces without it. I want you to use your power over me, to still the turmoil inside of me. I want you to crave me and need me and possess me, jealously, and best me with your strength so there is no question I am yours, and yours alone. I want you to *own* me."

Sliding from his lap, I sunk to my knees and rested my hands plaintively on his thighs, leaning close. Close enough to brush his rigid cock with the tips of my fingers, trace the shape of it, once more evident under his leggings.

"In fact," I murmured. "Now I have grown so wet trying to explain myself, I find I *want* all of those things... *right... now.*"

CHAPTER NINE

I ROSE TO my feet in one long, languid movement, vividly aware of the broad swaths of amber sunshine bathing the room. The links binding my shackles chimed softly; the bright arches of the window casements and the wide-open doors tickled me with a sense of exposure.

Bannon's guards still waited outside. They would have heard all I'd said, and if one of them looked in at just that moment they would see me slip the sarong from my hips, letting it cascade from my body and puddle, shimmering, at my feet. The pleasant afternoon breeze, light and sweet with the scents of agapanthus and grevillea, buffeted my bare flesh, raising goosebumps on my arms and my flush, stiffened nipples. In the slant of the light the gold studs through each pink tip winked and gleamed for him.

Bannon's gaze roamed over me, appreciative of my strong, lissome body scrolled with tattoos, scarred by ligature marks of past bondage. He rose, bringing one hand up to run it through my hair. Instead of combing all the way through it with his callused fingers, though, he seized me in a firm grip and jerked me closer to him. Burying his face in my blonde mane, running his other hand slowly down my side, he inhaled the scent of me with a soft sound of delight.

"Sadira..." he growled against my hair.

I arched to him. "How long has it been, barbarian? How long since you had a woman to warm your bed?"

"Too long," he murmured. "Since my wife died."

The weight of his erection pressed to my belly, and he slid his hand down to cup the roundness of my bare pink bottom.

"You have a loyal heart." I leaned into him, slow and sensual, relishing the heat of his skin and the scent of wild, luscious desire. "As long as we are together here, in this place, let us make each other happy."

"Aye... " His voice sounded dreamy, far away. "At least... that long."

Closing one hand possessively around my throat, he pushed me, silently compelling me to lie back on the table. With his other hand he unclasped the heavy iron belt around his waist, prying open the front of his breeches to free his ready cock.

Bannon loomed over me; his urgent, straining erection pressed close into the softness of my mons. Rough knuckles ran down the side of one breast, down my ribs and to my tightly resisting thighs. He shoved his free hand, like a spade, between my legs, grabbing hungrily for my wet sex.

"Let me see it, Sadira."

His fingers dug deep into me, like a potter shaping clay, drawing a shuddering gasp from my lips. I obeyed, spreading my thighs, baring myself to him. Everywhere our skin touched I grew hot with fever, electrified.

"Will you fuck me, barbarian?" I whispered. "Please?"

Bannon hoisted my leg over his shoulder and landed a fierce, stinging slap on my ass. "My new pet has such a dirty mouth."

"I can strive to be more modest, if you wish?"

"*No.*" He rocked against me, teasing me with the heft of his cock. "Say it *again.*"

I'd grown so wet I thought I might come the instant he touched me. He slid two big fingers into me, and I sucked in a tight breath, arching desperately under his hold. The first sweet blush of delight shivered through me as he stroked and teased.

"Please fuck me?"

"Louder."

"Please *fuck* me, Master!"

He withdrew his hand, replacing strong digits with the hot shape of his cock. I groaned as he nudged his shaft along my folds, pressing close in a gentle, fluid, grinding motion. Keeping me pinned with the hand at my throat, he entered me at last in one smooth, ferocious thrust.

I rolled my head back with a short cry of pleasure. Raising my bound hands together to his chest I pushed, as though to thrust him away, but he leaned in harder and his fingers dug into my waist.

"What a wicked, wet girl," he growled.

"Yes... " I moved my hips in reply to him, welcoming him deeper. "*Yes...*"

The scent of him lit a fire of hunger in my belly. Strong and delicious and darkly compelling, like steel and leather and the height of a burning autumn. A virile, sexual smell, wild pheromones, like a drug on his skin. I breathed him in, intoxicated, tightening around him.

Every thrust of his cock filled me with tight, sweet bliss, swelling up from my loins to my core in warm, luscious pleasure, heightened by his rough grasp on my hip, the possessive power of his hand at my throat. He growled in my ear, words broken in ravenous, lustful abandon, more like the grunts and snarls of his animal namesake.

Bannon seized my chin in his hand. "Come for me."

I moaned in response.

"Look me in the eyes and *come*."

"Oh... oh, barbarian—"

The rush of powerful, shamefully *good* pleasure swelled and climbed within me. I cried out, loud in my ecstasy, as the crash of orgasm overtook me. I came hard, squeezing my legs around Bannon while my mind soared high, high above it all. I was floating—*flying*—and it had never felt so beautiful before.

After some seconds Bannon withdrew, a smile on his face, nursing his cock and watching me. I groaned for him, pressing my legs together to try and contain the climax, but hot, salacious dampness bathed my thighs.

"*Oh...* " I breathed, twitching, quivering with the dizzy pleasure. "But... but you didn't..."

With a grin he grabbed me by the arm, sliding me roughly off the table and to my knees before him. He thrust his cock into my mouth, salty and bitter and sticky with the taste of my own climax. It took only a few quick thrusts before he spilled thick, sweet semen down my throat.

Once I swallowed down every drop, he allowed me to relax back onto my heels. Without being asked, I opened my mouth to show him nothing remained, as I expected he'd want me to do.

A glow of deep satisfaction tingled along my skin. He'd left me sated in a way I'd rarely had the luxury to feel.

Bannon knelt beside me and wrapped me in his arms. He cradled me to his chest, and he was warm.

"Sadira," he murmured softly. "Did that satisfy your... chaos?"

"Oh, yes," I panted.

"I can't say I understand these customs you embrace. But... I do want you. Goddess Sherida, I want you. And I want... *more.*"

Yes, more. The serpent's poison is ecstasy, in the beginning. But what will you do, Red Bear, when you see how deep it runs in me?

A thought for later. If such a time ever came at all. For now, our union might only last the length of his occupation. Perhaps soon, he would return to his homeland, and I must explore my options for a life after Alaric.

Later, though. Later.

"Did we come to an agreement, just now?" I rested my head on his shoulder, listening to his heartbeat. The steady rhythm filled me with a tiny, childlike joy.

"Yes. I suppose we did."

He glanced at the book still lying on the table. "We have some interesting conversations ahead, Sadira."

Perhaps at the same time, we remembered where we were. The bright, easy light had grown a deeper ochre; the evening birds chattered their quiet welcome back to the world. Bannon and I glanced at each other with sheepish grins as we recalled the doors to the library were still wide open, the guards still stationed just outside.

"What a terrible little brat you are," Bannon teased, rocking me in his arms. "Now I'll have to ply those two with liquor or else never hear the end of it."

From his pocket he produced a key and popped my manacles open. I gave a start, dumbfounded at the gesture, and rubbed reflexively at the sore, reddened flesh of my wrists.

"Put your skirt back on, go to your bedchambers, and enjoy a long bath. Refresh yourself and then wait for me. There are matters I must settle with my soldiers yet, and I want to speak with the boy who attacked my kinswoman. I'll meet you in an hour. I mean to have another taste of you before I put you to bed, Sadira. Perhaps *several* tastes."

HE MUST HAVE forgotten my anxiety over the bedchambers, and I'd forgotten to say anything when he'd ordered me back to them. It seemed a moot point, though: from the moment I shut the great doors behind me—also shutting out the vile disdain of my guards—the apprehension fled. My uneasy sense of isolation kept silent.

Gazing over the dark room, I understood why.

Bannon would come to me soon. I wouldn't be alone, trapped with my unhappy memories or the vile remnants of Alaric's presence. The mad king's scent, his whispering dead voice... gone. Like me—like everything—these chambers belonged to the Red Bear now.

I smiled. My body brimmed with the shivering sweet aftermath of our delectable tryst.

As I undressed though, preparing for my bath, a low, rasping moan made me jump. I blinked at my reflection, then noticed the window behind me. The golden afternoon light had darkened by degrees: its mellow glow now slanted to an ugly, burnished red. A familiar—and foreboding—sky.

My heart dropped. An unpleasant shiver ran across the line of my shoulders as I moved to the window. Below, the sand and scree beyond the castle walls scraped and whipped in a furtive wind.

Sandstorm.

CHAPTER TEN

THE WIND GROANED and wailed, hotter than ever, dry and scorching. Dark thunderheads crouched on the horizon, but they'd bring no rain. Leaning out the window, I watched them, trying to judge their distance, and how hard the storm might blow.

I should have recognized the sound right away. That awful, droning voice of the wind.

Vashtaren sandstorms played terrible games with the mind and body. People and animals turned strange. Sometimes morose, sometimes paranoid, sometimes manic. I'd known people to take sick with seemingly no cause. Others could fall victim to seizure or embolism. Now and then, someone took their own life.

Once, though I hadn't expected my regular cycle for weeks, I bled. It had seemed no different than my normal menses, except for the unusual timing. But that was eerie enough. As though the storm called it from me. As though it tapped my very womanhood to drink it like a demon in the night.

I drummed my fingers on the window casement and grumbled.

Don't let it bother you. It'll pass, as all storms do.

Half an hour later, the scrape of the door announced Bannon's arrival. I stood in the smaller of the two bathing chambers, staring down at the second strange surprise of the night: the stone tub where I normally bathed had been split by an enormous black crack.

"How?" I murmured to myself.

The ugly fracture reminded me of the jagged fangs of sunset vipers, the venomous desert snakes infamous for lurking in rooms warmed by the sun and stirring only at dusk. They struck any poor fool unlucky enough to enter without noticing them. I'd been bitten once as a child. The sharp-edged, savage break in the stone recalled the same jarring, merciless wound. Curt, abrupt, devastating.

Cursed.

Bannon came up behind me to peer over my shoulder. "Well. That seems problematic."

"It didn't have a crack this morning." I crossed my arms and tilted my head to the side. "I can't see what might have caused it. Not a quake. Someone must have taken a hammer to it, or a mace."

Probably my guards. I didn't voice the suspicion to Bannon, though.

Bannon pursed his lips. "Nothing to be done. I suppose we can ask for a wooden tub to be brought up, for now. We'll find an alternative arrangement for you tomorrow."

I hesitated to tell him of the master bathing chambers with Alaric's opulent fountains and pools—conditioning still told me to avoid the sorcerer's favorite places. When Bannon cocked an eyebrow at me, though, evidently noticing my caution, I nodded to the compartment within.

"Alaric's spa lies beyond."

A smile spread over his face. "Well, if there is yet a hot bath to be had, let's have it! Go on in, as I told you."

He returned to the main room, and I watched after him. As before, the weight of his instructions— not heavy or difficult, but instructions nonetheless— alleviated the tension brought back by the hovering sandstorm and the inexplicable destruction of my basin. The tub itself meant nothing, of course, but it *had* been mine. Like my dog pillow. Neither one held any sentimental value, but their mistreatment could only affect one person.

Yes, it must have been one of the guards. They smashed it, angry I'd run off from them in the courtyard. A reasonable explanation. And reason seemed easier to come by with Bannon near.

I want a lover who will bind me and hold me down... for I fear I will shatter to pieces without it.

Casting one final glance at the cracked tub, I stepped through the archway into Alaric's grand saunas.

Alaric, so far as I knew, *never* bathed in something so common as a washtub. I'd been allowed into this decadent pleasure hall before, but only to entertain. Two wide, white stone pools steamed with water heated in iron tanks off the kitchens below and fed into the spa via aqueduct.

The floor had been hewn of rough granite, left coarse and unpolished to prevent slipping in the lingering puddles and wet footprints. Condensation glistened and trickled down slender, ivory pillars standing along a raised colonnade. Fixtures carved onto these held silver trays of soaps, lotions, and oils, and a fountain of fabricated waterfalls formed an extravagant centerpiece.

I circled to light the glass lamps hanging in sconces around the room. The king had always added more of his sickening cinnamon and bergamot oils to the bath, but thankfully those days were over. With a flicker of vindictive joy, I plucked up two red phials from the tray of fragrances, then dropped them down one of the drains in the floor.

"Never have to choke on *that* reeking fog again," I muttered to myself. Considering the other aromas, I tapped a finger to my lips. What scent would Bannon prefer?

Just then, something smooth and dry slithered past my ankle. A sly hiss rose up from near my feet. I shot a panicked glance downward, but the steam obscured my vision. A dark, winding shadow glided across the stones.

With a short cry I stumbled, falling straight for the solid granite shelf of one of the waterfalls. I thrust out my hands and caught myself on the edge, narrowly avoiding cracking my skull.

Eye of Akolet! It was a snake. I felt its scales, it was a snake!

Again, I imagined the sunset vipers curled up in hidden places, lying in wait to strike the unsuspecting heel. But sunset vipers favored dry, hot rooms and desert sand. Humid, steaming sanctuaries were the lairs of a different serpent: the deadly delta asp.

But... there was nothing. No sinuous, winding reptile. No trailing ripples in the water where it might have disappeared. The musical trickle of the waterfalls and patient drip of condensation were the only sounds.

I... imagined it. I must have slipped on my own. Tripped over my own ankle.

Creeping doubt raised goosebumps along the backs of my arms. I scanned the room, half expecting the gathered sorcerers of the Order waiting for me amid the clouds of steam.

"It's just the storm," I assured myself. "Just an ugly sandstorm, scaring you like a child."

I shook away my dread and straightened. Selecting the first perfume my fingers closed on—aroma of desert rose—I added a measured dose to the fountain. As the sweet, light scent bubbled in the falls and down into the baths, I shed my clothing, picked a tray of soaps and exfoliants, and slipped into the steaming basin.

The tingle of hot water swallowed me up, setting my whole body to pins and needles, making me catch my breath. After a second, I let it out with a quiet groan of satisfaction and relaxed, tilting my head back to soak my hair.

"*Oh...*"

After a long, luxurious moment, all thoughts of vipers and asps and lurking cultists faded away.

Gradually my skin adjusted to the temperature. I slid onto a stone bather's bench set into the side of the pool. The next thing I knew, the great door to the chambers opened again, rousing me from my bliss. Bannon came to the edge of the pool and paused there, gazing down at me.

"Well," he said, voice soft. "Don't you look at home?"

Cool, watery reflections from the bath licked at his figure, illuminating smooth lines and muscle. He stripped off his vest and then, more slowly, his trews.

Shameless, I watched him. When he stood naked before me, I let him see my appreciative interest, conspicuously admiring the fluid beauty of his form. Wetting my lips, I spoke in a soft, throaty voice.

"My Master is most beautiful."

"Is he now?" Bannon replied in a tone that was half chuckle, half hungry growl. "Careful, kitten... I might have to hurt this man who captivates you so."

I laughed. How could I *laugh* so easily? In Alaric's world, I'd been so stoic, humor itself so... frivolous.

I scooted forward on the stone seat to let Bannon slide in behind me. As I did, it came to me. Humor, laughter, flirting—all required a give and take in a way Alaric never employed with me. They were interactions between equals, or near equals at least, and Alaric and I had *never* been equal. In his world, laughter belonged to him, and—as part of his purview to select each thing I may or may not have—he hadn't shared it with me.

Bannon settled into the water, sending a silent ripple along its surface. His broad thighs rested on either side of me, and he wrapped his arms around me, pulling me into his lap. His dusky skin still smelled of sweat and our earlier fucking. I tilted my head back against his chest and inhaled.

Bannon bent to kiss the top of my head as his hands wrapped around my midsection. Along his neck, the wild pheromones lacing his flesh smelled even stronger, and more delicious. I took a chance, pressing my lips to his skin.

So much of this scene clashed with what I understood of passion. Bannon's hands searched my body, gliding easily over the flesh of my belly, down my abdomen, and over the smooth swell of my hips. His palms, callused but gentle, stroked me, learning the rise and dip of my curves, exploring my brands and tattoos with his fingertips.

"You are such a beautiful woman." He pressed his lips to my earlobe and reached for the tray of soaps I'd put at the edge of the tub.

"Do you wish for me to bathe you?" I leaned from his lap to take the tray first, chagrin creeping up the back of my neck, but Bannon tugged me back into place.

"Another time." He picked up a cake of waxy soap and scrubbed it between his palms. I watched with puzzlement, until he brought his sudsy hands to my shoulders, and worked the lather over my skin.

"I was very hard with you earlier." His breath at my ear made me shiver. "And you endured so well. It is my turn to tend to *your* needs."

His warm, strong palms kneaded taut muscle, working apart the tension of days with smooth, skillful motion. Without meaning to, I let out a gentle groan, and Bannon shook with laughter.

"Relax into me, girl." He moved his hands lower, pressing thumbs firmly into the muscles of my middle back, then working his way under my arms to massage my studded breasts. As his fingers brushed my nipples, I gave a tiny gasp, and pressed myself to his touch.

"I said relax," he repeated. His lips found the back of my neck—the place just under my ear—and he kissed me. His hands eased me out of my arching position and drew me back to a soft, neutral place. "I will feast on your breasts again, little she-cat, but all in good time. I am taking care of *you* now."

"Barbarian," I protested. "I told you, I do not play the role of Master. It is my place to serve you—"

"This isn't service. My kitten was meek and yielding today, while I fucked her most lustfully. With these hands I pried apart your thighs and held you down by the throat. I know you like rough play, Sadira, but it doesn't mean you're to be left without some gentle care after."

"But I—"

He squeezed me to him, kissing my shoulder. "When I ride my horses hard, I give them a thorough cleaning and rubdown after. Now hush up and let me bathe you."

I fell silent. After a moment his hands found a spot of tension on my neck, and I let out a soft moan of pleasure.

"That's my girl," Bannon murmured. I closed my eyes and rested in his arms.

When he'd satisfied himself bathing me, Bannon allowed me to straddle him and wash his body too. Hungry anticipation filled me when the stiff shape of his cock nudged my sex, but Bannon made no move to enter me. I lathered soap across his broad chest and over his shoulders, leaning close to press my wet, slick breasts to him, and it earned me a knowing, mischievous smile. When I rocked my hips to him, though, inviting him further, Bannon slid his hands under my buttocks and held me up, shaking his head.

"No, no, kitten."

"But you said—"

"I know what I said. But I have other things in mind. We still must discuss the *terms* of this arrangement. Tell me what rules you kept before."

I pressed my lips together and resumed washing him, sliding off his lap to scrub his neck and back.

"I slept on the dog pillow, as I mentioned."

"We won't be continuing *that,*" Bannon assured me. "My woman sleeps in my bed."

My woman. A swift streak of pride warmed my chest.

"I was not permitted to wear clothes within the bedchambers. Not permitted to preen over my appearance. Not permitted to touch or be touched... "

I cited the many edicts Alaric had lain down for me, and the punishments and rewards he attached to them. Bannon nodded as I spoke, stroking his beard. By the time I'd explained the extent of my slavery, I'd finished washing him, and we sat face-to-face in the water, each leaning on the lip of the bath. I marveled to find I'd been speaking to him with a casual ease I'd never slipped into before.

I bowed my head. "I apologize, Sir, if I've rambled."

"Sir?" he repeated, rubbing his chin. "I do like that better than *Master.* Let's have you call me *Sir* from now on. And I admit I do like the thought of you slinking about, always naked. We'll keep that rule as well if you're willing."

I stared at him. "Willing? Of course, Sir."

"Is there anything else?"

I shot a quick glance over my shoulder, toward the hall.

"Alaric kept another chamber for pleasure," I admitted. "One for... more primal indulgences."

Bannon furrowed his brow and tapped his fingers on the granite lip of the pool. "Such as?"

A dozen explanations raced through my mind, but each one seemed too much. How would I explain to Bannon the spanking benches and the sawhorse where Alaric chained me down for long sessions of whipping, or dripping hot candle wax over my curves? What would my new Master think of the stocks where I'd been held immobile, while my breasts and buttocks were groped and pinched and fondled?

Perhaps Bannon sensed my hesitation. Reaching out to caress my cheek, he murmured, "We'll discuss it another time."

I had no chance to answer, as he scooped me up in his arms and rose from the tub. I shivered at the sudden cold breath of air on my wet skin, and wrapped my arms around Bannon's neck, pressing into his heat. He carried me back to the hearth in the main room and laid me down on a pelt of desert antelope.

A fire already crackled for us. He must have lit it while I prepared the bath, and though we'd taken our time and the flames had fallen low, he stoked them back to life with fresh kindling and a rousing stir of the poker.

Outside, the wind moaned and whistled against the castle walls. It rattled the shutters, but as I basked in the light of Bannon's crackling blaze and in the warm desire in his burning dark eyes, I barely noticed. The storm was outside. The barbarian, my new Master and new lover, was inside, with me.

He crawled over my body, kissing my belly, breasts, neck. He took my earlobe gently in his teeth

111

while his hand slipped up to my throat and closed over it in firm possession. Tracing the tip of his tongue along the curve of my pinna, he bumped his hips to mine, letting me feel his erection anew.

"We'll discuss other rules as we find the need for them, I expect. For now, though, I do have a few of my own."

His free hand stole down between us, and he traced the head of his cock up and down the cleft of my sex.

"This pussy," he told me, "belongs to *me*. Say it."

"Yes," I replied joyfully. "Yes, Sir, my pussy is yours."

"You wish to be my personal slut? Then if I tell you I wish to *fuck* this pussy, you will give it to me."

"Yes, Sir." I lifted my hips to meet his questing member. His harsh words, stripped of civil pretense, filled me with wicked delight. A sweet flush rose to my breasts and a yearning sigh escaped me. "Yes, it is yours to fuck."

"And your ass, should I want it." He ground against me, making me groan. "And your mouth. Any part of you that can be fucked belongs to me. You understand?"

"Any part of me that can be fucked," I agreed. "I am yours, oh Red Bear... your pet, your possession. Your *toy*."

He bent to kiss me. "Are you ready for me to make love to you?"

"Yes!" I reached up to cup his face in my hands, gazing adoringly at him.

Bannon laughed, a warm, sweet sound like honey and liquor to my soul.

"Goddess Sherida, you really are an insatiable beast..."

THE YOWLING OF the hot desert winds blasted open the shutters, startling us from our sleep. The sandstorm gales sent dry, scorching lashes in at us through the window casement. Clouds of yellow dust and grit rendered the sky outside an ugly, bruised ochre, and from the courtyard and the surrounding halls, startled voices arose.

I climbed from the bed to shutter the windows and slide a heavy stone panel across the casement. The hot winds still snuck in, licks and tongues of the Ruined Sands, but the panel shut out the worst of the storm. I ground at my stinging eyes. Swirls and feathers of golden sand made patterns across the floor.

"I will never get used to these blasted sandstorms," Bannon grumbled. He rose from the bed to knot a bolt of cloth around his waist.

"They are hell to endure." I toyed with the ring on my collar. "This one is bad. I've never seen one with winds this hot."

The storms drove everyone indoors. They closed you into *yourself*. These were the nights I'd begun to understand Alaric truly, and to despise him. Perhaps only the maddening excuse of the winds made it possible, or perhaps the restless claustrophobia pried open my heart to let my deadly emotions prowl free.

"Here now, Sadi, stop it. You'll give yourself bruises."

Bannon took my hands. I hadn't noticed I'd wrapped my arms around myself, digging my nails into my own biceps as I stared at the stone panel. I half expected it to shatter inward and pelt us with fragments of rock.

I schooled my response. Easier, with Bannon's permission. His instruction relieved the weight on my anxious mind.

"Come," he said, and gestured for me to sit on the end of the bed. I did, and he cradled my head in his hands, searching my eyes.

"Are you all right?"

I nodded. The warmth of his palms comforted me. Bannon brushed one thumb softly along my cheek, and I leaned into his touch. The simple motion of one thumb soon spread, and he massaged my temples. After some moments of this, I opened my eyes, and found myself so much more at ease.

"Better?" he asked.

"Yes." Taking his hands, I kissed each finger. "Thank you, Sir."

I gathered his hands into my own to rub my cheek affectionately over the backs of his knuckles. The ritual eased my mind from the storm, focusing me on the sensation of his skin, his scent, and his warmth.

"Little kitten," he murmured.

A scream of the wind outside made me jump, and he gripped my shoulders to steady me. Without a word, he lowered his face to mine. I tilted my chin up to kiss him, and—

Someone assailed the door, the violent screech of iron scraping stone like a razor down my spine. My guards rushed into the room,, gripping their weapons as though they expected attack. Behind them with her own deadly-looking halberd, came the tall woman who'd shackled me earlier.

"Captain," the woman began without preamble. "The young man from this morning—he's attacked again. This time he nearly killed our healer."

CHAPTER ELEVEN

I BLINKED. AT first the report made no sense to me, but then I looked again to the shuttered window. The wind gave a scream outside.

"The storm..." I breathed.

Bannon's lieutenant shot a sour glance in my direction, then switched her attention to Bannon. I hadn't bothered to cover my nakedness as he had, and this stony warrior evidently disapproved. Even though the woman wasn't looking at me anymore, I made a point of drawing back my shoulders in icy hauteur and gave all the guards the chilliest glare I could manage.

Bannon straightened and reached for his trews. "I'll be there immediately, Mara."

I rose to dress and follow him without a thought.

Mara gave me another ugly look. "Should the black magician's *witch* be coming? It will only complicate matters."

I cut a furious glare at her. To my relief, though, Bannon inclined his head in a nod.

"It's all right. Sadira defended our kinswoman from this young man before."

"Sir—"

Bannon raised a hand. "She comes."

Mara wrinkled her nose, but turned away, leading the other soldiers back into the hall.

I donned leather leggings and a boiled leather bodice—actual soldier's wear rather than my ornamental garb—and fell in at Bannon's side. He assessed me, and nodded approval.

Under Alaric's rule, the castle's place of healing had been an alchemical laboratory, overseen by the sorcerers. Bannon's people had appropriated a portion of the former slave's barracks, close to the castle's main hall, for the convalescence of those injured in the war.

"Our chief healer died during the first raids on your capital," Bannon explained.

I almost corrected him—*no, not* my *capital*—but held my tongue as we hurried toward the new lodgings of the injured.

"Three of his students survived the battles and have taken charge of triage. We sent word for another of the master healers, but her caravan is late... "

The way he trailed off, and the vague, distant cast of his eyes, pricked my attention. I didn't ask why this news troubled him. The night's attack concerned me more. Had Bannon's lieutenant said it was the same boy involved in the morning's altercation?

He must be an apprentice of the Order after all, I fretted, though it still didn't seem possible. When we reached the scene of the assault, however, all thoughts of *why* were abruptly replaced by questions of *how*.

117

The boy might have been fifteen years old, sixteen at the outside, and scrawny. I hadn't wondered about it before because I'd assumed he'd caught his earlier victim unaware. As I took in the sight of his handiwork now—and him, wan, wide-eyed, trembling in the grip of two of Bannon's warriors—it astonished me.

How could he have done... this?

One of the nurses from Bannon's army sat propped against a wall while another healer examined her. Her right arm jutted the wrong way at the elbow; her nose had been broken, too. One eye already swelled shut, but the other showed the unsettling red stain of burst blood vessels. Bruises bloomed on her throat where large hands closed to strangle her.

Something about those marks looked wrong to me. *Off.* My search moved from the nurse to the boy, then back again, as I tried to pinpoint the reason.

Too big. His hands aren't that size.

The boy's eyes had gone bloodshot, red-rimmed, and full scarlet around the iris. Thick, dark tears ran in tracks like smeared kohl from the corners. The stigmata of the serpent god. *Again.*

I gripped Bannon's arm in a quick, silent plea— *Don't hurt him, it's not his fault*—but I couldn't look away from the rest of the wreckage. The boy hadn't just beaten his nurse. The whole room—a small pantry repurposed to store medical supplies—lay in ruins.

The sharp fragrance of too many medicinal compounds made my throat tighten, and I coughed. Crates of bandages, broken open, lay toppled on their sides, contents unraveled and doused with kerosene; bottles of ointments and remedies were smashed, oozing and drying in tacky splotches on the floor; herbs had been flung from their jars and stamped into powders on the stone.

The expressions on the faces around me told me everyone had reached the same conclusion as I. There were still injured here. Now, how would the healers care for them all?

Mara and Bannon stood with their faces upraised, studying something above. A message had been scrawled overhead, on the ceiling itself, in a crooked hand.

The serpent god repays.

On the ceiling? My mouth dropped open in wordless disbelief. How in the world could this slim pup have done *that?*

The room had fallen silent. The eyes of all Bannon's people, and even the boy, now landed on me, standing in the middle of it all and gaping like a fool. I inclined my head and folded my hands behind my back in a neutral stance.

Bannon inhaled a long, deep breath, crossed his arms over his chest, and addressed his lieutenant.

"What happened, Mara?"

"Merysa took midnight watch over the ward," Mara reported. "She came to check the storage after strange noises caught her attention. Then she found the boy here destroying the supplies."

She gestured at the injured Merysa, who gave a stiff nod. After a pause, Mara added, "She did say she suspected him of sleepwalking. She didn't think it could be deliberate destruction."

"He's got to be one of Order, Captain," said one of the guards. So, the thought had occurred to them, too. "He should be locked in the dungeon with the rest of them."

Nothing about this sat right with me. I'd stand between the barbarians and this desert boy if I had to, until the truth behind his actions was revealed. I couldn't let them imprison him with the twisted, warmongering sorcerers below.

"May I speak?" I asked. Everyone in the room pinned their attention on me, and my skin prickled under the scrutiny. Bannon gestured for me to go on.

"I know the men in the Order of Akolet. I was made to witness many of their rituals. If this boy had studied with one of them, I would know. He can't possibly have undergone the fine discipline and *years* of cultivated study required for magic such as this."

"Then how do you explain the bleeding eyes?" one of the Sanraethi snapped. "You mean to say that's *not* the mark of black magic and evildoing?"

"Peace," Bannon cautioned. "What of the eyes, Sadira? Can you explain it?"

I considered the boy, then shook my head. "Perhaps the work of another. If one of the Order discovered the power to subvert a person's mind—"

The room broke into a rumble of angry, nervous grumbling.

"There's only one member of the serpent's cult still walking free," Mara kept her tone even, but her lips formed a thin line. I stifled the wild urge to snap back, meeting her glowering accusation with a fierce glare.

My heartbeat quickened as Bannon said, in a perfectly calm voice, "Sadira has said she is no witch, Mara. I believe her."

"What proof has she got?" Mara thumped her halberd on the stone floor. "The whole desert knows she was the black magician's most favored. We heard the stories, even back home! Why wouldn't he teach her his magic?"

"I *have no* magic," I repeated for what seemed like the hundredth time. "Alaric *wanted* to harness supernatural power in me, but I disappointed him in that regard."

"And made up for it in others," snapped an older woman, one of the slaves who'd worked as a seamstress for the Vash royalty. I whipped on my heel to retort, but Bannon interceded.

"I'm not interested in what happened when the tyrant Khan ruled this castle," he warned the old woman. "And I will not have anyone starting a fight over it."

More murmured disapproval.

"I beg you not to punish the boy," I said. "He's not to blame, I'm certain."

Bannon considered me, then cast a critical eye at the desert boy, then at Merysa. His silent grimace worried me—an unpleasant flutter of doubt upset my stomach.

He sighed and shook his head. "I can't allow two assaults to go unchecked."

"You can't have him in the dungeon!" I burst out. "Not with our oppressors!"

Bannon shot me a sharp look, cocking one eyebrow in startled rebuke. I recognized the expression: Alaric sometimes stared at me the same way if I surprised him with some thoughtless mistake. I withered and looked down at the floor again, clasping my hands before me and twining my fingers in the metal rings of my bracers.

"I *can't* ignore this," Bannon repeated. "I regret the necessity, and rest assured I'll investigate your suspicions. But for now, I have no choice."

He saw me opening my mouth to protest again and spoke over me. "*Especially* if he may be used again to do even more damage to my people."

Waving a hand at the wreckage of the room, he added, "Or our supplies."

I shut my mouth but pinned him with a rebellious scowl. Bannon returned it with grim authority, holding my gaze long enough to make a silent point, before shifting his attention to Mara.

"Imprison the boy," he commanded. "But put him in a cell *away* from the sorcerers. Bind his fingers in case he has magic of his own, but if I hear anyone has abused or abased him, they'll wind up in a cell, too. Understood?"

Mara nodded to Bannon, then to the guards holding the boy. "You heard the Red Bear. Get to it."

As the crowd broke apart and the Sanraethi moved in to obey—two taking the boy to his prison, two lifting Merysa to help her into the sick room—I continued to glare at Bannon. I knew I'd misspoken. I'd disrespected him, *and* in front of his people.

I also knew Bannon had done what he must. The same thing I would probably do if I'd been forced to decide. But it *hadn't* been my decision, and I was already in for a punishment anyway, so I indulged the luxury of petulance, glowering while the captain conferred with his lieutenant. They made no effort to keep their conversation from me, but I nursed my outrage rather than listening.

Once Mara marched off, Bannon fixed his attention on me again.

"My kitten shows her defiant side." He shook his head. "That was inexcusable, Sadira."

I lifted my chin. All my frustration twisted and wound in knots inside me, making me lightheaded and restless. I wanted to burst. Hot, hateful tears threatened to fall.

"Is this how you will handle us poor desert refugees, then?"

"Calm yourself," he said, using the same warning tone as before.

"Would you have done the same if he were one of *your* people? Or one of the prisoners from some other land? Is it only because he is Vash that you lock him away with those tormentors?"

"Sadira."

He took me by the arms, and even though my anger roiled his touch managed to ground me.

"I *hear* you," he told me. "I understand it frightens you. But *I* must consider what's best for all, *including* the boy. A prison cell may not be comfortable, but it is safe. If you're right and one of the cult is using him, they can make no more use of him now. If you're wrong, I've protected us from a future attack. I *must* be judicious."

Of course, he must, and of course, he'd been as fair as possible. Still, it angered me, and the howling sandstorm rattled my nerves, and above us those horrible words hung like an evil promise.

The serpent god repays.

"This is what I meant before," I whispered, trembling. "About breaking to pieces. Your people... how they scowl at me, how *sure* they are of what I am

123

and where I belong. I want to help, Bannon. I want to *do* something, but—"

"Stop talking."

I did. Still the words seethed inside of me.

"Breathe," Bannon ordered me. "One breath in, one breath out. Why are you *looking* at me like that?"

I hadn't realized I was still scowling. I hung my head.

"I'm sorry, Sir."

He took a step back from me and rested his hands on his hips. "What does a Master do when his slave is so insolent?"

When I didn't answer, I expected him to be angry. He opened his mouth as if he meant to do exactly so, but hesitated and fell silent. It relieved me. I only needed a moment to gather my scattered thoughts.

"He disciplines her," I said. "With a lash, or a switch. Or some other implement."

"Is that what you need right now?"

I bit my lip. I needed *something* to set me right again, something to settle me. The sting of his palm— a familiar comfort. A reassurance.

"Yes," I said in a tight voice. "Please, Sir."

"Turn around and put your hands flat on the wall. Spread your legs. Wider."

We'd examined an illustration in the book earlier demonstrating this form of punishment. I did as ordered, grateful at the firmness of his tone, the smooth yet harsh authority. Book or no book, I'd sensed this power in him from the beginning. He knew what I asked. He understood.

He loomed behind me and his big hand rested on my ass. My breath hitched, just a little, and his other hand came down on my shoulder to steady me.

"Eyes open."

"Yes, Sir," I whispered.

"You're trembling. Why?"

Shaking my head, I replied, "My mind is racing. I can't be still, there's too much... "

I swallowed. I did tremble, and it hurt, because at the same time I *wanted* to be still, and so tried to keep myself rigid.

"Don't do that," he said. "Don't stiffen. Are you afraid of me?"

I uttered an ugly, frantic laugh, focusing steadily on the floor. "No, Sir! Not you. It's... it's the storm. I am always afraid of these storms."

"Relax. The storm isn't important. I can't have you breaking down and especially not in front of the other soldiers. You can't speak to me as you did here tonight."

"Yes, Sir."

"I told you to relax."

"I'm trying," I answered in a soft tone. I couldn't seem to ease my shoulders of their tension.

He loosened my belt and tugged my leggings down to bare my naked rear. No one had shut the door to the storage room. If anyone came back to find us, they would witness my punishment. I didn't mind it, though. It would do, to be witnessed. I only wanted him to do it. Restore order to my mind.

The first stinging slap landed on me, hard, and I bit my tongue.

"You can cry out, if you need to," Bannon said. Then another sweet slap, and before I could catch myself, I gasped. A shudder slipped down my limbs.

"I told you not to be so rigid," Bannon growled at my ear. "Breathe in, and out. *Yield* to me, Sadi."

I remembered the night of his victory when I'd told him I would *not* yield until he proved himself. Tension; combat. Lust came with conquest. This, though... *now*, he instructed me to give over to him. He ordered me to obey.

No lust in this exchange. Not in this act of discipline I deserved. When he commanded me to yield—to submit—there came something deeper, more costly.

Intimacy.

I did as he said. Swallowing back my tension, I made myself breathe. Slowly in; slowly out. My body softened.

Then *slap!* His hand came down and I threw my head back with a startled, voiceless gasp. The wild, singing pain jolted me, rocking me forward on the balls of my feet. With his hand on my shoulder Bannon steadied me again. The next slap came a breath later. I jumped. Gasped.

The spanking pulled my mind from its distraction, pulled me into bright focus. As my round little bottom burned, I basked in the hot flash of his palm striking me, galvanizing me.

Alaric used to make me count each stroke out loud as he disciplined me. Bannon hadn't mentioned it, but out of habit I counted anyway, to myself. He spanked me twelve times, and by the end silent tears ran down my cheeks. Wonderful tears: cathartic, joyous, sweet tears. A release as beautiful as orgasm in its own way, because it softened me, broke me down.

When Bannon let go of my shoulder, he pulled me into his arms, where I quietly cried, and smiled, and relinquished myself.

"Did I hurt you, Sadira?" He took a seat on one of the crates and cradled me to his chest. One thumb brushed a tear from my cheek.

"No, Sir."

"Why are you crying?"

"I just am. It's all right. Really, I'm not hurt. It is... a relief."

I leaned my head on his shoulder, breathing in his warm, lovely scent.

"Do you feel better?" he asked.

"Yes. I'm ready to do what you need of me."

"Good."

He didn't rise, though, not right away. We remained together, him rocking me very slowly, very gently, stroking my hair with one big, warm palm. His other hand slid down, carefully easing slow, patient circles over my sore backside.

"Other soldiers," I murmured after several moments.

"Hm?"

"You said, 'I can't have you breaking down in front of the other soldiers'."

"Yes," he replied. "Circumstances are worse than it appeared. Evidently the regent's caravan and our medicine woman have arrived while we dealt with this matter, and now we have even more trouble on our hands. Congratulations, Sadira. You've been conscripted."

I blinked. "What's happened?"

"Mara's summoning the last apprentice healers and will be back any moment. She'll explain on our way. Are you ready?"

"Yes, Sir."

He slid me off his lap and helped me to my feet, then rose to his own.

"Very good. There's... one other thing you must know before we see the medicine woman."

I nodded, assuming my normal position of obedience with my hands behind my back. Bannon looked me over—assessing me, I realized—and the first sliver of unease slipped under my skin.

"She is my daughter."

CHAPTER TWELVE

STEERING US THROUGH corridors abuzz with curious onlookers, Mara led the way toward the stables. The sandstorm wailed, louder and louder by the minute, and set my teeth on edge. It had driven everyone indoors, except, Mara reported, the small contingent of warriors keeping watch on the walls.

"No one expected the caravan to arrive in the middle of such a squall," she said, never breaking stride. "Only twenty survivors, and most of them injured."

"*Twenty?*" Bannon demanded. "Lieutenant Canaan sent sixty warriors along with the king's brother. You're saying only a third of those forces made it here?"

"According to your daughter, they ran into an ambush at the far borders of Vashtaren. The storm caught them by surprise and gave the enemy the advantage. Others might still find their way to us if they've survived... but Ailsa doesn't seem hopeful."

"Has one of the desert tribes betrayed us after all?" Bannon wondered through gritted teeth.

I kept my thoughts to myself. *More likely the winds drove them mad.*

"What of the regent?" Bannon asked.

Mara frowned and shook her head.

The survivors of the caravan had been rushed into the shelter of the stables, and there a tall young woman with a blazing halo of red hair shouted orders at the uninjured travelers and wide-eyed stable hands, directing triage. The apprentice healers summoned by Mara hurried to help.

Bent over a man propped against a feed hopper, the redhead didn't even look up when Bannon approached with me at his heels. The smells of blood and sweat hung in the air, mingling with the bold whiff of horsehide, sweet hay, and dung.

A cautious, curious discomfort beat in my breast. Ailsa, who might have been only seventeen by the look of her, seemed unaffected by the gore and bloody bone. She resembled her father: they had the same brick-red hair, straight blade of a nose, and serious, thoughtful frown. An impertinent roundness of cheeks and softness of features lingered on her face, however; those, she must have inherited from her mother, along with a buxom feminine figure.

Handing her patient a thick strop of leather and instructing him to bite down on it, Ailsa made efficient work of setting his broken leg. The Sanraethi man's face contorted with anguish and he gave a muffled grunt. Ailsa straightened with a huff and pushed back a thick, damp hank of her messy curls.

"We lost some of our best sword fighters before we even knew it," she said to Bannon. "So far as I can tell they never saw what hit them. *I* barely saw anything through that storm. Forty-some-odd soldiers just swallowed up by the winds and whatever rat bastards ensnared us. I've got Willa with a serious injury to her left arm, and Carrow took some sort of bad blow to one eye. Might lose it. But I've done all I can."

"The king's brother?"

From the tone in Bannon's voice, I guessed he already expected the worse, especially after Mara's dark response.

"Dead," Ailsa confirmed. She swatted at a fly buzzing by her neck. "They say you're out of supplies? How can you be out of supplies, Da?"

"Not *out* of supplies, lass." Bannon crossed his arms over his chest. "Wrecked by a saboteur. Earlier tonight, as a matter of fact, which strikes me as... *convenient.*"

Ailsa pursed her lips, and a pert little line appeared between her brows. "Without more supplies, I've done all I can do here. Do you have anyone to find beds for the injured? Then you and I can discuss the attack."

Bannon nodded. "Stay here. I'll assign a team."

He stepped away to give the order. After he'd gone, Ailsa turned to me for the first time. I braced myself.

Ailsa peered at me, musing over the markings on my skin. Recognition dawned on the girl's face, and her blue eyes—also from her mother, no doubt—widened.

"Goddess Sherida. You're *her*." Ailsa said it with no hint of compunction in her tone. "You're the black magician's woman."

I pressed my lips together and exhaled a quiet sigh. Bannon's daughter continued her assessment, pausing to grimace when she noticed the leather collar and bracers.

"Lord Khan's infamous consort." Ailsa put her hands on her hips. "Allied with my father, have you?"

"I have."

Ailsa took a step closer, looking me straight in the eyes. She searched them, as though she could read in them some hidden secret.

"Careful, Lady Ailsa."

One of the guards joined us. I recognized him: the one at whom I'd thrown the platter. He stepped between us, nudging Ailsa a step back as though I carried a plague.

"You have it half right. She was the black magician's *whore*."

Oh, honestly. I didn't even hit *you with the stupid plate!*

"The saying is wrong," he continued. "A she-cat *can* shed her spots, if to save her hide. She'll mewl prettily for any tom who—"

I slapped him across the face. When he rebounded and looked like he might strike me back, I squared my shoulders, lifted my chin, and fixed him with a defiant stare.

"You know nothing. You know *nothing* about me, you arrogant, ignorant pig!"

"Stop!" Ailsa elbowed us apart. "*Goddess Sherida,* does this seem like the right time to assault each other?"

The guard scrubbed a hand across his face and spat at my feet. "Keep an eye on this witch, milady. She's working wiles on the captain. Has him giving her liberties when she ought to be jailed with the rest of the fanatics below. If you ask me, *she's* the one who put the desert boy up to ruining our supplies."

Ailsa's lips twitched, very subtly, but I caught it. Bannon's reappearance put an abrupt end to any further discussion, though.

"What in the name of all things is happening here?" he demanded.

I lowered my gaze but didn't relax my shoulders or bow my head. "This soldier and I had a difference of opinion. Sir."

"He earned the slap," Ailsa added, and I dared to smile at the other woman, relieved. The gesture proved premature, however. In a low, disapproving tone Ailsa added, "Apparently, *Da,* you and I have more to discuss than medicine."

THE SANDSTORM LASTED days, and the castle grew restless as it stretched on and on. The news of the ruined medical supplies spread quickly, and despite Ailsa's attempts to reassure the group, unhappy murmurs wormed their ways through the halls. Many who had been injured in the battle for the capital still lay in sickbeds and relied on the medicine for full recovery.

With the storm forcing everyone inside, where would we find more supplies? What if more were injured, or an illness swept through the ranks?

The worst were those who'd lost limbs, like the poor woman, Willa. Ailsa hadn't been able to save her arm after all, and the amputation had to be done without any calmative or proper remedies. I offered what I could, bringing the tinctures of cannabis and harmal from Alaric's stores, and teas of blue lotus and opium poppy.

Ailsa—she was nineteen, it turned out, eleven years younger than I—accepted the drugs to distribute among the most desperate sufferers. She hadn't seemed to make up her mind about me as the former king's whore and the Red Bear's new, transgressive bedmate, but she was pragmatic. Medicine bought at least a temporary peace between us.

Meanwhile, I made an effort to find my new place among the castle's inhabitants but met with increasing resistance. The soldiers grumbled when I joined their exercise or volunteered for shifts at watch. I offered to work on the castle reconstruction or the deployment of its resources with the other freed slaves, but only Rayya would speak with me. The others looked upon me with suspicious and dread. *They* had all cast off their leashes and chains and put their humiliation behind them. I still wore my collar.

Perhaps in their minds, I clung to it. They regarded me with confusion and careful distance in their expressions. There were no more desert masters—so why would I still wish to serve?

Whom did I still wish to serve?

I could have told them Bannon had taken my leash, but they still wouldn't understand. How could I blame them? Perhaps if I hadn't been slave to the most poisonous snake of all, I would be content with their gentler, emancipated life. But—as Bannon himself had noted—I was a deviant. I didn't know how to set aside the creature within.

Alaric kept me so well, I mused one evening, examining my naked body in the mirror again. *Alone. Concealed. Maybe I will find other Masters, but part of me will always be his and carry him with me. Like a black dog. Like an evil omen. That, I can never cast off.*

Though the sandstorm never truly lifted, at times the screams of the wind fell to moans, and the scorching, stinging heat mellowed to a tolerable level. Bannon and his lieutenants agreed to rotating small shifts of soldiers along the castle walls as lookouts, equipped for the changing temperature and torrential sand. I volunteered, and patrolled the ramparts from post to post, reporting to soldiers who eyed me and dismissed me quickly.

By the third such rotation, still no one had seen any hint of life beyond the castle. The streets of Vashtaren could barely be glimpsed outside the walls. There'd been no sign of the attackers who ambushed Ailsa's caravan, but still, an oppressive sense of disquiet hung in the air.

Because it hides in the wind. I shivered and pulled my balaclava close, covering my face and nose. *It hides... predator and scavenger. It waits in the sand for the mice, trapped in this castle, to run out. We will wait for the storm to catch its breath, and then we'll run. We'll run even when the wind howls again and the dead who lie in the streets of Vashtaren rise to stop us.*

Where had *that* come from? My fingers came up reflexively to touch my collar, but it was tucked under the woolen fabric of my tunic. My dream came back to me: the hands of the priests snatching and pulling at me, the yawning grave of the king hissing and rattling with a thousand hungry, unseen snakes.

The serpent god repays.

"It's certain *she's* the cause of it."

Coming to a landing on the steps to one of the guard's posts, I overheard a man's words from the walkway above. Wrapped in cloaks against the whipping sands, two of Bannon's people kept watch. Their faces might be hidden, but I recognized the voices. An older man called Jarl had spoken first; his partner, Chrissa, responded with a short, noncommittal sound.

"He shouldn't leave her walking free." Jarl scuffed his boots in the sand gathering by his feet, grumbling. He bore an old injury, a badly healed break which crippled one leg and gave him an uneven, twisting gait. When he stood, especially for long periods of time, I had noticed he grew restless, kicking his bad leg, shaking it, shifting back and forth from foot to foot.

"Damned concubine to the desert's craziest zealot. She belongs in chains."

"Captain says she's one of the slaves," Chrissa replied. "One of the people we came to free."

Jarl replied with an ugly snort, pulling his balaclava free just enough to hawk and spit over the side of the wall.

"You think so? How many of the free slaves act like *her?* Slinking and doting like a hungry cat? The slut is softening him by his cock. She whores herself to him, and he swallows her lies. Did you know the guards outside her quarters say she demands he beat her? They hear her crying out and begging him to strike her, or to be trussed and ridden like a horse."

136

His voice lowered, and I almost lost it in the sound of the wind.

"I think she has him ensorcelled. Maybe that *ritual* of claiming—she made him do it, you know—is really a means to sow the seeds of her spell. I'm telling you he's not himself since he bedded the bitch."

In a pique, I stalked up the stairway leading to the parapet. I shot the two Sanraethi a scowl, and even under my balaclava I knew they'd recognize me by the tattoos over my eye.

Striding up to Jarl, meeting him face to face, I jabbed him in the chest with one finger.

"You've got a lot to say, for someone so sure I'm a witch. Next time show some backbone and say it to my face."

Before he could answer, I spun away from him, continuing my circuit along the wall. Fiery indignation burned in my chest, and I furiously regretted not challenging the man to a fight right then and there.

But fighting won't help. It won't make them trust me.

A violent gust of wind pushed me back toward the fortifications, and sand showered down, obscuring the view ahead. Braced on the stones, I shut my eyes and uttered a growl to myself.

The serpent god repays.
Maybe they're right to fear me.

CHAPTER THIRTEEN

AFTER MY CONFRONTATION on the wall, I avoided Bannon during the daytime. No point in encouraging mutinous rumors with even more familiarity, so I found reason to be useful elsewhere, and let him captain his people.

Every night, though, I embraced him, grateful for the relief of his presence and the surrender of my will. We read more of the book on mastery and mused over its illustrated rituals. I sat on the floor by his feet while he stroked my hair, and I read to him the practices within. We selected simple figures and played them out, happy to exhaust our tensions with gluttonous pleasure.

I knelt for him as he tied my arms behind my back, testing patterns and designs reaching from my wrists to my elbows. Once he'd bound me, he teased me with tools from the bedside collection: tormenting me until I writhed with the touch of downy feathers or the strands of a velvety whip; delivering sweet, light slaps from a riding crop to my breasts, buttocks, and thighs; fixing weighted clamps over my studded nipples.

Afterwards, he'd unwind the ropes and marvel at the braided impressions left on my skin. He kissed the marks, followed them with his tongue, agitated them with a deep press of his finger drawn down their reddened lines. We'd fuck, or sometimes we'd make love—it depended on how harsh the day had been for us both. Then he'd wrap me in an embrace and hold me, telling me over and over how pleased I'd made him, and what a good girl I'd been.

I never asked him to stop. I wanted the ache, the tenderness, the unabated, animal need. I wanted him to climax deep inside of me, marking me in the most primal way. I wanted every ounce of his anxiety, tension, and worry, exhausted in the sating of his most savage, most beautiful desires.

After several nights of our playful games and tempting diversions, though, my barbarian surprised me.

"I think I'd like you to show me your pleasure chamber."

I looked up from perusing another of the Order's old tomes. "You... you do?"

He'd been pacing the bedchamber for quite a while, setting me on edge with anticipation. The storm had still not let up and tempers had reached a violent high, with two of the castle's former slaves breaking into a fight over the evening meal. No one had been hurt this time, but emotions flared. The pressure was worse than ever.

Bannon swung one arm in a circle, kneading his shoulder as he did. "Yes. I've been curious since you brought it up, and tonight especially, I'm in the mood to work my kitten until she can't walk straight. This chamber of *primal indulgences* seems a promising place to start."

A manic clash of joy and trepidation made my heart give a heavy series of thumps. I rose to my feet. As agreed, within the bedchambers I wore no clothes, so, naked, I went to him.

"Yes, Sir. I'll show you."

The hunger in him seemed sharper than usual. He stalked after me, like a predator after prey, as I guided him to the innermost heart of Alaric's sadistic secrets.

The instant I entered the torture room, instinct told me to kneel. Alaric had designated the very center of the room, amid the wooden pillories, crosses, benches, and tables, as the place where I must wait on my knees. I would recite the rules of my slavery as he stood before me in only his leather breeches, open to reveal his ivory cock at full attention.

Though the urge to obey the old ways pulled at me, I resisted. Alaric was not the master of this chamber anymore.

"Sadira?" Bannon rested his hand on my lower back. "Is something wrong?"

Coming to my senses, I shook my head. "No, Sir. Only remembering the rules of the past."

"And what were the rules, in here?"

The room, a gallery of devices, featured a raised platform straight down the middle, upon which the gleaming fixtures—some padded with rich, brown leather, others rigid frames of glossy, polished wood—stood in two rows, like sculptures on display. I climbed the short two steps up to this stage and led Bannon to the place where I'd so often kneeled.

"I waited here on my knees while my Master selected my torture." I gestured to the spot, then to the equipment around us. "I might be bent over the spanking bench, with my arms bound, to be paddled until it burned. Or in the standing stocks, I'd be locked in with legs spread and arms upraised, with every part of my body exposed to his whims."

The memory made me shiver. "*Beautiful* torture, my barbarian. Wicked pleasures which took me to my limits, and then further still."

Bannon took a walk along the gallery, rubbing his chin. He strode all the way to the end, then back to me. Hooking his index finger through the ring on my collar, he said, "Come."

He guided me down the aisle to one of the leather-padded bondage horses: a wide beam, edges blunted and smoothed to make it subtly rounded, set on solid struts. This one had two smaller, secondary beams along the sides, allowing the master to arrange the slave in a variety of positions. Shining rings built into the design, and a latticework of metal bars along the base, provided anchor points for ropes and chains.

"Show me this," he instructed, releasing my collar.

I smiled, delighted, as I stepped forward and laid one hand on the supple leather. "Yes, Sir."

So many poses to choose from. As I mounted the bondage horse, first I straddled the beam, throwing a glance over my shoulder at my barbarian to see his expression.

I rocked my hips, mimicking a rider in the saddle, and Bannon flashed me an approving grin. I moved forward on the beam until I reached the end, stretched my arms over my head, then leaned back until I lay supine along it, my legs bent and resting on the lower beams on either side. My hair dangled over the end of the horse, and I smiled at Bannon upside-down, like an innocent cat stretched out on its back in a ray of sunlight.

He gave me a grin like a fox who's just found his way into a rabbit pen. "I think I get the idea."

"Will you bind me down, please, Sir?"

A pair of shackles hung from a ring on the front of the horse: iron bracelets linked by a very short chain. I offered Bannon my wrists, and he closed the bracelets around them.

"Are you comfortable, bent backwards like that?" he asked.

"I have trained," I assured him with a wink. "Remember, I am a *chorremachi* fighter. And I have been tied down maybe a few times before."

A soft snort of laughter escaped him, and he began a slow circle around the bondage horse, running his hands over it, and me, with careful consideration. Leather belts attached to the beams, and he seemed to guess their purpose without any trouble: he stretched one over my midsection and pulled it tight. Two more secured my legs, spread wide, ankles bound beneath my thighs.

"Will it hurt in the morning?" he asked, running his big, warm hand over the flat plane of my belly. His touch spread a sweet, suffusive tingle to my flesh.

"Only in the loveliest way, Sir."

"You are so soft," he marveled. "So flexible and pliant, to bend so prettily and treat me to such a display."

He circled me again, slower this time, sliding his hand up my right thigh and giving it a deep, deliberate squeeze. Then he did the same to my hip, my waist, up to my breast, savoring the tautness of my whole body as I uttered a breathless moan.

"My desert kitten..." He squeezed my bicep, then leaned in to kiss my shoulder, my neck, my cheek. "I thought I would never take another lover after Ailsa's mother. I thought I had savored all I ever would of passion."

"Were you ever like this?" I asked. "With her? Did she ever get to taste the Red Bear's full, ravenous imagination?"

Slipping around the front of the table so I could stare directly up at him, Bannon gathered up my thick mane in one fist, twisting it into a knot. "Even if I'd known of these practices, it wouldn't have been right for me. Or her. Not then. It seems I have different needs, now I'm older. Different appetites. And Aileen... I don't think Aileen would have liked domination as you do."

He selected a pair of slim metal chopsticks that were lying across a dish on the device beside us and used them to pin my hair in place. When I laughed, he took me firmly by the chin and forced me to look him in the eyes.

"What's so funny?" he demanded, though he smiled.

"Those are for *other* purposes, my barbarian."

"Oh?" He released me and bent down to kiss my neck. I shivered beneath his touch and he moved down my body, planting kisses along the curves and planes of my flesh. "How should I be using them, then?"

He settled between my thighs, and his breath warmed my smooth vulva. I licked my lips and tried not to writhe with impatience.

"Bind them together at each end with twine," I explained. "Very tight... with the slave's nipple between them. Or you may use them to torment certain pressure points, pressing them deep into sensitive muscle."

"Well, isn't that clever?" he murmured, playful. "Any other *complaints,* slave?"

Before I could answer, he flicked out his tongue and teased the jewel studding my clit. I gasped, arching along the unyielding spine of the bondage horse. He lifted and teased the slim gold rings piercing my labia, then with slow attention tasted his way along the valley of soft, tender flesh.

"Well?" he pressed. "Speak up! Any other *corrections* you'd like to make?"

"None!" I let out an urgent sound of delight. "I am sorry, Sir... please forgive me!"

I opened to him, welcoming him to devour me, and a hushed breath escaped me when his lips pressed to my taut clitoris. Bannon's tongue stroked and savored the deep heat of my pussy; I writhed as he circled my clitoral piercing, kissed it, and pressed it with the flat of his tongue. Like fire kindling from low, dark coals, pleasure mounted within me.

"Beautiful, sweet slut..." With two fingers he entered me, stroking, thrusting, toying with me in a gentle, come-hither motion. "*My* sweet slut. My needful, shameless, *cock-hungry* slut."

His words raked me with a naked humiliation and excitement, an arousing sense of exposure. I strained under the leather belts, legs burning with tension. The tips of my breasts stiffened to perfect tiny stones, aching for their own attention: a touch, a squeeze, a long, firm pinch.

Withdrawing from me, he straightened, and reached out to take ahold of my chin. He slid his fingers into my mouth, letting me taste the bitter wet hint of my own arousal. I sucked obediently, running my tongue along them to reclaim what he offered.

I didn't even notice him slide his breeches down his legs, unleashing his erection, until he guided his cock into me. I gave up a cry that trailed off into a desperate moan.

"Oh, Sir..."

"You're so tight!" He quickened his pace, looming over me, thrusting hard, shaking me against my bonds. "No doubt it is all the shameless orgasms you enjoy. Or perhaps you've learned the secret ways of the ancient tantra. Tell me who this tight pussy belongs to, you hungry little she-cat?"

"You." The simple word brought on a wild, blushing shyness, though we both knew very well how I craved the hot, coursing culmination of his lust. "My body—any part of me you desire—belongs to you."

"Let's hear you beg."

"Please, Sir! Please claim this pussy as yours again, as you did our first night. Mark me, renew your claim on me."

He moved a hand down to where our bodies joined, and his thumb found my studded apex. A new shock, bright and light and joyous, shot through my core, as Bannon flicked and circled, tormenting my clitoris as he fucked.

"Oh, Sir! It's too much! I'm—I'm going to—"

"Go ahead," he taunted me. "Make it good. Make it *wet*."

The orgasm came quick and strong, sweeping over me, sending me into a shuddering wave of pleasure.

"*Good* girl."

His words sent a vibrant rush of joy through my body. The raging, firebrand glow of his gaze simmered along my skin.

"But I'm not done," he growled.

He picked up his rhythm with a yearning, bestial grunt, until his breath came in a ragged, heavy exhale, and he pressed himself deeper, drawing out the motions, expertly stroking that perfect sweet spot inside me. Bliss mounted in my core as he picked up speed.

The first throb of his orgasm sent a swell of greedy joy through my body. With a wild, eager cry I struggled, calling out for him, savoring the feel of him deep inside me. I shut my eyes, and in my mind, colors burst and popped—my head and chest alight with effervescent joy while my hips, my sex, my legs shivered into a sharp, arcing pleasure. I tipped, tipped, until at last the final rush of ecstasy took me, filling me with brilliant bliss.

I raised up a long, lustful moan, relishing every pulse between his body and mine.

I floated on the rapture for a long, long time. Eyes now open, I stared up into the ceiling, but saw nothing. My mind drifted far, far into a field of lush, violet heather. Bright stars lit up my sky, and sparks came falling down, and now they were sweet, fragrant flowers all around. I lay in their plush tranquility, basking in it.

He remained there, suspended above me on his arms, panting, until finally he relaxed and lowered himself to kiss me. He held that kiss for several warm, lasting seconds, prolonging the union of our bodies, and even as our lips parted, we kept still, gazing at one another's glistening faces.

Bannon kissed the lobe of my ear. "You're shivering, Sadi. Are you cold?"

"Yes." My own voice sounded very far away. "But I don't mind."

"Let's get you to the bed."

He unbound me, bracelets first and then belt after belt, and helped me off the bondage horse. My legs, weak and trembling, nearly gave out beneath me, and so once again he scooped me into his arms and carried me, as if I were a sleeping child.

Bannon put me into bed and stretched a blanket over me, crawling beneath it to join me. He curled his body around mine, took my hands in his, and drew me to his chest. I hovered in my bliss, grounded in the warmth and scent of him beside me.

Presently a silent stirring pulled me from my doze. I reached to draw him back to me. Laying a finger across my lips, though, Bannon climbed out of bed, tugging the blanket up around me.

"I'm not leaving," he assured me. "I'll be right here."

I tucked myself deeper into the plush animal furs. I listened to his movements. Quiet footsteps. The scrape of a wooden chair across the stones as he shunted it aside. He slid back the shutter I'd drawn over the window several nights before, and only then did I realize what I *didn't* hear.

Bannon sat on the window casement, peering out into a dark, clear night.

"The storm's passed," he murmured, as if to break the hush would bring back the squalling winds.

"Maybe. Sometimes they only pause to catch their breath."

He came back to bed and sat, tilting my chin up to kiss my lips. "Maybe in the morning you'll be free to enjoy the sun."

I smiled and raised an eyebrow. "Free?"

"I see no point in pretending you're my prisoner anymore."

My lips parted in a shy, but relieved grin. "So, you trust me?"

"I do."

We lay beside one another, and Bannon stroked one broad hand over my belly. He wore a thoughtful look, and as he caressed me his fingers gradually found their way down to my sex.

"Will you not conceive soon? The way we fuck, I'm surprised you haven't already."

My cheeks burned. I looked away.

"No, Sir. There will be no children."

"You don't need to call me 'Sir' in matters such as this," he said. "It makes me feel... distasteful. I'm not your master when it comes to bearing children. *That* is something we discuss as equals."

I shook my head. "No. It isn't something we will discuss at all. There will be no children, Bannon. At least, not with me."

He paused. "You... are unable?"

"Alaric tried for years. The great king required an heir, after all. No seed ever took."

"Sadi... I'm sorry."

"Don't be." I sat up, brushing back my hair. "I never wished to be a mother."

"Maybe the trouble lay with him?" Bannon offered.

"He enlisted other men to act as stud when he failed. No, Bannon. I cannot conceive."

For a moment he looked as if he'd start offering sympathy. He lifted a hand to stroke my face, but I stopped him.

"Please, don't," I told him, terse. "Don't act as though it makes me pitiable. I've had very little liberty to decide anything for myself, but the one freedom I've always had is *not* to be made a brood mare. Nothing Alaric did terrified me more than trying to make me bear a child. I'm too self-centered to make any sort of mother, and I am not ashamed of that. I would not change it."

Bannon searched me with a dark, thoughtful gaze, in a look of puzzlement.

"Perhaps it is this desert." I relaxed beside him, temper cooling. "So tainted and barren. Or the rituals of the Order, or the magic he worked on me. Alaric poisoned me in so many ways over the years, my barbarian. I've always believed this was just one more."

"Poisoned you." His fingers ran over my wrist, following dark red paths of ink across the delicate flesh. "Sadi, how am I to know if I hurt you?"

"You've done nothing to me I didn't desire. I've told you so."

"But if I *did* hurt you? Truly hurt you, not as a matter of play. If I did it without knowing, would you tell me to stop?"

I opened my mouth to answer but found myself unsure.

"Would you know *how* to tell me?" His voice dropped to a low, patient murmur, but his words were firm.

I nibbled my lip. "The slave does not dictate what the Master does."

Bannon's expression darkened. He stopped tracing his finger along my wrist and closed his big hand over mine.

"You extend a great deal of trust to me, Sadira. Trust and responsibility. If you want me as your Master, you *will* damn well tell me if you are in real distress."

"To what end?" I asked. "I am for your pleasure, whatever pleasure it may be."

"Didn't you tell me Khan kept you in fear? That your loathing of him stemmed from his pleasure in terrorizing you?"

"Yes, but you are not the same—"

"Right," he agreed. "I am not. And I won't have my *lover* in unnecessary fear or discomfort in this arrangement. What you desire, what you need, I'll give, but you will *tell* me if something is wrong."

I considered him. "All right, Sir. How will I tell you?"

Bannon combed his fingers through my hair. "Say *atala*. If you say *atala*, I'll know to stop."

"*Atala?* What does it mean?"

"A word for mercy, in the old pagan religion of the north." Bannon scooped me closer to him, kissing my forehead. "It means I must do no more to you."

"How clever of you."

Bannon ran the backs of his knuckles over my cheek.

"I'll be your Master, Sadira. But I'll be caring for you just as hard as I fuck you. *That* is how a barbarian loves his woman."

Loves. The declaration—and it *was* a declaration, not a request—softened me. I didn't respond at first, but after a quiet moment I took his hand in mine, kissing his warm palm.

"Very well, Sir. I will do so."

"Thank you."

He pulled me close, cradling me to his chest. "If the storm passes, I'll soon be on my way home to Sanraeth. My king will send another regent here. The people Lord Khan enslaved—"

"Will go home," I finished for him. "Each to their own country. But what about me?"

"You?"

"No one knows where I came from. I've belonged to Alaric all my life. I don't know where home *is,* if not here."

Bannon fell silent, though he continued stroking my skin. He didn't have an answer.

Neither did I.

CHAPTER FOURTEEN

I STOOD ON the wall alongside the other soldiers. We all stared, baffled, at the sands below.

Bodies. Two dozen or more, scattered across the sand around the castle and the ruined city streets. Some wore the sigils of Bannon's forces—the people missing from Ailsa's caravan. Others might have been soldiers and warriors from the last days of the war, and some, the people of Vashtaren itself.

I had already visited the other side of the castle grounds and seen the same thing there: the bodies of Alaric's enemies and his broken people, strewn around his fortress. A bloody offering to Akolet.

An odd geometry accompanied the sight: all the bodies lay within about fifteen yards of the outer walls. Gazing down over the ring of them, I guessed thirteen might be more precise. Thirteen, because it was a dark number, a shadow number. A favorite among Akolet's sorcerers. Thirteen, fifteen, or ten, though, it mattered not. The corpses circled the castle like fallen leaves at the base of a dead tree, but in a perfect, symmetric circle.

Within that circle, the streets of Vashtaren, its buildings, merchant stalls, and alleyways, had all been blasted and ruined by the storm. Dwellings were left in strange cross-section, bisected neatly into the destruction as though by a great curved blade.

The unpredictable chaos of a sandstorm never left such order in its wake. As I stared down at the scene, the sense of many eyes weighed on me from all around.

Unnatural, the onlookers seemed to say with their stony expressions. *Dark work. Witch's doing.*

They were right.

The sound of quick footfalls across the stone below drew my attention. One of the young pages from Bannon's folk. He rushed to climb the stairs to the rampart, where Lieutenant Mara gathered with the other guards to assess the omen of the corpses.

I watched, silent in my curiosity, as the boy delivered his message. A short message. A summons, I imagined, as Mara and two of her warriors detached from the group and made way for the main castle keep.

Without bothering to explain myself—none of the soldiers wanted me there, anyway—I followed.

The page guided the group through the open golden hallways now crowded with restless onlookers. I caught sight of Rayya gathered with the team of wall-builders: she'd shorn her hair in a new style, trimming the sides down entirely and leaving only a single broad strip of short, dark curls down the middle of her scalp. A nervous, rabbity twitch crossed her face: the same shy, frightened look animals took on when they sensed bad winds or tremors in the ground.

The sandstorm had crept under everyone's skin. The sandstorm and the evil omens rising in its wake.

I followed Mara and the others down to the kitchens, where they met with Bannon, Ailsa, and a small group of guards and kitchen hands. Bannon, flanked on one side by his daughter and on the other by a somber-eyed Vash refugee, watched with a grim expression as the castle's kitchen hands carried up various food stores from the cellar.

I didn't have to come any closer to find out what was wrong; the smell left no doubt.

The food—almost all of it—had spoiled.

JEERS AND ANGRY hollers preceded me down into the underground dungeons reserved for Alaric's enemies and, more often, his victims. The last sorcerers of the Order of Akolet awaited their sentencing here in rows of iron prison cells, until the regent from Bannon's home country arrived to oversee judgement.

Though I wore my leather bodice rather than my ornamental garb, and my cloak and balaclava from shifts on the walls, the sorcerers recognized me. They called to me before I'd even entered the space between chambers, and cold voices warned me to go back.

"You have no place with us, apostate!"

"Akolet's lowest whore, whore to his whoresons, comes to us more welcome than you."

"Hide your face or bring it before me so I can spit upon you."

I did go to them, and I drew back the balaclava to face them without fear. A man I knew—Rikhi, one of Alaric's high viziers—waited for me at the door of his cell while his companions crowed and hissed behind him.

Rikhi regarded me with a humorless frown, and when I refused to drop my gaze, it deepened to a sneer of disgust. In the cell next to his, another vizier named Bhrune rose from his seat on the floor to come watch our exchange. Bhrune had been Rayya's master, the man who dressed her as his little toy girl.

Neither man looked as frightening to me now, with their scarlet robes gone and their frail, bleached skin unpainted and unadorned. The conquering Sanraethi had stripped them of their jewelry and precious silks, and now they wore plain muslin shifts, their hands tied fast with simple rope, more naked than if they'd worn nothing at all. They had nothing, and they were nothing, without their king or god.

Except both Rikhi and Bhrune had once possessed me, given leave by Alaric to humiliate and shame me. They'd also been among the men he'd used to stud, trying to get a child on me, and that bred a deeper fear in me, a *real* fear.

I'd been traded and received enough in my role as sexual plaything and that, I understood. I didn't like these men, but I'd been Alaric's to give. When I'd embraced my role as his slave, I'd accepted *he* would decide whom I'd fuck, and how. But to bear a child from either man—from *any* of Akolet's dark order—would have been terror I couldn't bear. It was one thing to surrender myself in exchange for twisted, addictive pleasure. It would be another to sacrifice my body to nourish life on behalf of these men.

I faced them now, men to whom I'd been slave and toy and chalice, and I hoped for cooperation. Cooperation required respect, however. As yet, Rikhi and Bhrune didn't even regard me as human.

The prickle of goosebumps rose all along my arms. Even the fires of the torches failed to chase away the subterranean chill in the air. My shivers, though, came not from cold.

They frightened me. They frightened me because they knew me. To these men I would always be Lord Khan's personal pet. They'd witnessed my induction, seen me wrapped up in the rituals and dark magic alongside them. These men, too, would suspect me. They knew of the poison Alaric fed me and my violent, audacious appetites, all the ways in which I'd never truly escape the beast I was inside.

They would also know what must have transpired for Bannon to cement his victory. My dream returned, the angry mob of Alaric's followers coming for me, howling to see me punished, to bury me alive with the Master I'd betrayed.

Coward! Adulteress! Witch! Queen!

Only seven of the Order's favored sons survived the battle for the castle, and two of those had died of injuries thereafter. Five men in cages shouldn't frighten me. They could do nothing to me.

But...

What if one of them... or *more* than one of them... harbored some reservoir of power even now? Had they seeded hidden apprentices among the castle's population, who channeled their will to bring down the conqueror and all the slaves he'd liberated?

Someone used the boy to destroy valuable supplies. Someone fouled the food stores. Someone might even have held the sandstorm over us, stirring foul weather to ensure our entrapment.

Dark work. Evil work. Everything a man like Alaric would appreciate.

I ran a hand through my hair. The five remaining sorcerers occupied three cells, one on my right and two on my left. Though the last of these had room for a second prisoner, it heartened me to see the boy whom Bannon had imprisoned occupied his own cell far from the others, out of their reach. My barbarian made good on his word.

The boy glanced up at me as I passed, then snapped his head sharply away, as if to look at me caused him physical anguish. I faltered in my steps and brought a hand up to my chest. Perhaps I should have expected disdain, but still... from him?

I sighed and moved on from his cell to the others.

Their eyes crawled over me, helping themselves to my body even now, when they were chained and divided from me by bars of iron. A foul taste rose at the back of my throat. They made me quake inside. Had I really believed they couldn't scare me? All they'd done was aim their knowing, greedy stares my way, and already I wanted to vomit.

I swallowed back the feeling and straightened my shoulders. "I want to know which of you is behind the attacks on the Sanraethi."

"*Sanraethi,* now," mused Bhrune. "Listen to the fancy whore. *Sanraethi,* she calls the barbarian savages. As though they've given her some place among them."

"Your only place is underneath." Rikhi spat on the ground by my feet. "Underneath the heel of your

Master, underneath his divine form. Underneath the ground where he now sleeps."

"Lord Khan isn't buried in any grave." I hoped they couldn't hear the quaver in my voice or see how the subject of graves and burials made me dizzy. "The Red Bear and his men sundered the body and left it out among the sands where the jackals and carrion birds could find it."

They laughed at me, a patronizing round of ugly chuckles and dry, husky cackles. I ground my teeth but struggled to keep my expression calm.

"One of you—or maybe all of you—brought dark magic down on the people who've saved me. I'm no fool. I know what your dark arts look like, and the boy in the cell back there is no magician. So, which of you is doing it? Do you really expect it to save you?"

"Stupid thing," Rikhi replied. His voice, cracked and mewling, made me think of an old toad, maybe the great-grandfather of all toads. "You're not free. Your last chance at freedom died when the Lord Khan plucked your sweet cherry and tasted your first blood. A slave like you has no freedom. A vessel has no freedom. And that is what you are, *all* you are, and all you will ever be. Lord Khan's pet, servant, and slave."

As long as you live...

"The Red Bear killed Alaric," I hissed. "He took Alaric's kingdom in fair conquest."

"You mean he wet his cock in you," another said. "What is it to us? Maybe those who have never sought out the ascendant edicts of the seven-headed serpent are compelled. *We* know you, vessel. We knew Lord Khan, and we know you."

"We know what you are." When Bhrune grinned at me, I could think of nothing but bleached bone or an old patch of sand. "The savage has done nothing to you Lord Khan did not already do, nothing we, his followers, were not invited to do under his own sight. You are forged for men to fuck, slave. Your choice is irrelevant."

"Aye, fuck the barbarian if you like." Rikhi flashed me a cruel smile full of eerily straight, square, white teeth. A hideous toad with abnormally perfect teeth. "Fuck *all* the barbarians. None of them, no one anywhere, will release you. You are the king's. Always. Anywhere you go, anyone you go to bed with, you will always be his possession."

The words sent a creeping, crawling disgust up the back of my neck, from under the buckle on my collar, marked with Alaric's symbol. The first grim fingers of a headache pressed on me, just beneath my temples.

Then, from behind me, back in his lonely, single cell, the imprisoned boy gave a snort.

I spun toward him, heat blooming across my cheeks.

"Join a nunnery, witch," he scoffed. "Beg for forgiveness."

The sorcerers burst out laughing. I only stared. After several seconds, I clenched my fists at my sides and lifted my chin. Thank goodness for the flickering torchlight, though, because I didn't want the boy to see it if I lost my grip on my tears.

"These snakes can say what they like," I hissed at him. "But I defended you. You were a prisoner here, like me. I wanted to *help* you!"

"A nunnery wouldn't do her any good!" one of the other prisoners guffawed. "Khan's whore is a hungry monster, and she knows it. She needs what he gave her, what he trained her to love, what she gratefully and greedily took from him and his proxies. If the savage sends her to a nunnery, she'll only spread her madness and have the whole place turned into a brothel by season's end. She is the hungriest whore you'll ever meet, boy."

The boy glowered, but his disgust was aimed at me, not the crude exclamations of the cultists. I glared back, sure now he would see the tears, but too angry to retreat. Retreating would be to admit through cowardice that the priests were right, and I was a whore. A craven sexual beast, a predator, and a freak.

But I am, aren't I? I am hungry. I am needful, and... and shameless. *Am I not? What I crave, what I yearn for and require... doesn't it make me exactly what they say?*

I swallowed the lump rising in my throat, frozen in place between the boy's disdain and the mockery of the Order, feeling like I might burst from humiliation. *How could I ever survive without Alaric? Alaric, who knew me, who saw my darkness and tasted this poison, and found it good. Alaric who trained me, who saw the way to tame and punish such a wicked, carnal beast?*

My nails cut into the meat of my palms. A certainty fluttered through my head, that if I could have seen my own tear-streaked face in the glass, I would see blood there. My eyes, bleeding like the eyes of the possessed. It wasn't possession, though: it was a curse. A curse on me for deviating from Alaric's path, for betraying him, failing to throw myself on the enemy's sword after him.

What am I doing? What place is there in this world for me, if not in the bed of the serpent? Who can contain me, command me, if not him?

"Sadira."

I blinked.

Bannon stood before me. When had he come? I blinked again, halfway expecting him to disappear. He didn't. He stared down at me with stony disapproval.

"Why did you come down here?"

I opened my mouth to answer, but the sorcerers interrupted.

"She wanted to relive old times, Red Bear," Rikhi jeered. "Hoping for a bit of bodily worship. Perhaps you'd care to join in? Maybe she'll convert you to a new religion."

My stomach lurched, and I glanced down at the floor. I didn't miss the sneer of disgust curling Bannon's lip, however. As the prisoners resumed their mad laughter, I worked to regain what composure I could.

"I'm sorry, Master," I whispered. "I wanted to find answers for our present struggles."

Bannon took my chin in his hand and made me look him in the eye. "And why would you come here for such a thing?"

"I have no magic of my own, but I know the ways in which they may employ theirs. I thought one of them—"

"They're locked up," he said. "Have no tools."

"Yes, Sir, but—"

"You shouldn't have come down here without telling me."

The steel in his voice relieved me. I swallowed, focusing on him.

161

"Forgive me, Sir."

His frown shifted into something more contemplative, and he examined my face. Did he believe the cultists, and think I'd come to them in pursuit of something sexual? Perhaps they had no tools for their arcane channeling, but the body of a willing slave, the physical and emotional energy they could generate in the heat of sex ritual, could be as good or better than any lifeless fetish or foci.

Do you believe them? In my frantic unease, I thought he must. How could this secret meeting appear to be anything else?

Bannon's dark look crushed me inside. He stepped past me to stand between me and the cultists' cells.

"Sadira is *mine*," he declared in a low snarl. "You know how I claimed her. I'll do it here, now, before all of you, if you doubt my right."

My spine stiffened. I tried not to gape at him. Not because the threat bothered me. It didn't, not in the least. In fact, it thrilled me, but would he really? Had he come around to craving exhibition so quickly?

Or did he understand the importance of the gesture, to me, and to those who had shaped me?

Bannon paused, leaving the men time to answer, but they said nothing. Peevish, angry scowls were their only reply.

"Come here, Sadira."

I did as he asked. Bannon seized the ring of my collar and jerked me close, until we were nose-to-nose, and his dark eyes burned into my own.

"Kneel," he instructed, and released my collar. I dropped to my knees.

162

"She is *mine,*" he repeated, circling me, making each word slow and deliberate. "Her body, her heart, her mind, are for me now. She is a fine creature, is she not? Beautiful. Ardent. Even powerful. I take great joy in this treasure I have plundered from your king and his so-called god. I'll not have crass and ungrateful words spoken of her."

He tangled his fingers in my hair and tugged, forcing me to sit up straighter, making my breasts jut and my soft, flat belly tighten. The deep red of my tattoos seemed to glimmer in the torchlight. The scrutiny stripped me down, and I held my breath.

"You lot may look on her one last time. Look at the prize I stole from your master. Understand I will never be as careless as he in his keeping of her. Look at the lovely treasure he left for me. Once I've punished her for her foolishness in coming down here, there won't be a thought left in her head of him, or of you, or of the ways in which you squandered her. Once I take her back to my chambers, she leaves this unfortunate history behind her, and her perfection is out of your grasp forever."

Having completed his circle, he stooped and took the ring of my collar. I rose in one smooth, graceful motion and faced him. He tugged, and I followed without a word.

"And you." He thrust a finger at the imprisoned boy. "Sadira defended you and very well may have saved your life. You will apologize for your part in her shame just now."

"Yes, captain," the boy murmured, glancing askance. "I apologize, Sadira."

I nodded my acceptance.

"Drink from that well if you wish, usurper!" Rikhi called out. "Alaric Khan poisoned the waters long ago. She'll spread his curse to you and all the others she opens to. Her true lord lives through her, and until you put her in the ground, she will pass his word on and on. She'll be your corruption and your downfall, sure as the serpent strikes at the heel. Cursed! She has cursed you all!"

Bannon didn't bother to respond. He pulled at my collar again and led me from the prison, to whatever punishment   awaited.

CHAPTER FIFTEEN

HE FORBADE ME to bow my head. Instead, I was to stand straight, keeping my shoulders back, looking up and ahead.

"I'll not have you hiding your face like a pouting child," he told me, and I did as he said. He took my cloak, leaving my arms and shoulders bare, and commanded me to fold my hands before me, not behind. He didn't put me in manacles. Looping a short length of rope to my collar for a leash, he paraded me before the servants and soldiers who walked the halls along our way to the bedchambers. The castle inhabitants stared, raising eyebrows, murmuring to each other.

"Sir?" Mara stepped forward from a cluster of onlookers. "Has the prisoner done something? Do you need a set of chains?"

"Sadira is not a prisoner, Mara," Bannon reminded her with a sharp note of reprimand. "She's only been a bit foolish, and I aim to correct her."

Mara drew up a scowl, switching her look from the captain to me. I knew too well what she must see: a woman flush with heat, her skin pinkening at the attention on all sides, her eyes bright. Because this display filled me with need.

Could Bannon know what he did to me, flashing me about like this? Did he see the flush of red at my throat, the set of my jaw, the tightness of my thighs? The sheer awareness, the attention on me, the dark edge of *warning* in his voice. He frightened me like this, but I wanted him. The anticipation electrified me, and I struggled to keep still.

Mara shot me one last look of disdain—oh, how I wanted to *laugh*—and then she stepped out of the captain's way. Bannon guided me onward, and every glance at my humiliation lashed me with a beautiful secret shame, which to me became a pleasure.

When we reached the master chambers, he closed the great iron doors behind us and crossed his arms over his chest.

"Well?" he asked.

I blinked. Glanced around the room as if he'd asked me to find something.

"I... I don't understand you, Sir."

His grim expression darkened further. "What do you have to say for yourself?"

My thrill fizzled. I hung my head, staring at the floor.

"*Look* at me," he commanded. "And tell me why, by Sherida, you thought it wise to stir up the simmering crock of filth those men keep hot."

I met his gaze right away. "I'm sorry, Sir. I only thought... I hoped they might give something away, give some clue where all these misfortunes are coming from."

"And you didn't for a moment think about what they might do to you?"

"Do to me?" I cocked my head to one side. "Sir, they're locked up. What could they possibly do to me?"

"Exactly what they did."

Seizing me by the shoulders, he spun me to face the looking glass.

I beheld my own bright, tear-reddened eyes. No tracks of blood, as I'd feared in one anxious moment, but the ghost of heavy tears, heavier than I imagined. My hair, tangled and mussed. Had I run my hands through it in my anxious fit? Along one collarbone, where I'd clasped my hand when the boy spoke to me, there now appeared a raw set of small pink marks. I'd dug my nails into my skin, scratched myself and left stinging little gouges.

I'd gone down into the dungeon proud and neat, full of the high intention to impress the Order into giving up their schemes. Now I appeared anything *but* neat. Bhrune and Rikhi had left me shaking like a scared rabbit.

How had they done that? When they were locked up, and I walked free?

"I... I see, Sir."

"I've brought you into my guard and into my confidence. If you take it upon yourself to go meet with my enemies and then return looking like a keening mourner at a funeral, what am I to think? My people already suspect you, but they *are* coming to see your strength. You can't cast away their confidence now."

"I apologize, Sir," I said.

"*And,*" he continued, "haven't Khan and his disciples hurt you enough?"

I looked down at my hands. "I'm afraid I don't follow."

He lifted my chin.

"You are strong, Sadira. You know it. You are a soldier, and willingly endure torture, even enjoy it. You *never* bow your head or skulk away when one of my people insults you. You are proud."

He gestured at the mirror. "How do a half-dozen captive, powerless mystics reduce you to tears?"

I studied my reflection. The back of my neck and shoulders tingled with shame. He *had* taken me into his confidence, and I'd made him look like a fool when I slipped away to a secret meeting with his enemies. I'd never intended any such thing, but my Sanraethi detractors would come to the worst conclusions regardless.

The sorcerers frightened me. Men who'd born witness to my nakedness, to the marking of my body, and the discipline I received. Men who, at Alaric's bidding, used me as a table or a footstool, or ordered me to hand-feed them their meals. Men who owned a part of me still.

Why? I'm not theirs! They can't touch me! Can't— can't—

Can't get under my skin. Can't run their fingers along the fault lines of my spirit.

Or so I'd hoped.

"I am *not* strong, barbarian," I admitted in a small voice. "Not when it comes to them."

"This is exactly what I mean," he snapped. "You walked into a pit of scorpions with a mission, and instead you let them sting you until you grew sick. For what purpose? You owe them no chance to punish you further. You owe them nothing. You need never look those men in the face, so why allow them any opportunity to hurt you more?"

"I thought... if I could just get them talking..."

One look at his grim expression, and all at once my plan seemed so stupid. So obviously stupid.

"I'm sorry." I whispered, cheeks burning. "It was impulsive, and careless."

"It helps no one to have you subjected to insult and abuse. Now of course, you know, you'll have to be punished."

Punishment. Not play. I'd upset him. I'd made him really, truly angry.

"Bend forward and put both palms flat on the wall. Either side of the mirror. I want you to *see* why I am doing this."

I obeyed, assuming the position. I studied my face in the mirror: my fever-bright cheeks; the remnant tracks of my tears. My gray eyes, dark as a storm, held a deep, wounded grief.

Before Bannon began, I drew in a deep breath and let it out in a slow, steadying exhale.

"Count out the strikes," he instructed as he slid my leggings off, baring my bottom. He'd read more on the subject of spanking since my last punishment. "And tell me you will be a good girl from now on."

I almost wanted to laugh. *Can I promise that? Really?*

"Are you ready?" he asked.

"Yes, Sir."

"Tell me why you are being punished."

I considered my haggard reflection. I thought of Bhrune, and Rikhi, and how loathsome they were. How loathsome they made *me* feel.

"I visited the sorcerers of Akolet without permission," I answered. "And I let them... "

I couldn't think of the right word for it. When I struggled, Bannon helped.

"Let them abuse you. Let them abuse *my* beautiful, precious kitten."

His. The word gave the punishment fiercer meaning. I'd allowed others to denigrate *his* pet. And it made him angry.

Because he cares.

The first strike came down and I jumped, giving up a cry of surprise. He'd caught me off guard, and I almost forgot to recite my apology as promised.

"One, Sir. I will be a good girl from now on."

Bannon made a sound of approval. His hand lingered on my bottom, moving in gentle circles to diffuse the ache. Then, without warning, the second slap came.

"Two, Sir! I will be a good girl from now on."

He continued, his strikes growing harder with each repetition. The tension of my confrontation with Rikhi and Bhrune twisted up inside me, tighter and tighter with every blow, and soon it grew too heavy and burst within me. I swallowed back a sob as I counted out the eighth strike and promised again to be good. Then the tears came. Beautiful tears, washing away the filthy feelings stirred up by the cultists, cleansing me.

Bannon hesitated. "Do you need me to show mercy, Sadira?"

"No, Sir." I shook my head without looking at him. "Please... it helps. Please complete the punishment."

I cried as he administered another slap, and another, and counted them off, basking in the fresh outpouring of emotion. He finished me off at an even twelve spankings, and then pulled me from the mirror to take me in his arms.

"Very good," he whispered, stroking my hair. "Very good, kitten. Now let's have you bathed and put you to bed."

Together we entered the baths, and he washed me with soaps of lavender and chamomile. When I moved to do the same, though, he denied me.

"Not tonight. You've misbehaved, and you'll not be having the things you enjoy for the rest of the night. No tending my body. No play. No lovemaking."

A rush of dread rose to my chest, and my eyes must have gone very wide. He touched my cheek.

"Don't worry, I'm not going to leave. I'll remain with you—and you'll be sleeping in the bed, not on the floor—but I'll not follow up your punishment with any pleasurable reward. You might forget how serious I am about the lesson."

I relaxed, but I couldn't ignore a pang of disappointment. I watched Bannon bathe himself, forbidding me to touch him. The intimacy in the act of washing had become one of my favorites ever since our first night together in these pools, and all fear and discomfort in the saunas had fled while we made it part of our bond. His denial stung as much as the spankings, and I resolved I would *never* drive him to such measures again.

After the bath, he lit a fire in the hearth and ordered me to bed. I climbed beneath the covers as instructed, and within moments, he joined me.

"There now." He reached out to take my hand, and I grasped his fingers gratefully. "Don't worry, my girl. I'm right here, and here I'll stay. Once your lesson is over, everything will be back to normal."

"How long will it be?"

"You are a smart girl." He studied me and nodded as though confirming something. "Just one night of denial should be enough. Tonight, you sleep beside me but without satisfaction. Tomorrow things will go back to the way they were."

"It's an effective punishment," I told him. "I hate it."

Bannon shook with warm, rough laughter. "Well, lass, I suppose even *you* have a limit to your tolerance!"

Smiling at me, he stroked a thumb across my cheek. "Please tell me why you are still so scared of those men, Sadira?"

As I contemplated the question, I shivered, and drew the animal furs closer. He might deny me the comforts of sexual closeness and the carnal pleasure of body heat, but he would stay. He'd assured me of it: he would not abandon me, even though I'd angered him. He'd come so far, to understand the importance of these gestures and tokens I craved.

"It... " I swallowed back a lump in my throat. "It is difficult to explain."

"Try me."

A frown crossed my face. How to tell him what the Order had done to me? How to explain what I'd been to them, and why? He'd followed me partway down the dim and perilous path into my world. Could he stand the truths behind *these* questions?

Perhaps he understood my hesitation. "Can I tell you a story myself?"

"Anything you like, my barbarian."

He withdrew his hand from mine, and brought it to his own chest, where a series of white, ragged lines marked him. "When I was only Ailsa's age—and she, still a wee little pea in my young wife's womb—I fell prey to an enemy faction from the far north. Giants, if you can believe it. They captured me, along with the whole war band in which I served. Killed our captain in front of us and bore us away into the frozen wastes."

I wanted to touch the scars, run my fingers over them as he spoke. I resisted the urge, though, as he'd not given permission for me to initiate contact. My hand slid over the raised flesh of my own scars, though—a smooth series of three fine lines, paralleling the diagonal ridge of my collarbone up to my right shoulder—while I tried to imagine Bannon as a young man, less than twenty, carried away from his young, pregnant wife by mythical giant-folk.

"Three more of our soldiers were killed before they got to me." He shifted onto his side, and we lay face-to-face as he continued. "Once they'd had their fill of killing, they entertained themselves with torture. They beat me, and then cut on my flesh with their iron knives."

Bannon paused, running his thumb in gentle circles over my knuckles. "You are a student of masochism, Sadi. I do not think I need to explain how it hurt."

"No. I can imagine. I remember."

"The northern giants are not universally torturers and sadists, mind you, but *this* clan had a great love for it. Perhaps they, like your sorcerers below, served some twisted, brutal god who demanded it of them. In any case, they marked me with these scars, not for any ritual reason but because it pleased them to watch me bleed. Then they imprisoned me with the war band and left us to stew in our fear."

In my mind I saw glistening ice caves and spears of frozen stone, barring Bannon and his people from escape. "Do barbarians fear?"

"Oh, we do, when circumstances call for it. The giants did not make me afraid, though. They made me *angry*. I worked with my fellow soldiers to break loose. We planned, nearly until the next dawn, then slept in shifts to replenish ourselves as we could. When the enemy came again the next day, they selected a different warrior—a sister of one they'd already killed—for torture."

He stroked my hair, but his look had grown distant. Seeing those same cold blue caverns, perhaps, and the furious defiance of the Sanraethi girl the giants meant to break.

"I led the war band in an ambush on the one who came for her: we aimed for the whoreson's eyes, and beat him blind with fists, and with shards of ice or stone we gathered from within our prison. When he fell back, we fled, but other giants pursued. I commanded the war band to scatter while I and three others—those we could arm with some manner of weapon—covered the retreat. We blinded and killed *six* of the giants that day, Sadira: one for each soldier they'd stolen from us, and two more for good measure. Two more of our number were maimed, but we all survived. This is how I came to be called the Red Bear and given my tattoo; a badge of honor over the place where I paid in blood."

This time he did guide my hands to him, to let me feel the place where his tattoo covered a portion of the old injuries. His skin, hot and dry, grew smooth and tight where the giant's blades had cut him, and the subtle swell of raised lines filled me with pride.

"Now, will you tell me of your scars?" he prompted me.

I touched my upper arm. The first weals I'd been given stretched across the backs of my shoulder blades. I'd never even seen them for myself.

"These," I whispered to Bannon, running my fingertips over them. "These were the first. The king carved them into my back with a blade when I reached maturity. He said he'd waited a long time for the pleasure of... of *engraving* me. They were to be my first lesson. They hurt so much, Bannon. I wasn't prepared, I... I cried."

"Let me see."

I rolled over to allow his inspection. His fingertips traced Alaric's complex designs, and he said nothing. After long moments, he touched my arm, and I shifted to face him again.

"After the scars came this tattoo." I touched the spiraling red design around my eye and down the side of my face. "He said it would heighten powers of insight and spiritual vision. But, as with everything else he branded on me for magical purposes... "

I lifted one shoulder in a shrug. "Nothing ever manifested."

"And when you weren't able to produce the magic he desired?"

"He grew angry. He resorted to punishment, not because he believed I denied him but because he thought the rigors might spark some unrevealed talent."

The memories brought with them Alaric's horrible, husky whisper. *I know you don't understand why you are being punished. It is not your place to understand. In this way, we will find the power you are hiding.*

Bannon's face twisted into a look of disgust. "Did he honestly believe he could beat you until you displayed some magical talent?"

"Alaric made himself look shrewd and witty, and blessed with a godly intelligence. He could make his followers believe anything. After all, the sacred serpent favored his forbears for generations. But did he believe it himself? I have no idea."

"You endured, though."

"I did." I followed the tattoo from my cheek to my neck, down to my collarbone, where it spiraled into other designs. "At the same time, I discovered my own secret. I learned of the bestial desires in my heart, and what was required of me. I learned to endure."

A thoughtful frown crossed his face, and Bannon stroked his beard. "Tell me of that."

I closed my eyes with a soft sigh. "The bite of the needle, the aching burn of ink and blood on skin... all release a kind of bliss. I surrender to it and revel in the sweet pain. Perhaps it isn't really *pain,* and I only use the word because I don't know another. But it *changed* me."

"So, you learned to love pain even before you loved sex."

I nodded. Sitting up in the bed, I brushed my fingers over the gold barbells piercing my nipples. "Strain, pressure, tension, burns, stings, needles, blades... each can and has been a source of ecstasy to me."

"And what of the sorcerers?"

He wanted to guide me back to talk of the Order. Even the mention of the priests made my mouth run dry, though, and my heart thump.

"Please, Sadi." He caressed my naked arm. "*Why* do those men hold so much power over you still?"

I drew my legs to my chest and wrapped my arms around them, avoiding his scrutiny.

"The ringleaders down there—Rikhi and Bhrune—they were Alaric's favored loyalists, and sometimes he rewarded them... with me."

"You mean you—"

"Played whore to them, yes." Shame made me shudder. Before Bannon could respond, I rushed on. "In passion, as in fear, and suffering, and pleasure, there lies power and energy. I had no talent of my own, but my body and my emotions could still be a source of power to others. So..."

I held out one hand palm up, as though the conclusion should be obvious.

Bannon made a thoughtful sound. I feared his next words, but rather than saying anything, he laid one big, warm palm on my back and ran it in gentle, reassuring circles over my skin.

"You must have known," I whispered. "Your people say it often enough. That I am a craven, lascivious bitch. Debasing myself not only for Alaric, but for all Akolet's men."

"*I* do not think so," he said. "I know nothing of the rituals you were made to participate in, but I have learned something of you. You may enjoy rough play and subjugation, my kitten, and may burn with a ravenous desire for good sex, but neither of those is a sin. And neither is license for any person to harm you. You were a slave, Sadira. You had no choice in the matter when Khan traded you to others. That was *his* crime."

When I didn't answer, Bannon sat up. Throwing the matter of my punishment aside for the moment, he gathered me in his arms and held me close.

"You are no one's bitch." He gave me a chaste kiss on the top of my head. "And *slut* or *whore* only to me, and only so long as it pleases you to hear it. Whoever was your master before and whatever he chose to do without your consent, that time is over. *I* will not discard you to the will of others. As I said to those dogs in the prison, you are mine now, and I care for that which is mine."

I lay my head on his chest, saying nothing, listening to the soothing beat of his heart. After several moments, a smile came to my face.

"Would you really have taken me there, in the dungeon before them?" I asked.

"Would you have liked me to?"

A salacious shiver rose to my chest, making the tips of my breasts tingle. "I think I would. Let them see how beautifully my barbarian Master fucks me."

"Careful, lass." He stroked my hair. "You're still being punished, after all, and I may have to be angry if you get me riled up with that language of yours."

"Yes, Sir. I will be good."

My smile grew, though. The warmth of his arms relieved me.

"Rikhi and Bhrune," I said. "They were two of the men Alaric employed as studs when he could not kindle a child in me. They frighten me the most. As Alaric's personal slave, I had no leave to deny him. He dictated everything, from my clothing to the times I could bathe or sleep or relieve myself... down to the weight of the food I ate. But he *could not* make me bear a child. *That* power was out of his hands."

I sighed. Bannon tightened his arms around me, and kissed my temple, but said nothing.

"I endured nearly thirty years being a slave in this castle, and ten of those being Alaric's personal toy. I lived with it. I became an active part in it. But... the *thought* of him... *any* of them... planting his seed in me so I must bear his progeny..."

Emotion overcame me; I paused to choke back my fear and disgust and hugged myself even tighter.

"Shh, Sadi." Bannon rocked me in his embrace. "You don't have to think of it anymore. Those men have no power over you now."

"No," I agreed, thinking of our earlier conversation.

Will you not conceive soon? The way we fuck...

"Now it is *you* who holds that power."

Bannon withdrew his arms, though not in any chastising manner. He gave each of my shoulders a quick, deep rub before lying back down on the bed, and gesturing for me to do the same.

"I hold only the power which you give me, Sadi," he told me. "I admit I like these dark desires you stir up in me. I like the way you submit, allow me to sate my most bestial needs with you. But everything I have done, you have requested or agreed to, because it brings you pleasure, too. I wouldn't ask to have it otherwise. That is why I have given you the word *atala,* if you wish to stop. I don't care what it may look like on the outside: you are *not* my prisoner."

I slid back onto my side to face him. "Are you angry I will not bear you a child, either by chance or by choice?"

Bannon stroked his beard. "Children are precious to me, Sadira. I suppose I and all my soldiers were raised to want a passel of bairns to make their house a home. Even Mara has three of her own and speaks of bearing another once we venture home. But I have Ailsa, and at nearly forty I think my childbearing years are behind me. If I'd been meant to father more, I'd have done with Aileen. She and I weren't exactly modest when it came to fucking, either, only if she heard me say so she'd slap my mouth right off my face."

His smile, when he spoke of his late wife and of Ailsa, was the charming smile of a young man. It warmed my heart, and I folded my hands under my head, gazing at him.

He brushed a few strands of hair behind my ear. We lay beside one another for long, long moments, until a distant, droning howl from outside drew our attention. Together we looked up toward the window.

"Another sandstorm?" Bannon murmured.

Lips pressed in a thin line, I shook my head. "The same one. I told you, sometimes they only stop to catch their breath. It's coming back now. Perhaps in a day, perhaps in three. But it's coming."

He rose and crossed to the window. Staring out over the desert below, he frowned, and clenched his fists on the casement.

I could guess what he was thinking. "We have to find a way out."

"Aye," he agreed in a grim tone. "But even if we abandon the castle, we have sick and injured to tend to. I won't leave the prisoners to slowly starve, but it does not please me to think of killing them without trial."

"If one of the sorcerers is behind these misfortunes—"

"*If*, Sadi. *If.* I'll not execute helpless men with no swords in their hands. As long as I am captain of this castle we will abide by the laws of my king, and in times like this the laws are more crucial than ever. If I kill the priests and the troubles continue, then what?"

He closed the shutters and slid the stone panel across the casement to keep out the wind. He leveled a somber gaze at me, running a hand through his wild red hair.

"I can't set a precedent for killing on suspicion of ill intent," he said. "Don't you see where that would lead?"

I did.

It would lead directly to me.

CHAPTER SIXTEEN

I WOKE TO a throbbing ache in my temples all the way down to the base of my neck. I groaned, rolling over in bed, away from the window and the howl of the wind.

Bannon stirred and came awake. "Sadi? What's the matter?"

"My head is in misery," I mumbled into my pillow. "I apologize, Sir... I have suffered such sickness all my life. The sound of the storm is... like *needles*."

He shifted. A hand touched me gently on the cheek. "You don't feel feverish."

"It is no fever. An old Vash physician called them megrims. When they come on me like this... oh... *oh,* it hurts so much."

He rubbed my shoulder. "What can I do to help?"

"Nothing. I gave Ailsa my entire supply of cannabis."

"Perhaps she has some left. Stay put."

A moment later the door to the bedchamber scraped open, then closed, and I was left alone. The sandstorm outside howled and I cringed, the sound scratching at me like a knife down the knobs of my spine.

I didn't know how much time had passed before Bannon returned. It was difficult to keep track of time, or anything, when I couldn't ignore the throbbing in my own head. The door scraped across the stones again, and a moment later Ailsa looked dispassionately down on me.

"The old physician called it megrims, did he?" she asked, crouching to look in my eyes. She held first one open, then the other, studying my pupils. The room remained mostly dark, with the window shuttered and covered, so the healer struck a match to see by. I tried not to wince. Then she shook it out and put her fingers to my temples, moving them in slow circles with gentle pressure, and watched me grimace.

"Hmph." She rose to her feet. "Unfortunately, I don't think it's wise to use what medicine we have left for headaches. I sympathize with you, but we are so limited—"

"I understand," I said, voice barely above a whisper.

"Stay here for today. Leave the room dark. Drink cool water—*cool*, not *cold*—and dip your hands or feet in hot water to draw blood away from your head."

"Ailsa, there must be more you can do than *that*," Bannon grumbled, keeping his own voice hushed.

His daughter rounded on him, planting her hands on her hips. "*Not* for headaches. I'll not be using what little medicine we have on something so mundane."

"She can barely open her eyes!"

I grated my teeth—he hadn't spoken very loudly, but the edge in his tone stabbed at my brain like a spike.

"And staying here in the dark, she'll barely need to. I'm sorry but I have patients recovering from amputation and serious head injuries."

She tossed a glance back at me. "Sadira can endure."

"She's right, Sir," I offered before Bannon could become angry. I held out a hand to him and he relented, taking it and giving it a reassuring squeeze, before addressing his daughter.

"You have nothing to help her?"

"Cool water," Ailsa repeated. "Hot foot bath."

"Give me an hour, Master," I murmured, trying to sit up. I didn't miss the troubled expression on Ailsa's face when I called him *Master.* "I'll be well enough and can join you."

"Absolutely not," both of them told me at the same time. They traded a quick glance, and in that instant, even in the dark I could see how alike they really were. Ailsa gestured to her father, indicating he speak first.

"You'll stay in bed, as Ailsa tells you," he commanded. "Don't worry. I'll come up when I can to check on you. You'll not be left alone. But you'll *rest,* as you're told."

I uttered a long, low groan, but didn't try to rise. Bannon stroked my cheek.

Ailsa had discreetly turned her back to us. "Is there anything else, Da? There are others who need me."

"Aye, and me, too." Bannon straightened, giving me one last affectionate stroke of the hair. "I'm going to send a scouting party out before the sandstorm is fully upon us. We must hope they reach one of our allies, the desert clans who fought with us to take Vashtaren. I'll send someone with the water basin for you, kitten."

I nodded, and he and Ailsa left the room.

The wailing, screaming wind outside seemed worse than ever before, and I didn't think any scouts could get through such a squall, even if he sent seasoned Vash. I tried to bury my head under the furs and block out the noise, but still it reached me, yowling and screeching like an angry wildcat, sinking deep into my brain.

I didn't even notice when someone entered the room to drop off the steaming basin and a pitcher of cool water to drink. All at once, a warm, brown hand had taken mine, and Rayya sat beside me, expression full of sympathy.

"Here you go."

Rayya guided my hand into the basin, then tipped a tin ladle of the drinking water to my lips. I whispered my thanks, then buried my head under the blankets. Rayya ran a hand in smooth, reassuring caresses up and down my side.

My old friend stayed with me for a long time it seemed, periodically giving me more to drink and checking the temperature of the basin until it had cooled. Then I felt soft, dry lips touch my brow, and Rayya was gone, taking the basin away.

I imagined a good portion of the morning had passed when I finally stirred awake, headache still lingering but greatly lessened. I sat up and ran my fingers through damp, messy blonde tangles, and grimaced at the tension in my shoulders.

Outside, the ugly croak of a crow seemed impossibly close, as though it perched right on the casement on the other side of the stone panel. Maybe the wind had blown the shutters clean off.

What's a crow doing out there, then?

No wind. No scraping, wailing claws of any storm outside. In the grip of my migraine, then, had I imagined the awful noise?

I rolled my head back, tilting it side to side, and straightened my spine into a meditative position, drawing my legs into a lotus pose. I took several slow, deep breaths, and tried to imagine the desert outside, a smooth, pale sea of sand. No storm, no gales. No circle of destruction around a battered castle, no eerily silent town beyond the walls.

I thought of the sand, like a perfect pane of glass under the sun. The *warm,* delightfully soothing sun. The sun I hadn't enjoyed for days, grinning down on my skin and baking away my tight, coiled strain.

The shutters gave a loud rattle, and a splintering *crack* rocked the inner stone panel. I jumped: a fresh shot of agony pierced my skull like a spear, and I bent forward over my crossed legs, moaning.

The crow I'd heard gave another chiding cry, and with a flutter of wings, left the casement.

When the newest ache had faded, I slid from the bed, finding a simple sarong to wrap around my naked hips. Desperate for silence and stillness, I retreated to the inner chambers. No windows in there—no screeching wind or croaking birds, imagined or otherwise. I thought of visiting the baths for a hot soak, but then, with a flicker of interest, found myself instead in the torture chamber.

Alaric's torture chamber stood like an altar erected to the glory of agony and pleasure. I lit the lamps in sconces along the wall, admiring how the molten light glided over leather cushions and rich, dark wood.

I strode across the room, soothed by the smells of resonant desert oak and clean, oiled hide. I trailed my fingers over the tools of punishment, Alaric's collection of whips and crops, crafted imitation phalluses, shackles and gags, tiny jeweled clamps and silken masks.

This place had been a place of worship, of carnal exultation. Punishment, reward, training, and most of all, pleasure. He'd tested me to my limits here. When I satisfied him, he'd spoiled me, mind and body, with sexual excess.

I liked the torture chamber. I'd spent so much time here learning the ways of a good pet and floating on blissful tides of satisfaction and affirmation when I'd done well. It had become a place of comfort for me. It wasn't always so; sometimes Alaric really had hurt me, past the point of catharsis and to the point of trauma. But when it was good, it had been my favorite place in the world.

The sweet perfume of orange oil, used to clean and polish the fine furnishings, soothed me despite the headache. I crossed the room to a cabinet where the oils were stored and withdrew a stoppered bottle and a soft rag. Guided by the solace of a familiar routine—it had been my job, of course, to keep the chamber immaculate—I dampened the rag and went to work on the devices. The ease of the simple chore swept aside other concerns.

I'd worked for over an hour, and closer to two, making my way to nearly the center of the room when all at once a bark of bitter laughter startled me from my reflection and made me jump. I dropped the rag and knocked over the bottle of oil as I shot to my feet, fists clenched and jaw set.

Two of the Sanraethi—my familiar old guards— stood in the archway, staring into the torture chamber with expressions of ugly, sneering disgust.

CHAPTER SEVENTEEN

"WHAT IN THE name of Sherida are you doing?" The older of the two men ventured two steps into the room and snatched up a flogger from the table of toys. "Do you see this, Gregor? I didn't think it could be true, the tales they tell about her."

The younger guard, Gregor, grimaced with something like embarrassment. "By Sherida, get up from there, woman. Fawning over crucifixes and pillories."

"Perhaps she'd like to demonstrate their use." The older guard had seized a carved stone phallus decorated with ridged designs and smooth, subtle knots. "Show us how she's captivated the captain with her whore tricks and sorcery."

He made a move toward me. A swell of rage stiffened my spine, and I straightened, sneering at them, fists balled at my sides.

"Get *out* of here!" I snapped, though it brought a fresh throb to the back of my head and neck. "You had no right to enter the master chambers without invitation, and you had no right coming in here! Leave, or I *will* show you the use of that object, and you won't find it as pleasant as you think!"

The guard put down the phallus and growled at me, reaching for his axe. Beside him, Gregor's hand hovered over his own blade, but he stared at his partner, not me.

"What is this?"

Mara appeared behind the two men. Taller than both of them, she crossed her arms over her chest and scanned the room before her. I couldn't read her expression, as she pushed past Gregor and stalked up the aisle of the gallery. Her glance shot back and forth over the various devices of play and punishment before settling on me, in my plain sarong and nothing else.

I thought Mara might have something to say to me, but instead she pivoted back to the guards.

"What are the two of you doing in here? No one stationed you on these rooms."

"We were making rounds on this floor," Gregor replied. "The door to the chamber was ajar, and Olson heard chanting and dark incantation from within."

"Liar!" I snapped. Fury blazed in my chest, and a flush of heat rose to my breasts, neck, and cheeks. "There was no chanting, nothing! As though *you* would recognize dark incantations even if you heard them."

"Quiet," Mara advised me, putting out a hand. "Put my mind at ease, then. What were you doing in here?"

I gestured to the spilled orange oil now sweetening the air with a powerful aroma. "Just *cleaning.* Sacred serpent, you invaders will make everything into some sort of evil ritual. I came in to escape the noise of the wind, and I found the scent of the oil soothing."

Scowling at Olson and Gregor, I added, "*These* two entered uninvited and then—"

I faltered, cut off by sudden embarrassment. The fire in me guttered and my shoulders slumped.

"They... thought they might have a... *demonstration* from me. On the use of—"

Mara stopped me. "I can imagine. Olson? Is it true?"

"An idle threat." Olson clenched his teeth and glanced askance. "Only meant to scare her out of whatever mischief she had planned."

Planting my hands on my hips, I growled, "I didn't plan any mischief!"

"Right, you came to *escape the wind,*" he jeered. "What wind, sorceress? Brew up a tempest in your teakettle?"

"The *sandstorm*—"

Mara cut us both off, slicing a hand through the air.

"The Red Bear posted no guard on these rooms or on the lady." She pointed them toward the door with her halberd. "Go."

"Lieutenant, I tell you she was conjuring—"

Mara shot Olson a cold glare. "Are you prepared to argue your case in front of Bannon?"

"No," I interjected. "No, don't call him away from his duties. He's got more important things to do."

With a sigh, I crouched to mop up the spilled orange oil. "I'll clean this and then go back to the bedchambers. My headache's back, anyway."

The lieutenant considered me, then the guards. She gave one grave nod. "I think that would be best, Sadira."

At least she called me by my name this time.

BANNON WOKE ME early in the evening. I'd been dreaming of something huge and terrible, shaking and rattling the doors and windows of the castle, screeching like a primordial draconic beast. And eyes: eyes everywhere, carved into the stone pillars and walls, shining at me from mirrors, peering at me from cracks in the floor.

The warm caress of my Master's hand delivered me from these visions, and I rose from sleep to find him sitting on the edge of the bed beside me.

"You were groaning," he told me. "Has the headache improved at all?"

I sat up, stretching. "I think it may finally have passed. I'm sorry, Sir. I lay here all day instead of serving like the other soldiers."

"You fell ill." He shifted and began rubbing my shoulders. "Plenty of others have as well today. You were not the only one Ailsa confined to quarters."

"The storm," I began, and Bannon nodded.

"Yes, I know. It'll be back by morning, the others tell me. They say it's not uncommon for people to take sick when one is about to strike."

"It hasn't even begun yet?" I pressed the heel of my hand to my temple. "But I've heard the wind all day. It nearly made my ears bleed."

"There's been no wind yet, Sadi. No great gales... only the occasional dry, warning groan ahead of the squall."

I scrunched up my nose and gave an ugly growl. "*Ugh!* I feel so useless. I could have been keeping watch, or at least helping ration some food."

"Speaking of which... "

Bannon leaned over to retrieve a plate he'd set on the bedtable. "Not much, I'm afraid. We're trying to extend the rations by working them into stews. Luckily, the wells have not gone foul. Yet."

He tipped the bowl to my lips and I drank. A weak broth peppered and seasoned with bits of beef. Dried beef, I thought. Probably from the leftover supplies Ailsa's caravan had brought with them. I drank obediently, and with gratefulness.

"We sent scouts to seek aid," Bannon told me. "I thought we'd better get them out before the storm renews. We can only hope they manage to evade the worst of it and can reach one of the other desert clans. That man Rayyan is a rare asset; it was he who helped plot their course to our allies."

Despite my grim mood, I managed to chuckle. "Bannon. *Rayya* is a woman."

He cocked an eyebrow. "Really? Well, she's never bothered to correct me, and I've been calling her "brother" for days now."

"Probably she's too shy." Finishing the stew, I relaxed into his arms.

He wrapped me in a close embrace, leaning his head on mine. "Mara said you had another *difference of opinion* with Gregor and Olson."

I nodded. "I was in the pleasure chamber trying to clean the equipment. The scent of the orange oil was soothing my headache before they barged in."

Tilting my head up, I gazed at him. "The older one, Olson, suggested I demonstrate the use of the toys for them. I think, before Mara interceded... he might have become forceful."

Bannon blew out a harsh, weary sigh, and tapped his fingers gently on my arm. "That isn't our way. Not our clan, and not Olson, I think. I've known the man for years. He's happily wed, and even if he *were* so despicable, his wife would have him gelded. And she's serving on the wall today. I could have her here with a knife to do it herself if I wished."

"So... you do not believe me?" I twisted my ring in its shackle.

"I believe you." He rubbed at his mouth. "The storm is having an evil effect on everyone. Even a man I've trusted so long as Olson is... not right, like this."

Perhaps it is me. Perhaps the Sanraethi, the Vash, they are all right. I do carry a curse in me.

I closed my eyes and hugged Bannon's arm tighter.

The serpent god will repay...

"You're tense as a wire, Sadi." Bannon kissed the top of my head. "You said the scent of orange in the pleasure chamber soothed you?"

I perked up. "Yes, it did."

A sly grin spread across his face. "How convenient. I was just thinking it's time you demonstrated another of your captivating apparatuses for me, kitten."

For the first time that day, a flicker of delight made me smile. I rose from the bed, taking his hand, and led him into the inner rooms once more.

"Stay here," he ordered me, stationing me beside the collection of toys.

"Yes, Sir."

Once again Bannon strolled up and down the center aisle of the room, laying a finger on each device as he passed, considering them with a critical scrutiny. Sweet anticipation rippled through my body as I watched him.

At last he reached the metal frame with shackles hanging from the crossbar. "Yes," he mused. "This one, Sadi. Select a suitable toy and bring it to me."

"Yes, Sir."

I knew which one to choose right away: a whip of red-and-black suede tails, with a handle shaped deliciously for full penetration, should the Master wish. I forced myself to move with decorum as I took it, though I trembled with the desire to hurry to him, hastening the moment.

Bannon took the whip, tucking it into his belt. "Stand here."

I did as asked, taking my place in the center of the frame. Without being told—though maybe I *should* have waited, since Bannon was still learning the ways of a Master—I folded my arms behind my back. Bannon took my first wrist and raised it over my head, closing it in the shackle above; then repeated the action with my second wrist. I hung bare before him, balancing on tiptoes. Though he couldn't see it, a private, pleased smile touched my lips.

"Be good, Sadira, and don't make a sound." He touched a finger to my lips. "And just what do we have here?"

His hand dropped to my bottom, caressing first one round cheek, then the other. I let out a long breath, warmed by his gentle, tender attention. Soon he worked with both hands, stroking in slow, sweet circles, drawing a titillating flush to my skin. His touch moved up to my hips and around, stroking the gentle swell of my belly, making me tremble as his fingertips tickled in their passing.

I sucked in a soft gasp as he found my breasts. He moved his palms over them, running thumbs over my jutting, stiffened nipples. I couldn't help myself as the swell of delight tingled through my chest: I gave out a hushed groan.

"Bad girl." His whisper came right at my ear; his lips brushed my earlobe, and his beard rasped my neck. "I told you to be quiet."

"Forgive me, Sir."

"Such a bad little kitten..."

His right hand cupped my breast and gave a careful squeeze, tugging my studded pink peak until I bit my lip to resist making a sound. With his other hand, he explored between my thighs, stroking my mons, sliding his hot fingers along the folds of my outer lips.

"Spread your legs."

I expected him to slip his fingers into me, finding me ready and wet, but he didn't. Instead, he circled my clitoris with a teasing slowness, before withdrawing his tender touches altogether. I shivered, my whole body primed for more.

Keeping my eyes closed, I listened for Bannon and tried to sense his presence near. I *did* sense him, in a wonderful and gratifying way, feeling him with me, watching me, contemplating my body.

The first slap of the whip struck my left buttock, and I gave another ragged gasp. It stung with a beautiful, wicked delight, swift and exciting. He followed it up with a second quick slap on my right buttock, a technique I knew he'd read of in our book.

Not as stark or solid as a spanking, the whip delivered a sparkling burst of bright sensation. Bannon lashed the leather tassels back and forth across my bottom until my skin grew hot. Then he moved up the smooth planes of my back, whipping left then right in a practiced motion. My breaths came in hoarse, heavy pants, and my pussy ached for attention.

He circled me and whipped my front, slapping the tassels across my naked breasts. It made me jump but I held my tongue, and my nipples throbbed with delight. When he went down low, though, and snapped the whip between my legs with a hard, quick blow, I gave a yelp.

"*Atala!*"

Bannon stopped. "Did I hurt you?"

I'd said the word before I'd even though about it. A lump rose in my throat.

"Sadira?" He stepped closer to me, and his hands rested gently on my hips. "Are you all right?"

"It was too hard," I whispered. Shame made my voice quake. "I'm sorry. It's only... my piercings—"

"I understand." He slid his hand down to give me a gentle caress, soothing the spot. "I apologize. You did good to say the word and tell me to stop."

"I don't want you to stop, Sir. Just... please... softly, there."

"Very good, my pet."

He tugged me by the collar—affectionately—and claimed a kiss. He flicked the whip with much gentler force against my inner thighs instead, in a teasing, glancing blow.

"Better?"

"Yes," I breathed. "I like that, Sir."

He kissed me, then let go of me. Seconds later, the whip came, and I surrendered to the suffusing pleasure.

After several moments, Bannon came around behind me, and the click and slither of his belt slipping free of its clasp sent a shiver through my body. He rested one hand on my hip; with the other he lifted my thigh, holding it aloft, as he pressed himself to me. Skin aglow, hypersensitive from the hot lash of leather, I grew tense with anticipation at his touch. The unmistakable shape of his cock pressed like an enemy sword into my flesh.

"You may moan now, if you like," he whispered in my ear. Then he entered, sliding up into me. I let out a shuddering groan and he thrust, filling me until it seemed too much, and my thighs shook.

"Goddess Sherida!" He groped my tender breast and tugged at my nipple, eliciting a joyous cry.

I stretched my leg higher, inviting him deeper. "Yes, please... "

"Whipped up and down until your tits and ass are striped so pink," he growled. "And all the hungrier for barbarian cock."

His body rounded to mine. I arched to meet him, tugging the shackles, and my chains rattled as his pace increased. His firm, flat abdomen smacked against my sore buttocks as Bannon had his way.

"Please, Sir! Don't hold back!"

"Don't *you* hold back," he commanded. His hand came up to tangle in my hair, and he gripped it like reins, pulling my head back until I cried out. "I know you're close, Sadira. I can feel it all over you. You're ready to come, all right. So, go ahead. *Come* for me, my kitten. My sweet, wet she-cat."

I let out a long, heady moan, melting at his words, lost in a shimmering, rising bliss. The shudder of my orgasm shook me to the core and my balance faltered, but he held me steady. Tilting my head over my shoulder, I kissed him again and again, murmuring his name as our lips parted.

"Good girl," he snarled in my ear. "Now let's see how many times we can make you do that again before you've had enough!"

His thrusts grew fiercer, driving into my tight sheath, fragile with my climax. It was too much, it was overwhelming, but I bit my tongue to keep from saying the word that would stop him. I didn't *want* to stop him—I wanted more, even as it made my legs quake and my pussy shudder. I wanted to see just how much he could give me before I went insane.

He grunted, letting go of my upraised leg to seize my sore buttock in one greedy hand. I held the leg in place in his stead, bracing myself on the metal stand and groaning as his fingers groped my flesh. My mind succumbed to a delirious inebriation as he fucked me to a second overwhelming peak, and a third, and all I knew was that my pussy would be so beautifully sore in the morning, so wonderfully, achingly sore...

"No more!" I begged, but it wasn't the right word, and I knew it. "No more, please, Sir—I can't! I can't!"

Bannon didn't stop. He planted both hands on my hips and held me fast. He grunted like an animal now, ravenous with one desire. I gave a short, mindless shriek as I approached my limit, a dizzying, terrifying, obliterating joy.

"*Atala!*" I finally gasped, teetering on the edge. "Sir, please! Please, I can't take it anymore!"

As if he'd only been waiting for my surrender, Bannon gave a last, adamant thrust and then withdrew. A final, hard, harsh surge of pleasure wracked me, and my pussy convulsed, sending a wet rush of fluids down my thighs in fierce jets, like a man's own climax.

My head spun. Bannon slipped the pin holding my shackles to the frame and I sunk, ragged, to the floor. Then he was in front of me, stroking his glistening shaft at an urgent pace. He gripped my hair again, forcing me to tilt my face up. His own orgasm hit him, sending hot jets of his seed across my cheeks, neck, breasts as he rolled back his head and groaned.

I sat in a heap on the floor, heaving, shuddering, even after he'd let go of me and stepped away. I barely knew where I was anymore: my mind and body were wrecked, intoxicated. My legs were jelly; my arms ached.

His warm, wet semen glistened on my skin, a primal and instinctive sign of ownership. And I loved it.

After some time, a woven quilt was wrapped around me. Strong arms gathered me up and held me close to a broad, warm chest. I leaned my head against dusky, sweat-dampened skin, and breathed in the scent of my male. I touched him, laying my fingers just over the dark red tattoo. I wanted to speak, but no words came.

Bannon carried me to the hearth in the bedroom. He laid me down, still wrapped in my quilt, and retrieved the clay pitcher of water from the bedtable. I smiled up at him—it was all I could do—as he sat beside me and poured a bit of water from the drinking pitcher onto a clean rag to wash my face.

"You were stunning," he whispered to me as he worked. Gently he moved the corners of the quilt away, ran the rag over my neck and breasts, then paused to fold and rewet it, tending to me with its clean side.

"So stunning, my beautiful one." He bent down to kiss my brow. "Like the wild lionesses of this land, lissome and strong."

After each gentle pass with the washcloth, he kissed my skin, and tucked the blanket back around me. I shivered when he reached the place between my thighs, but Bannon touched me with slow, attentive care. He planted one warm kiss on the swell of my mons and covered me up.

"Are you comfortable, Sadi?"

"Yes," I murmured.

He stroked my hair. "How's your headache?"

"What headache?" I smiled at him, and he smiled back.

"I'll return shortly," he promised, and rose to take pitcher and washcloth to the inner chamber. I blinked and rolled to face the fire to await him.

He'd just come back from the baths, drying his naked body with a fresh cloth, when a shrill scream of terror cut through the night.

CHAPTER EIGHTEEN

BANNON DONNED HIS breeches in a hectic rush, as I rose from the floor to find my own. My body swayed and I staggered, still weak, but the scream acted on me like an alarm, charging me with adrenaline. I found my sarong and my ornamental breastplate, fitting them on before sprinting out the door after Bannon.

"This way," I told him, tugging him toward a hallway on the left. Bannon moved ahead and I kept pace beside him. A moment later, muffled cries, a pleading woman's voice, led us down a second hall, and with a flash of dread I knew where the sounds were coming from.

I tapped Bannon's shoulder and pointed to an archway flanked by serpentine sculptures. "The shrine room."

From within the room came the dull, hard thuds of fists, accompanied by savage growls and grunts and the woman's diminishing cries. Pulled by vibrant horror, I reached the room's doorway first: it took me a fraction of a second to assess the scene, and I lunged at the hunched figure looming over a limp guard.

Raising my clasped fists, I struck the attacker in the back of the head. He whirled on me, and I recognized the man named Jarl. His dark eyes bore the same red, bleeding rage as the boy who'd destroyed the medicine stores.

He's possessed! I thought, just as Jarl wound up and threw a punch at my face.

I jerked back in time to avoid a broken nose, and his fist collided with my shoulder like a hammer. The wind went out of me in stuttered surprise at his astonishing strength; Jarl sent me reeling back, and I had to duck before he followed the first hit with a second from the other side. His punch crashed into a stone pillar behind me, and I winced at the sound of his bones cracking. Throwing a glance over my shoulder, I saw with horror he'd cracked the *stone* as well.

How? How could he do that?

I ducked, moving in the other direction. Jarl lumbered toward me, while Bannon swept to the side of the victim. I recognized her, too: Jarl's usual partner at the watch, Chrissa. Her cries had stopped, and her glassy eyes rolled in their sockets. Jarl had beaten her bloody, leaving her arms and face swollen with horrible dark bruises and oozing scrapes before Bannon and I arrived.

I tried to see if Chrissa stirred or spoke, but Jarl charged at me, and this time I didn't move fast enough. He sunk a deep punch into my gut, forcing me toward the wall. I clutched at my midsection, hissing out a sharp breath.

When I met Jarl's reddened berserker gaze, though, a sure, steady calm came over me. I touched my tongue to my upper lip, staring into his bleeding eyes. I'd fought men his size before, and larger— Alaric's enemies. Swallowing my dizzy, distracted emotions, I scanned his body for a weak point.

He didn't seem to notice his own injuries, or the way he wobbled when he lurched forward on his bad leg. I dropped into a split and his swollen, bleeding hand swept candles, sticks of incense, gold coins, and another of the seven-headed serpent sculptures to the floor. Jarl yowled in fury, and I ducked in close enough to ball up fists together again. This time, though, I threw my force to the side, thrusting one sharp elbow into his groin.

Jarl made a gagging sound. Before he could rebound on me, he drew a short, straight dagger from his belt.

I hopped up onto the shrine he'd just cleared. Jarl ran at me, blade upraised, and I bounded straight up, letting the shining weapon slice through the air beneath me. Landing in a crouch, I kicked out one heel and caught him in the teeth. Jarl snorted, blood bubbling over his sneering mouth, and I kicked him a second time, smashing his nose.

The frenzied guard reached out both hands and stumble-stepped toward me, but Bannon grabbed him from behind, wrapping one muscled arm around Jarl's throat, pinning him in a chokehold.

I watched, heaving, as Jarl struggled in Bannon's grip. Bannon dragged Jarl back from the shrine, avoiding his flailing hands snatching and grabbing.

After a long, tense moment, Jarl's struggles weakened, and he slumped in Bannon's grip.

I climbed down from my perch, studying the man, waiting in case his struggles renewed.

They didn't. Bannon released Jarl before his breathing stopped altogether, and the man crumpled to the ground in an awkward heap. I met my captain's gaze over the fallen soldier and flicked a quick glance at Chrissa.

"Alive," Bannon assured me. "But very badly beaten. She needs to go to Ailsa ri—"

Pounding footsteps in the hall interrupted him, and Rayya appeared in the doorway along with a second soldier, another of the Sanraethi. Rayya, too, now bore the leather armor and weapon of Bannon's people, and I surmised both of them had been on patrol elsewhere on this floor.

"We heard the screams," said the soldier I didn't know. "But we couldn't tell where they came from."

Rayya crossed to me and gripped me by the shoulders. "Are you all right? We tried to come as fast as we could, but every time we came down one hall it seemed we heard your voice coming from another."

"Not me," I assured my friend with a shake of my head, and gestured to the unconscious Chrissa, lying on the floor.

"Eye of Akolet," Rayya said in breathless horror.

"Take her to my daughter," Bannon ordered. "Both of you, and with great care. He's concussed her, for certain, and I'm afraid he may have also broken several of her ribs. Before you go, give me a pair of your shackles. Jarl must be restrained."

Rayya handed Bannon a set of chains, staring. "*Jarl?* Jarl did this? But—"

"Take Chrissa, and for the sake of Sherida, take *care* when you move her."

I knelt before Jarl, inspecting his bloodied face.

How did one of the Sanraethi *fall prey to this madness? A castle boy might have served one of the cultists or at least been somehow accessible to their manipulation... but Bannon's own soldiers?*

Glancing up, I scanned the room. Rayya and the unnamed soldier, with Bannon's help, got Chrissa supported between them and carried her away. Bannon looked down at himself with a grim string of muttered oaths—blood streaked his chest and hands, and Jarl had managed to claw four ragged, ugly lines across one bicep. But I noticed these things only in periphery; as I rose to my feet, looking up toward the high ceiling of the shrine room, an ugly, uneasy dread stirred in my gut.

Why Jarl? I peered down at the soldier, as Bannon stooped to cuff Jarl's wrists together behind him. Jarl's bad leg should have made any sort of altercation difficult for him. Even if he could pummel Chrissa, all she'd need was one good opening to dart past him and run away. He wouldn't have been able to catch her.

Yet when I pounced him from behind, he whirled on me like a puma. He came at me with no trouble whatsoever, so what had hold of him?

"Sadira?"

I turned to Bannon. "Sir?"

"What are you thinking of?"

I considered the shrine and its implements scattered all over the floor. "I don't know."

I touched him. I touched him, too, on the wall.

More footsteps outside. Mara appeared, filling most of the doorway, halberd in one hand. Bannon beckoned her in, and two more soldiers followed.

"Confine this man to one of the empty dungeon cells," Bannon told them. "Keep him separate from the sorcerers, *and* the castle boy. If one or both of them is inflicted with some illness of the mind, I don't want them murdering each other."

The soldiers carried Jarl away, and Bannon led me and Mara back into the hall.

"What else do you know of the stigmata our violent offenders have displayed?" he asked me.

"I have told you everything already." I pinched the bridge of my nose with a sigh. In the aftermath of the fight, the adrenaline rush now fading, the exhausted weakness in my limbs resumed. My arms shook, and I worried my legs might abruptly give out beneath me. All the pleasure in soreness had run out, though, and now I just ached.

"The sorcerers," I mumbled, defeated. "The sorcerers have cast some spell upon us."

No, argued an ugly voice inside me. *Not the sorcerers.*

I didn't say it aloud.

The serpent god repays.

Bannon scowled and began to pace. "How can they? How can they steal the senses from my own warriors?"

"Foul serpent worshipers!" Mara spat, nose wrinkled in disgust. "This whole land and everyone in it, *poison* to the core."

Too weary to bother with manners, I buried my face in my hands and groaned. "Not all the Vashtarens, nor even all the Vash in this castle, served the serpent god. That would be why they call us *slaves.*"

"Slave or not, those who lie down with snakes will be bitten, and their wounds grow infected." Mara narrowed steely eyes at me. "And there are always *more* snakes hiding where we do not see."

Though worn out, I rose again to face off with the lieutenant, stepping up to put myself nose to nose with Mara. "If you are once again implying—"

"Why would Jarl attack his partner?" Mara demanded. "He's as steadfast and loyal a guard as you could hope to have at your side. He's mentored Chrissa for years! What could cause him to beat her nearly to death, and on an altar to that vile god of yours, no less?"

"*Not* my god!" I shouted.

"*Somebody* bewitched him." Mara jabbed me in the chest with her finger. "And just how many of the *sacred serpent's* followers are there still left walking free in this castle?"

209

What happened to the woman who only hours ago treated me for the first time with some dignity? "I have *told you*—"

"*Enough!*" Bannon yelled, pushing us apart. "You will *both* compose yourselves, right now, or I'll have you confined as well!"

I fell back, seething but swallowing my pique. Mara glowered at me and crossed great muscular arms over her chest, but she obeyed the captain's order.

Bannon drew in a deep breath, nostrils flaring. "Sadira, what do you think?"

An ugly flash of betrayal darkened Mara's expression. I scanned the hallway around us, as if I might somehow find an answer there, and rubbed at the back of my neck.

"If... if the sorcerers somehow had access to him. If he took a watch over them in the prison, if one of them touched him—"

I touched him.

"—maybe they could have... planted some suggestion. Jarl might not even be aware of what he did. Like the boy when he attacked the worker in the courtyard. He didn't recall the attack even seconds after it occurred."

Dropping to sit on a prayer bench set against the wall, I added, "Jarl might not attack Chrissa. But the Order of Akolet thrive on the violence. Any violence at all. Like the seven-headed serpent they are predators and carnivores. This is why the Khan dynasty is favored by Akolet: they are the hunters stealing eggs from the nests of ground birds. They are the killers striking at the heel."

And they are the poisoners. I've always known Alaric changed me... I am poison, too. But am I poisoning others now? Has Alaric truly laid a curse upon me, an eternal punishment for breaking his rules, even after his death?

Is this my fault?

Or, in the absence of its most powerful avatar, perhaps the sacred serpent really had come. Come to punish the invaders.

Come to repay.

"I can search the archives again," I offered Bannon. "Maybe I missed something before."

"Are you certain you want to be seen lurking about a bunch of dark spellbooks and evil prophecy?" Mara jeered.

My lips twisted. I clenched my fists and cautioned myself against bouncing to my feet and socking the other woman straight in her broad, handsome nose.

"Mara," Bannon warned. The lieutenant backed down, and Bannon gave me a stern glare as well.

"I apologize, Sir," I told him softly.

He nodded, then turned to his first-in-command. "Let the others know Jarl is being imprisoned for his own safety. Afford him whatever ease and comfort we can. We'll have to keep a sharp eye on anyone who has already succumbed, and those who might yet fall prey."

"Aye, Sir."

Mara spun and retreated down the hall. I rose again, letting out a soft grumble. The activity had spoiled my sense of lingering bliss, leaving an unhappy exhaustion in its place. All I desired was a long, deep sleep. We'd have to go down to Ailsa's quarters first though, to find out Chrissa's condition, and then Bannon might wish to check on Jarl, if the man had already woken. Resigned, I slipped my arm through Bannon's and gave him a gentle squeeze before we made our way downstairs.

Before we left the hallway, however, a figure appeared coming our way. Rayya again, wearing a frightened expression.

"Captain. Sadira. We took Chrissa downstairs as you asked, but... "

Rayya glanced askance. In that brief gesture, I saw all the old doubt, anxiety, even *fear* my friend had endured under our old, malevolent masters. I didn't like to think about what could make poor Rayya look so troubled and uncertain again.

Bannon's tone was firm, but not unkind, as he asked, "What is it, soldier?"

Beckoning us to follow, Rayya led the way down to the castle's main stairwell. At first, I didn't know what my old friend meant to show us, as the stairwell stood empty and there seemed no evidence of other trouble. Rayya wasn't pointing us down the stairs, though. Instead, with a hopeless grimace, the former slave pointed at something overhead. I followed her motion, and cold dismay filled my chest like a rush of icy water.

Three dead ravens hung above the archway. *Hung* there, by no visible means, no rope or nails or other binding, as though gravity itself inverted to arrest them pinned to the stone. Across the arch, *burned* into solid stone, was another message.

Die for him.

CHAPTER NINETEEN

THE SANDSTORM WHIRLED to life again before sunrise. With it came a growing desperation.

Sweltering hot days left even the shadiest inner hallways and deepest, windowless cellars nearly unbearable. The wells still gave clear, clean water to drink, but it came up from the earth as flat and warm as the thick, stifling air. When the winds of the sandstorm wailed outside, desert dweller and barbarian alike sought shelter on sleeping cots in dim rooms, wearing as little as possible, and moving only when necessary.

When the storm blew too heavily to post soldiers on the watch, I volunteered in the kitchens to give others a break from ovens and boilers. I hadn't done scullery work for twenty years, but we didn't have much to prepare anyway. We were approaching the last of our good rations, and people had started catching rats and even scorpions to stretch provisions further.

As supplies dwindled, more and more of the castle inhabitants grew tense, irritable, even belligerent. Workers snapped and jabbed at one another in sharp displeasure. Arguments broke out over the size of rations or the share of space one person received over another. The Sanraethi eyed the Vash with wary suspicion; the Vash bristled under the expectations laid on them by the Sanraethi.

"Very few people in my homeland practice magic," Bannon explained to me one evening as we reclined in our rooms. "Dark portents like those birds, they're the things of fables. Only stories. Until we came here and faced Khan's armies, the only *magic* we knew of came from the prophets of Sherida and invoked healing or comfort."

Those refugees of other nations and tribes strove to avoid the clash, reverting to the silent, unobtrusive mien they'd relied upon during Alaric's rein. Dim, drab shadows filled the castle halls once more.

Two more injured soldiers from Ailsa's caravan died of their injuries. Merysa, the second victim of the Vash boy, lost her life as well, to Ailsa's despair and confusion. Merysa had seemed to be getting better.

If there is *a curse,* I pondered, watching from an upper landing as Ailsa and Bannon oversaw the removal of the bodies, *it's getting worse every day.*

I hugged myself, running my thumbs over the tattoos on my upper arms.

All these marks, all the rituals Alaric invoked over me... He changed me, inside and out. Used my body as a talisman, my spirit as a vessel.

Had he made me a dark plague-carrier? An instrument of his vengeance?

The serpent god repays.

Every day, I paired off with Rayya, the only person in the castle who didn't look at me as though I were some slimy, slithering reptile. My old friend didn't mind spending time working in a mostly empty kitchen or clearing the tower rooms of previous owners 'belongings. The only job Rayya wouldn't perform was entering any of the shrines, or the living quarters she'd shared with her master, Bhrune. When the soldier giving out assignments tried to send Rayya to these tasks, I interrupted.

"Respectfully," I said to the taskmaster in an even tone, "have another worker clear those old rooms. Someone who was not made to serve within them against her will."

After a silent, awkward pause, I added, "Please. Don't make Rayya go back to her master's chambers."

The soldier peered at me, then at Rayya, face screwed up in doubt. He issued us a different assignment, though, sending us to one of the upper towers instead.

"I wish they'd stop looking at me that way," I grumbled as we climbed the steps. "They could extend some benefit of the doubt by this point."

"It wasn't you," Rayya said. "He was confused because you called me *her*."

"What?"

Pausing between stairs, I considered my friend. Rayya had put off any last vestige of femininity and begun putting on muscle in arms and shoulders. Her once-delicate hands now bore calluses from work, and she no longer looked slim and supple. She'd become strapping, approaching brawny. Yes, I supposed if a person hadn't known her in her life before, it would be easy to assume she was a fine-featured young man.

I leaned against the wall, crossing my arms over my chest. "You know, I remember when Bhrune dressed you in nothing but veils. You're almost an entirely different person now."

"I hated that," Rayya snapped, cutting her gaze away from me. "I hated *everything* he made me do. Since I turned eleven, dressing me like a doll, putting everything on display. Painting my face, making me keep my hair long like a... like a—"

"Like a woman?" I finished.

Rayya's jaw clenched, and her cheeks colored.

"Is it easier to let them think of you as a man, then?" I tried to soften my tone. "To avoid more lechery?"

"No." Rayya started up the stairway again. "That's not why."

I gazed after her, brows knit. "Rayya, dear heart, I didn't mean to upset you."

"I want them to think of me as a man," Rayya declared. "I'm happy when they call me *brother*. Do you think I couldn't correct them if I needed to?"

I hurried after my friend, taking the steps two at a time to catch up.

"Tell me what is on your mind," I coaxed Rayya. "I will understand."

"Will you, though?" Rayya scoffed. "You say it so easily. As if you could change your whole view of me when you have seen my utter nakedness. When you speak of my dancing in veils, and you remember the way *he* made *everyone* see me. Humiliating!"

I resisted the urge to say anything. Rayya rarely spoke as it was, and certainly never like this. The other slave had always seemed terrified of her own voice.

The storm? Or was this something Rayya had been holding inside much longer?

"Before Bhrune took me as his personal slave, I dressed as a boy," Rayya said as we climbed. "It wasn't perfect, but almost. Everyone mistook me for a boy and treated me like one."

I brought a hand to my mouth. "That's right, I remember. Everyone thought you were the miller's youngest son. Even *I* thought so."

"Yes, and they called me Rayyan, just as if I'd been born a boy and named as one. Then Bhrune found out what I hid beneath my boy's breeches."

Rayya shuddered in disgust. "It was like he *sniffed* me out. So many girls among the slaves, proper girls who dressed and acted as they ought. But he chose *me*. The last girl in the world who wished anyone to know her true sex. Perhaps Bhrune selected me because he wanted to expose me. Force me into the role I rejected. And so, I became his whore, with breasts and ass and—"

She wrinkled her nose and spat out the word as though it had burned her. "—*pussy* on display for everyone. As though—as though he thought it would *fix* me."

"Fix what about you?" I asked.

Rayya didn't answer. "You are right, Sadira. I could be a whole different person now. So, *let* me be that person."

My friend stayed grim for the rest of the day. I didn't ask any more questions.

I wasn't sure what to say.

The second morning after Jarl's attack, the winds died down enough for the guards to resume watch on the walls. The first shift hadn't even made it across the courtyard, though, before a new grim omen revealed itself. Mara had just dispatched us to the southern rampart when a wild gust kicked up, sweeping and scattering sand, uncovering the corpses: three desiccated warriors and one of the castle servants. They'd been sundered as though drawn and quartered; their limbs bore the marks of a predator's teeth.

"But... but we saw them out of the castle gates!" one of the Sanraethi soldiers protested as I crouched down, inspecting the bodies scorched by blistering winds and scouring desert grit. "These are the scouts the Red Bear dispatched. How did they end up back on this side of the walls?"

"Back inside the walls, and half-eaten," I amended. The dead scouts' skin had decayed to a ghastly black—lines of a horrible illness spread like gangrene, eating at the edges of their injuries. I scanned the barriers for breaches, but workers had erected heavy fortifications during the last lull in the storm, and they'd all held. No more holes in the great old stones, peeping into the empty streets of Vashtaren.

So how did four dismembered corpses get back in?

As though some brooding giant plucked them up for a snack and threw back the bones.

Mara summoned Bannon, and by the time we'd gathered up the bodies and arranged them to be better inspected, he'd arrived, stone-faced and grim. He seemed to reach the same conclusion as the rest of us in just one glance; these were indeed his scouting party, and they still bore the messages he'd sent along with them. However far they'd made it after leaving the castle, they hadn't reached their destination.

I had never seen Bannon become truly angry. On the battlefield he'd been ferocious, an indomitable beast with battle axe and shield. As temporary lord of the castle he'd shown displeasure, but never fury. With me, he'd been flustered and frustrated, but he'd never raged.

Now, his eyes grew dark and a muscle in his jaw ticked; he clenched his fists until his knuckles turned red.

Snatching up one of the axes from the fallen scouts, he let out a furious bellow and flung the weapon, one-handed, into the great castle gates. The axe spun in flight as if it were no more than a simple hatchet to him, and it struck home in the heavy desert ironwood almost to the eye.

"*Sherida!*" He fell to his knees, smacking his balled fists to them. "Lady who sees all! Seeker of Truth! Will you let your people starve to death in these badlands?"

"This isn't like him."

I glanced over my shoulder to find Ailsa had joined us. She'd grown ragged and thin, and her chapped lips pressed into a fine line. She seemed about to say more, but only shrugged.

"Captain!" came a cry from above. One of the men on the wall leaned out over his rampart, scanning the sands below. "Come see this, Sir!"

Bannon rose, clasping hands together before his face as though in a brief prayer, and then crossed to the steps mounted into the walls. I sprinted to join him, and Rayya and Mara followed.

Outside the wall, weaving and stalking among a ring of other dried out bodies on the sand, roamed huge, muscular black jackals. They dug about the corpses, pausing to seize a calf or hand or part of a nose, before resuming their restless circles. Some glared up at the castle inhabitants lining the wall, and bore their bloodied teeth as though laughing. The reek of their wild, sour hides rose in the heat, all the way to the assembled soldiers and lookouts.

Hyenas loped and hobbled around the field of the dead as well, along with dirty, patchy opossums, snuffling and chewing at withered flesh. As everyone watched, a hunched, crooked vulture dropped down from the sky and landed right on the rampart, snapping its hooked beak at one of the soldiers.

"Don't!" I lunged forward as the soldier beat the buzzard away with the shaft of her spear. The bird wheeled back into the colorless sky, and the woman spun on me, anger sparking.

"*Think* a minute, why don't you?" I snapped. With a sound of frustration, I grabbed the spear from her hands and set my gaze on the vulture overhead. Two more had joined it. I didn't have to wait very long before another one dove down, giving an ugly screech as it landed right before Rayya—*Rayyan, remember, Rayyan*—and raised up its wings in threat.

I tossed the spear to my friend, and Rayyan jabbed forward to plunge it right into the bird's tatty breast. Squawking with outrage, thrashing its wings, the creature struggled to pull back, but Rayyan held it down, pinned to the rampart, until its struggles ceased.

"There," I said to the soldier, pulling the buzzard from the tip of the spear as Rayyan handed the weapon back. "It's not pretty, but it's meat. Maybe you should take it down to the kitchens."

Rayyan gave a harsh, humorless bark of laughter. The other soldiers glanced back and forth, uncertain.

"Could be diseased," one of the men muttered.

I crossed my arms. "Then you die quickly of bad meat instead of slowly by starvation. Your choice."

Mara pushed forward through the group. "Take it," she instructed the spear carrier. "The workers in the kitchen will determine if it's edible. With stores running low, we can't be picky. The rest of you, don't hesitate to spear another of those birds if they come close."

"There's more." I pointed down at the pacing carnivores below us as the soldier scurried off with the buzzard. "They may look like omens to the rest of you, but I see valuable game."

Bannon joined us. He stared after the runner who'd taken the bird for butchering, then rubbed at his beard as he peered at the sands below.

"I'm not certain how safe it is to venture outside the gates, even during a lull in the storm. I don't know if the next people I send out there will be sent back to me in pieces before they reach the first beast."

"We can kill them from here." Rayyan put both hands on the rampart and leaned over it, considering the jackals and hyenas. "I grew up in the river valley, Captain. The fishermen speared crocodiles this way. We tie ropes to the arrows, then drag back the corpses."

I nodded in agreement. Bannon slowly nodded his head, as though picturing what Rayyan described.

"All right, it's worth a shot. Will you work with the archers to do this?"

"Aye," said Mara, at the same time I said, "I will, Sir."

We glanced at each other, and I saw the familiar steely glint of disdain in the lieutenant's eyes. Perhaps the same unhappy gleam shone in my own. Neither one of us amended our response, though.

The rest of the morning, while other soldiers patrolled the walls in pairs, wrapped tightly in balaclavas and loose desert garb to shield against the wind, I worked with Mara and the archers to adapt the spear fishing technique. Mara tasked me with carving arrowheads into barbed hooks along with two others of the Vash. Rayyan inspected the modified arrowheads and advised the carvers on how to preserve the swiftness and accuracy of the arrows.

"We'll have to wait until the wind dies down more," Mara mused. "But I think this will work."

I grabbed another arrowhead and began to carve it. Rayyan did the same. Neither of us said anything, but I imagined my friend was thinking the same thing I was.

There might be real food tonight, for the first time in days.

CHAPTER TWENTY

TWENTY-FOUR HOURS later, though the problem of meat and provisions had been somewhat lessened, Bannon's foul mood hadn't improved.

The spear carriers and archers had managed to bring in several buzzards and a handful of the ugly opossums, and as I suspected, none of the castle inhabitants turned up their noses at the meat. None had grown ill, either. Yet more trouble made itself evident, when three young desert children from the scullery snuck into King Alaric's solarium, a wide worship chamber in the western wing of the castle.

Grand and golden, before the fall of Vashtaren the solarium had been a glittering marvel: a crystal cathedral in the light of a bright desert sun. Golden rays poured down through breathtaking thick glass windows overhead, sparkling through gemstone hues and designs delicately etched into the panels. This had been the one place in the castle where the serpent worshippers desired bright illumination: here they basked in the strong heat, stretched across golden divans like reptiles in the sun.

Everyone had left it mostly alone since the Order collapsed. To keep out the intense, overwhelming heat it gathered under its crystal eaves, the refugees had closed the doors and barred them shut. The desert warlords who aided in Bannon's victory had laid claim to the treasures within the room already,

and Bannon's people had already scoured it for supplies. Nothing had been left within worth mentioning, or worth retrieving.

A few of the younger refugees had wanted pomegranates, though, and convinced themselves the ornamental trees in the chamber would be ripe with them. Of course, had there been any fruit worth harvesting, Bannon and Mara would have had workers in already to claim it. The hungry, impatient boys discovered *something,* though, dangling from the decorative branches. Whole, ripe, nearly-bursting bounties, swollen red pods fat enough to make the trees lean from their weight.

But when they'd cracked open the husks, the insides were spoiled, crawling with beetles and stinging black wasps. The youths ran, full of screams, their hands and faces bloodstained from the syrupy crimson fruit juice. As they fled, snakes poured out of the corners, and poisonous adder fangs found unprotected feet.

Only one of the boys escaped the grand sunroom, and he'd haltingly explained the scenario to his uncle before collapsing in a heap. He died of snake poison hours after.

The bodies of the other two were retrieved from the solarium, which bore no evidence of snakes or wasps. The foul fruit were there, though, cloying and fermented, a sickeningly sweet aroma ruined by the low undertone of blood.

Not pomegranates, I confirmed as I crouched to inspect the broken, oozing husks. *No, they look more like little, split-open skulls. And that* smell...

Not pomegranate at all. Nauseating and foul, a stench of spoiled wine and death.

I'd known these children. At least, I knew them by association. They'd served as page boys and attendants to Alaric's fighters, cleaning and fetching weapons, delivering orders, even sometimes sparring with apprentice warriors. *I* might have even trained with one. Maybe the boy who made it out. I didn't remember.

But I knew them. We'd survived Alaric's rule. We were meant to be free now.

Not dead.

The solarium entrance was sealed again and barred with iron in place of wood. *Black magic,* whispered the people in the halls. *Witchcraft,* muttered the Sanraethi. But this time the Red Bear would not allow the rumors to run unchecked.

"We *need* to know what brings these misfortunes on us." With an angry scowl he paced back and forth across the central dais in Alaric's throne room, while Mara and I stood by. "There may be no help on the way. The king's regent is dead and so far as we know, the forces on the coast don't even know we're in trouble. Unless this storm clears up completely by tomorrow, there's no chance of getting another band of scouts out to our allies in time."

In time. He meant before we all starved.

"Assuming they make it out of the city," Mara added, grim. Dark circles hung under her eyes, and despite her strong physique, she seemed to sag, shoulders slack.

"Aye, the city." Bannon rubbed at his beard. "Which has remained silent since these storms began."

"The Vash in the city are dead, Sir," I said in a hushed tone, feeling strangely ashamed. Everything about the situation made me ashamed, as I grew more and more fearful it had all been brought on by *me*.

The serpent repays. Die for him.

Above the throne, sculpted along the top of the wall high overhead, a marble frieze of purest white loomed over us. The elaborate, winding coils of a massive snake, whose sinuous scales split to form six angular viper's heads, gazing in all directions in observance of its domain. The seventh division became the torso, arms, and head of a man, menacing and ominous, right over the king's place on the throne.

The sculptors had fashioned the human face in the likeness of Alaric's great-grandfather, rumored to be a descendant of the god himself. It looked like Alaric, too, hovering over his domain, ever watchful, ever condemning.

"I'm certain they are dead," I repeated, forcing myself to look away from the hideous likeness. "I would say the people of this desert are used to sandstorms, even of this magnitude, but I think we all know by now this is no natural occurrence. We've seen no one and heard nothing on the other sides of the walls. The people in the city lie dead in their homes. That, or they are simply... gone."

"There is talk of a curse on this castle, Captain," Mara said, startling me as if she'd just jabbed me in the back with her halberd. "The prisoners murmur about it when they think the guards don't hear. A death-curse laid down by the king when you cut him down on the battlefield."

Bannon sat himself on one arm of the throne, drumming his fingers along the shaft of his broad axe. I didn't like the way the gruesome serpent above seemed to wait over him, a predator ready to strike.

"Sadira?" he asked. "It looks as though you've been right all along. I find it difficult to imagine the men in our dungeons—naked, stripped down, pitiful as they are—could mount such a devastating revenge. At least not without help."

A shiver of fear weakened me. Had *he* changed his mind about me too, now?

He rose again and crossed the floor to stand in front of me, tilting my face up to his. At his touch, my shoulders eased. I wished we could be gone from this room, horribly wide and open, with its soaring high ceiling and echoing marble floors. And that awful, awful snake. I wanted him to myself, alone in the plush, warm safety of our bed—*our* bed, *our* rooms, no longer stained by Alaric's horrible touch— where we could shelter from the storm together.

"You've suspected the cultists since the beginning. I should have listened. But they must have help outside the bars. Who could be carrying out their will?"

Unseen by him, Mara shot a withering expression our way. I swallowed and bit my lip. As much as I wanted to lash out at the lieutenant, what defense did I have? I *had* been Alaric's most prized possession, his favored pet. No one else in the castle, besides the imprisoned sorcerers, made such a likely conduit for the dangerous and destructive spell of revenge. Even I'd run out of other explanations.

"Sir, I—"

I hesitated, glancing at Mara, then back at Bannon again. "I know only a little of the power Akolet's favored magicians could wield. I did witness many of their conjurations, but... "

The wail of the sandstorm cut through, silencing me. I didn't realize I'd flinched until Bannon's gentle fingers on my bare shoulder soothed me.

"With no magic of my own, I'm afraid I only understand so much." I spread my hands out before me. "There were others—slaves in the Order's harem—who might know more."

"What sort of help do you think they can offer?" Mara asked.

Bannon and I broke away from one another. Running a hand through my hair, I replied, "They might have been used as I was, as vessels and conduits for the sorcerers' energies. Their bodies, blood, passion, pain, would have been subjugated for the sorcerers to channel arcane power. Yes, Lieutenant," I amended as Mara opened her mouth to interrupt, "we were their *whores,* if you must think of us that way. But we were used, as toys *and* as tools, and their ceremonies were part of our reality."

Mara curled her lip in an expression of disgust. "*Animals.* Those men are fortunate I did not get to them before they were clapped in chains."

She shot an unhappy look at Bannon. "And fortunate the Red Bear insists on a trial."

I turned back to Bannon.

"Ask Rayya—uh, Rayyan—to summon the others. But be gentle with them, my barbarian. Whatever the Order did to them, they were victims, not accomplices."

"Mara?" he addressed the lieutenant, without looking in her direction. "You know the one called Rayyan, don't you?"

"Aye, Captain."

"Find him and ask him to gather up the slaves who served in the harem. Bring them here, and let's see what they have to say about our prisoners and this supposed curse."

As the lieutenant marched off to obey, I looked up to Bannon. I silently begged for him to hold me, and he seemed to understand, because in the next moment he drew me close and cradled me to his chest.

The other slaves arrived in twos and threes, until all seventeen who had survived the war gathered before the great Red Bear, some for the first time. I sympathized with the wary expressions they traded with one another.

Alaric's thirteen sorcerers had all been male, but their tastes in sexual playthings didn't run in the same direction. Most of the Order's slaves were women like me. Some were men, though, and some—like Rayya, who wished to be Rayyan now—might have been either sex. Two of the former slaves were perfectly androgynous, a set of pale, dark-haired twins born male and female, but by all significant markers, interchangeable in their roles. They had belonged to a single sorcerer who died during the war.

They'd all discarded the trappings of their slavery, though. No more collars or bracers or jewelry put on them by their Masters. Rayyan was not the only one to have completely altered their appearance. Some of them, I knew, had started going by other names, names from before their imprisonment, or names which suited their tastes instead of their former masters.

But I keep my collar, and my scars. I keep my name, though I know it is not my name. No wonder I seem strange, even to them.

"Is this everyone?" Bannon asked.

"All who have survived," Rayyan responded. I met my friend's gaze across the group, and Rayyan crossed the floor to come stand beside me. She—*he, now*—took my hand. My earlier, clumsy obliviousness seemed forgiven.

"You have my sympathies." Bannon held out his hands to the assembly. "I dislike asking any of the prisoners of this castle to relive the circumstances of their internment. It's been my goal to have you all free of this place and far from these old ghosts and shadows. Back on your way home, wherever your homes may be."

He tilted a brief nod of recognition at two of the slaves who were obviously Sanraethi, like him, bearing the same tawny complexion and colorful, warm shades of hair.

"Unfortunately, of all those held captive, I'm told you seventeen were closest to the black magician himself, and his sorcerous allies."

"We're not the cause of this storm!" piped up one of the girls, a tall spitfire whose younger sister, also a slave of the Order, clung to her side. "We're not like them, not... not conjurers or witches!"

"So I've been told," Bannon assured her. "And I don't mean to imply you are. What I want is your help determining what *has* brought the storm, and all the evil being done within these walls. We have all become the victims, and you may be the only ones who can help me find the cause."

Too many eyes oriented on me. I tried not to let my feelings of hurt and betrayal show. Rayyan squeezed my fingers.

"Sadira has told me of some of the rituals you were forced to take part in." Bannon took a seat on the floor and gestured for the others to follow his lead. After a few cautious looks back and forth, they did, settling cross-legged in a circle one-by-one.

That's good. I stepped back from the group. *He meets them eye-to-eye. He petitions their wisdom as an equal, not a conqueror.*

Mara was back. I retreated to her side, letting Rayyan join the circle of the others. The lieutenant and I kept watch from the back of the room, like guards. Maybe we were.

"Tell me honestly," Mara muttered under her breath, not wanting to disrupt Bannon's discussion.

"What's going on here? It's all fine and good to seek opinions from the other slaves, but *you* were privy to the works of the king himself. You are not as lost as you pretend to be."

"Oh, but I am, Mara," I murmured back.

The former slaves were already growing more comfortable speaking with the Red Bear. Guarded looks softened; tense shoulders and spines eased. I hoped they could suggest to him something more fruitful than I could.

Still, in my heart, the cold, sharp light of my true suspicion remained. This was not the vengeful work of scorned men in the dungeon, or even the combined efforts of many of them. It wasn't malicious spirits, or a hex set loose in Alaric's final hours.

I worried the Sanraethi had been right all along. *I* was the cause of it. The cause of everything. Alaric had tied his vengeance up in a dark, deadly package, a black spell fouling everything it touched.

Me.

CHAPTER TWENTY-ONE

ANOTHER MIGRAINE JOLTED me from sleep, somewhere in the darkest hours of the night. I lurched over the side of the bed, reaching for the chamber pot, and managed to find it just before I lost the stew I'd eaten at dinner.

There it is again, the cinnamon and bergamot. His *smell, his favorite oils and incense. Eye of Akolet,* why *does it reek so?*

But as soon as the violent retching had passed, so had any hint of the hated aromas. The agony in my head, on the other hand, throbbed on, like iron nails driven into my skull. With great care, I shifted to sit on the edge of the bed, the torment curling me in on myself with my head between my knees. Eyes closed, I took a slow, deep breath and centered myself on the flow of clean air into then out of my lungs. In. Out. In—

"Sadira?"

Bannon, muffled with sleep. He reached one arm out and groped for me. Without turning toward him, I took his hand in mine.

"I'm all right," I whispered. He might not even have heard me. The slow, even pace of his breath resumed almost immediately.

Sacred serpent... has it ever hurt so badly?

I rested my elbows on my knees and kneaded my temples. *Like a spike. An enormous spike right between my eyes. I think my head might* explode.

I measured my breaths in and out, tuning myself to focus on the rhythm. My fingertips moved in small, alternating circles at my temples. Still the migraine thudded on like the fist of some angry ogre, and this time the screaming winds outside were very real, each rising shriek like a saw on my nerves.

When it eased enough for me to rise, I did, scooping up the soiled chamber pot. It hurt to move, but I forced myself to go to the bath chambers.

The humid steam of the baths gave me some small comfort. The bunched, aching tension in the back of my neck eased a tiny bit, and the warmth of the room was welcoming and quiet. I emptied the pot and gave it a rinse from a spout on the fountain, swirling the water in it and then emptying that, too, down the drain. The weight of even such a small chore did me in, though. Exhausted, I dropped the chamber pot on the floor and sunk to my knees, focusing on slow, steady breaths.

No, it never hurt so badly before. Pressure clutched and hammered my brain, as if to squeeze it from my skull. An unsettling prickle ran along my spine like a serpent winding, winding. *Constricting.* My mouth still tasted of vomit, but I couldn't find the

236

strength to even scoop a handful of water from the fountain to rinse it out.

Any moment, something inside me would burst, and I would die there on the sauna floor, blood trickling from my ears.

What is wrong with me? I've had these headaches all my life, but they've never been as bad as in these last few weeks. Never so constant.

The dream came back to me: the yawning grave, the maw of the serpent, the rattling of a thousand venomous reptiles. Hands all over my body; dry, slithering, legless coils sliding up my limbs.

Alaric's voice, beckoning. *You were meant to die for me.*

Maybe I was. I hunched onto all fours and crawled forward on the roughened granite to the border of the sunken baths, then laid out on my stomach, breathing in the steam. *Maybe I was supposed to die when Bannon cleaved Alaric's head from his body, and it's only taken this long to catch up.*

I'd been crying and hadn't noticed; a generous rush of tears escaped me as I lay my head gently down.

The cool, wet puddles of condensation on the sauna floor felt good on my naked skin, at least. I rested for a long time beside the hot bath, counting my breaths in and out, praying for the grief to go away. I didn't know how long I'd been at it before I thought of Ailsa's previous advice and dipped one hand into the hot water.

Oh... that feels good, at least.

Time passed. The headache thundered on, sometimes receding, then renewing in full force until more tears came. I wanted to sleep, but fatigued as I was, the pain wouldn't release me. Somewhere on the back of my neck, a hard, buzzing strain had started, boring down deep.

So, I rolled onto my back on the floor, letting my hand dangle in the water. I couldn't guess whether I'd been there for hours or only minutes. All I knew was the headache hadn't shown any signs of lessening, and if I was going to die of aneurysm or embolism, at this point it would be a relief.

Will it only continue to get worse?

Would this dark supernatural siege go on forever? Jackals and vultures acting as jailers while a sickening blight poisoned our food and stirred madness in our brains?

And if it does end? What comes next?

I wondered again where I would go when the castle was no longer my home. Where would I hide from screaming winds and blinding light then? If the headaches continued to worsen, when they left me crawling on the floor like a dog, tears spilling, where would I find shelter?

I'd been a prisoner in an inaccessible tower of Alaric's making. I'd been beyond the castle walls, of course, armed with blades and tasked with protecting his life. I'd even followed him to battlefields and to raids, where he reaped other prisoners like me: children too young to resist, stolen from farmers and fishermen with no warriors to fight back. All along, though, I'd been with him, bound to his side. And when I was with him, I was still his twisted prisoner, locked in his tower, away from the wide-open world.

I'll find work. There are cities beyond Vashtaren, cities planted all throughout the sands. There will be work in one of them. A guard post, or gamekeeper.

A nasty voice in my head—*Alaric's* evil, vengeful voice—whispered a different suggestion.

Whore.

But would that even be so bad? It had frightened me as a girl: strangers prodding and groping me like fruit in the market, lying down with partners who were utterly unknown. As a woman, though, I hesitated to reject the idea out of hand. *Why not? I told Bannon I worship carnal indulgence. Why not become a priestess of my own castle? The castle of my body?*

My head gave another throb and I rolled onto my side with a long, pleading groan. My free hand came up to tug and fiddle with the ring of my collar. Around me, the dim, flickering light in the steam baths seemed to shrink away by degrees, as though I were slipping, sliding, *falling* into a deeper darkness. The pit before the cairn in my dream. The gaping grave of the fallen king. The rattling of the snakes.

Somewhere far away, a voice called out a name. A woman's voice in a foreign accent. A cry full of despair.

Seren! Seren, where are you?

Not snake's rattles. Drums. War drums, pounding under a dark, alien sky.

I blinked. My eyelids had grown heavy, and the flickering lamps now seemed like pinpricks of light in the distance. Dancing orange flame and shadows...

shadows of people moving back and forth across a dark, swelling divide. Cries of anguish. Screams of grief, or suffering, or surprise. Sobbing.

Another voice... a man's voice. *Seren!*

"*Madrēn...*" my lips formed the old words, hardly cognizant as I did. "*Seunda...*"

Mother... grandfather...

Dark night. Sky full of clouds. Not the horrible, ochre, burning clouds of the desert sandstorm but bruised purple and blue and black, hiding an unfamiliar field of stars. The scent of strange, sweet trees mingled with smoke and ash.

Drums.

Seren! Sweet goddess, don't take my Seren!

I knew those drums, didn't I? I groaned and rolled over. War drums. *Alaric's* war drums.

The world rocked and swayed beneath me. Somewhere close by came the creak of wood and the slap of oars in the water. Stinking, burly bodies, rife with sweat and blood, above me. Small, shivering ones at either side. Behind us, the cries of the people onshore—

Onshore?

—began to fade.

"Ugh..." I croaked. "That *goddamned smell...*"

Cinnamon and bergamot. It practically choked me.

But didn't I throw those oils away?

When I put my hands down on the floor, I'd come back to the puddle-strewn granite of the baths. I squeezed my eyes shut against the steady candlelight and pushed myself to my feet. I *had* thrown away the oils, I knew it. I remembered the clink and rattle of the glass tumbling down the drain.

I pressed my hand to my brow as I searched for the stand holding the selection of perfumes. When I found it, I searched through the phials, setting aside lotus, amber, patchouli, and sandalwood. I sifted through desert rose, dragon blood, and anise, but there were no ampoules left of cinnamon or bergamot.

But it's everywhere...

Phantom scents and visions could sometimes accompany the worst migraines. I put it down to the agony in my head, and returned to my place on the floor, to soak my hand again. Ailsa's recommendation, simple as it was, had proven to be the only comfort I could find.

The instant I dropped my hand into the water, a searing, scalding flash shot up my arm. I screamed.

The bath *boiled*. I snatched my hand back up, clutching it to my breast, staring wide-eyed. Bubbling, violently roiling, the baths had become like a great, wide pool churning with a malicious tentacled monster beneath the surface. My hand throbbed and stung. But I couldn't move.

The water. Churning and churning. Shifting, rising, falling. *Rolling.* Bubbles burst and sent hot droplets flying, stinging my naked skin.

A person could fall right in.

Shaky, I climbed to my feet. I couldn't pry myself away from the water rolling... rolling...

A sharp stab jerked me out of it. I'd grabbed my own burned hand and squeezed it, shaking myself out of my stupor. The fresh pain doubled me over and I gave a harsh, guttural cry.

Cold water! Douse your hand in cold water!

Blisters already broke out along the surface, and skin had begun to peel. I rushed toward the fountain, the only source of water not fed from the kitchen pipes. But it, too, boiled, pouring bubbling jets of more steam, more scalding water swirling around the basin.

"Sadira?"

Bannon appeared at the other end of the chamber. I glanced up, meeting his gaze across the room.

"The water—" I tried to explain. "It just—and my hand—"

He stalked toward me, and I met him halfway before the steam clouded the room completely. His arms slid around me, and I rested my throbbing head on his chest, still holding my scalded hand, protecting it from contact. The baths warbled and churned around us, the violent rush picking up pace. The whole room, hot to begin with, had grown scorching. Soon the steam would cook us alive.

Together we escaped, rushing from the thick fog into the passageway, where cool, sweet air awaited us.

"My hand," I said, holding it up, reddened, raw, and shiny. Bannon took me by the forearm, avoiding the blistered places and the peeling skin, and pulled me to the bedside table. Snatching up the ewer of drinking water, he plunged my hand into it. Not cold—probably not much better than room temperature—but it spread a small relief through my stinging, tingling palm, and that was good enough.

"How did it happen?" he asked.

"I don't know." I ground my teeth. I had suffered burns before, even bad scalds, but none so quick or so deep. And my *head...* my head still *pounded.*

More tears came. I couldn't take it. Choking, I dropped to my knees, resting my head on the side of the bed. "*Dae Cator!*"

Bannon quirked an eyebrow. "Eh... what?"

"I—I don't know." I sucked in a sharp breath through my teeth. "I don't know, it just... it's nonsense."

He stooped to take me under the arm and draw me back to my feet. "You need to see Ailsa. You're pale as glass, kitten. You've got bruises under your eyes like somebody punched you straight in the face."

"Can you help me?" I leaned on him.

"Of course. Here, sit down and let me get you dressed. Then it's straight down to see my girl."

He tossed a grim glance over his shoulder, back toward the entrance to the steam baths. Even from here, the burble and rush of the water sounded loud... and somehow *angry.* It had started dying down, but like a growling beast, it seemed only to be waiting.

Not gone. Just waiting.

CHAPTER TWENTY-TWO

BANNON LED THE WAY downstairs and to the healer's quarters. Though I knew where to find Ailsa, anguish and dizziness blurred my vision. Bannon kept one strong arm looped around my waist, but still I made him pause when I thought I might throw up again.

It's not just a migraine. My mind raced, running in frantic, senseless circles. *I am dying. Alaric's vengeance has come. Any minute now, my heart is going to stop—*

Dae Cator, I'd said. What did it mean? Where had those words come from? They weren't of the desert language. They'd come into my head like panicking birds.

The sharp knock of Bannon's fist on a wooden door shook me from my distraction. We'd reached the medical ward. I straightened, slipping from Bannon's supporting grip to stand on my own.

Bannon knocked harder and called his daughter's name in a low voice. It wouldn't do to wake the others in the ward, especially the injured, whose best chance of recovery now relied heavily on bedrest and hope. After several minutes, the door swung open with a creak, and a bleary-eyed Ailsa blinked out at us.

"Da?" Ailsa rubbed at her face and gave herself a quick shake. "What's wrong? Has there been another attack?"

"An accident." Bannon nudged me forward. "Show her your hand, Sadi."

Wincing, I obeyed, lifting my scalded red hand up for Ailsa to inspect. Ailsa reached out with tentative, delicate fingers to take hold of me by the elbow, and gently moved the arm one way and another, examining the damage.

"Come in," she said, and opened the door wider. She guided me to a stool beside the room's long wooden table. "Hold it up while I find a cloth."

Bannon followed us in and shut the door behind us. Ailsa disappeared into an adjoining room. From within came the even breaths of several sleepers, and a rustle of someone rolling over in their bed. It took Ailsa only a moment to come back with a smooth, folded length of bandaging. She spread it on the table before me and then gingerly lay my burned arm down on it.

"What happened?"

Dizziness renewed itself in a sickening wave like too much wine. I pinched the bridge of my nose with my good hand and waited for the feeling to pass.

It didn't. "Ailsa, do you have a pot? I think—"

I pitched forward in my seat and vomited, retching a mouthful of sour bile onto the floor.

"She went into the baths," Bannon explained for me, while Ailsa rose to dig through her meager collection of medicines. "I woke up when she screamed. I don't know how the water came to be boiling hot but when I followed her in, the whole bath bubbled like a pot on the fire."

"I had a migraine." My chest stung as I spoke. "I took your advice, Ailsa... dipping my hand into the water to draw the pain away from my head."

"Looks like you succeeded." From a woven basket, Ailsa produced a vial I recognized: one of Alaric's tinctures of cannabis. She must have been rationing the medicine very closely to still have even a little bit left.

"Not entirely. It still feels like someone has driven a nail between my eyes and planted a foot on my chest."

Ailsa poured a measure of the cannabis oil into a spoon and dabbed a finger in it. Without needing any instruction, I opened my mouth and allowed the medicine woman to dab a few drops of it under my tongue.

"The burns are very bad." Ailsa poured the remaining medicine back into the vial and stoppered it. "But I do have a salve for them. We haven't needed it yet, so it's still in the saddlebags with my horses, in the stables."

"Please retrieve it, then, and see to her." Bannon stroked my hair and bent to plant a kiss on my brow. "I'm going back to the bath chambers to find out what caused this."

"Don't!" I protested, grabbing his wrist with my good hand. "Please, my barbarian... I... What if—"

He sank to his knees and cupped my face in his hands. "I will take care. I'll take Mara with me, to be safe. Other soldiers, too. We'll not risk another strange possession."

My nervous stomach gave an uneasy flutter. "Rayyan, too? Please. She—no, *he*—he knows the saunas as well, and will recognize if anything's amiss."

Bannon didn't seem to notice the self-correction, or my shift from my earlier assertion on Rayyan's sex. He nodded his agreement and rose, then disappeared back into the hall.

"We'll head to the stables in a moment, once you've had a little time for the medicine to work." Ailsa replaced the vial of cannabis oil in the basket alongside similar bottles and deposited the basket on a tall shelf. "I'd let you wait for me here, but after Jarl's attack on Chrissa, I'm not sure I want to leave anyone alone anywhere."

"Agreed." I rested my head in my hands and took a deep breath.

Chair legs scraped stone as Ailsa took a seat beside me. "You'll forgive my asking, but I thought you were famous for your perverted love of pain."

Letting out a rough sigh halfway to becoming a groan, I moved my head gently side to side in a negative. "Not like this. There's no sweet edge to this."

"What kind of pain does one like you find *sweet?*"

How to explain this to Ailsa? Bannon's own daughter, who'd certainly draw some very brutal, but very honest conclusions? Ailsa had a sharp mind, and she already regarded me with troubled cynicism. I preferred it to outright disdain, but still, we shared a very fragile, difficult peace. Did the barbarian girl really need to know more about my twisted desires?

"What can I say?" I mumbled. "There is a beauty and release in pain which is sought out and embraced.

It isn't the same when pain is suffered against your will."

"Hm." Ailsa touched my arm, above the scalded flesh, gingerly lifting it from the table and holding it up for inspection. "And what of the desert claiming ritual my father undertook to win you as prize? Would you call it willing or unwilling pain?"

Looking up, I met Ailsa's eyes.

"It was necessary," I said. "And it was not what you think."

Ailsa snorted. "Sanctioned rape. And you call *our* people barbarians."

"Bannon did nothing I did not demand. Believe me when I say he won his victory on *my* terms."

With a wrinkle of her nose, Ailsa released my arm. "Come on. Let's get down to the stables and find the burn medicine."

"I know how I seem to you, and your people," I said as I rose from my seat. "Even the other refugees think I must be mad."

"What troubles me is how you've ensnared my *father* in your madness." Ailsa grabbed a lantern from its sconce and motioned me out the door. "I don't like the way this desert seems to be changing him."

"Is it?" I asked. "Changing him?"

"Before this crusade, I'd never have believed my father capable of publicly humiliating a prisoner by leading them through a crowd by a dog's collar," Ailsa spat. "They call him warlord but even in war, he's never been a tormentor. And *you* are not even a true prisoner. You're his..."

The word seemed bitter to her, as she screwed up her face and said, "*Lover.* You're his lover. A conquered enemy, a prize of war, and now warming his bed."

"Is that really so strange?"

Ailsa gave an ugly grunt of a reply.

But wasn't I always that to Alaric as well? I cradled my scalded arm gently to my chest as we made our way through empty stone hallways down to the stables. *Sometime before my memory, I was taken from a fallen people he'd defeated, wasn't I? A spoil of war, and later chosen for his bed.*

My headache seemed to have receded a little, chased away by the medicine. Or perhaps purged along with most of my stomach contents when I'd vomited. The hazy half-dream I'd imagined as I lay on the floor of the saunas drifted back to me.

Seren! Sweet goddess, don't take my Seren!

In over two decades, I'd never remembered the night of my abduction. Of course I'd always known how Alaric and his ancestors reaped their slaves through raids on unsuspecting kingdoms, and as I bore no trace of desert blood, like Rayyan, it only made sense I'd come to Vashtaren as a hostage. I'd only been too young, and too confused, to recall anything before it.

That voice that came to me, I wondered. *Was it really the voice of my mother? Was it a true memory, or just the muddled scraps of a dream?*

"What was your mother like?" I asked Ailsa.

Bannon's daughter came to a stop, shooting me a look of confusion. I didn't know how to explain the question—I hadn't even realized I meant to ask it, until it was already out of my mouth.

After a moment, though, Ailsa softened, and started walking again.

"She was... different from my father and me. Not a warrior. A very soft person. The daughter of a clan councilman. More of a speaker, a negotiator, than a fighter, like we are."

"I don't even remember my mother." I touched my collar, brushing the embossed leather with the pad of my thumb. "I don't even know what it's like to have a mother. Or siblings, though I suppose I might have some, somewhere. Do you have any?"

"Siblings?" Ailsa shook her head. "None. My mother and father had only me."

We came to the tall double doors leading to the stables. The familiar and comforting scents of hay, manure, and horse hide mingled faintly in the air, and muted wails of the storm outside rose and fell beyond. Before going in, however, Ailsa paused, and spun to me.

"Be honest with me," she demanded. "Have you conceived a child with my da?"

Startled, I balked. "No! I can't—There is no—"

Ailsa cocked an eyebrow.

Starting over, I told her, "I have not. And I will not. That isn't part of our arrangement."

The corners of Ailsa's mouth twitched into a shrewd frown, her brows knitting together. She peered into my eyes, perhaps probing for the truth. Whatever she saw seemed to satisfy her, and she pushed open the stable doors.

A girl of about twelve years uttered a quiet squeak as we entered. She'd been curled up on a thick pile of hay, and now bits and pieces of straw stuck out of her hair.

"Oh!" She covered her mouth with her hand. "Lady Ailsa! I'm sorry, I didn't mean to fall asleep!"

Ailsa patted her on the shoulder. "No worries, child. Doesn't seem to be any harm done, and we all need some extra rest right now, I think."

While Ailsa and the girl spoke, I wandered down the corridor of horse stalls, admiring the creatures within. Bright black gazes glittered back at me out of every compartment. One of the beasts uttered a soft whicker as I passed. Another scuffed his hoof on the raspy, hay-strewn floor, and tossed his head prettily when I stopped to reach out my good hand toward his muzzle. It was soft and supple, like very fine velvet, and his warm breath fogged over my palm.

"What a lovely boy you are." I stroked the horse's nose, and when he sidled closer, I scratched his pert, flicking ear.

All at once, the stallion gave a rough, wet snort. He shook his head and whinnied, startling me into stumbling backward to barely avoid a chomp from his huge teeth.

"All right, all right!" I waved him off with a dismissive huff and began my search for Ailsa's saddlebags.

I found the two surviving wagons from the regent's caravan stationed at the far end of the stables. Just beyond them, the wide, tall double doors to the open courtyard rattled and wheezed under the storm's assault. Fine wisps and flurries of sand found their way in between cracks in the boards. I gritted my teeth at the sulfurous, moldy stink of slowly fermenting chaos.

It took only a few minutes of searching before I discovered Ailsa's saddle bags among the other surviving supplies. Ailsa's were full of smelling salts and mostly used wads of bandages covered in the dust and dirt of the trail. Soiled though they may be, Ailsa must have kept them for emergencies. Surely there'd been other medicines, but the medicine woman had cleared out the ones she would need most.

At the very bottom of the second bag, I found a small metal tin. Twisting it open, I discovered a viscous, waxy yellow substance smelling sharply of bitter herbs and something floral.

"It's the only medicine left in here," I reasoned. "It's got to be the salve."

I climbed down from the cart.

A sudden sharp *crack* made me jump, dropping the tin of salve to the floor. As I stooped to retrieve it, another *crack* sounded on my left. I shot a glance at the horse stall and quickly ducked out of the way as the creature within reared, giving a wild shriek, and thundered heavy front hooves on his stall door.

"What's wrong?"

I clamored to my feet and approached the horse's door, reaching out with my good hand to calm him. The poor beast tossed its head back and forth, bashing at the wood.

Spinning, I stared as a second horse brought its weight down on its door. Up and down the corridor of their stalls, the animals were going mad.

Eye of Akolet!

A quick movement caught my eye: slithering under one of the compartments, a thick, black, scaly tail.

Oh, no...

Clutching the tin of salve to my chest, I ran for the stable entrance where I'd left Ailsa and the stable hand. I'd made it almost halfway back when a second stable hand, a young man, stepped out from a space between stalls and I collided with him. We fell in a heap of limbs to the floor. I gave a short shriek as I landed on my scalded hand.

In a burst of noise like a thundercrack, a dozen wooden doors burst off the horses' stalls with an explosion of shattered planks and enormous splinters. I pressed myself closer to the floor, holding the stable boy down with me, as debris rained down on us in a pounding clatter.

"Back behind the stalls!" I shouted at the boy, rising to a crouch and pulling him after me. Somewhere in the din, Ailsa cried out, and the first horse raced past us, coming perilously close to trampling us as we ducked for cover.

"No!"

The stable boy jerked away from me. I spun, keeping low, and made a grasp for his arm.

"We need to get out of the way! The horses are about to—"

The boy backed away, staring at me, full of fear. *Why is he shying from* me? *I'm not the threat here!*

More horses poured out and galloped down the corridor. I yanked my hand back and ducked into the farthest corner of my shelter, losing sight of the boy as powerful equine bodies blurred past.

The stampede couldn't have taken more than a few seconds, but I shrank back as far as I could, covering my head and clapping my hands over my ears. The migraine flared back in full force—or was it just the quaking, thunderous sound of frantic animals all around?

When the last of the horses had run past, I shakily climbed to my feet. Dizziness made me sway, and I seized one of the vertical beams dividing the stalls. The shrill whinnies and furious snorting of the animals hadn't ceased—when I wobbled back out into the corridor, I saw the herd had caught up at the back of the stables, crashing into the doors to the courtyard. Horses thrashed at them, rearing, kicking, but an iron crossbar prevented their escape.

One of the carts from Ailsa's caravan had been smashed to splinters. Some of the animals had collapsed under the raging panic of the others and screamed as they were kicked and trampled. Taking a deep breath to galvanize myself, I made my way toward the frenzy.

Ailsa had already reached the outer doors along with the horses and had climbed partway up the wall to crawl along a thin shelf where livery was stored. *She's working her way to the bar from the side,* I realized, and hurried to the opposite position to help work the crossbar free.

Horses seethed and pitched; I managed to duck aside just as one fiery-eyed charger reared, churning at the air with sharp, gleaming hooves. A rope dangled on my side of the doors, looped over a beam high above—probably for lifting and moving bales of hay back and forth across the floor. I seized it and leveraged myself up on the wall, wincing as the rough hempen weave chafed my injured palm.

I reached out for the crossbar just as Ailsa took hold of it from the other side.

"Slide it my way!" I shouted.

Ailsa nodded, and together we worked the iron beam toward the right. Straining against the searing agony in my hand and the unwieldy weight of the bar, I let out a sound somewhere between a groan and a scream, but at last I managed to pull the bar out an extra few feet. I closed both hands on the rope and rappelled myself higher—then brought my weight down on one bare foot, hitting the very end of the bar.

The iron levered up, out of its traces, swinging and sliding down on my side. The stable doors burst open under the weight of the herd, and the horses broke out into the howling, scouring winds.

Ailsa and I dropped down from our positions and fell back from the open entryway. Hot gusts of sand blew in, chasing us down the corridor as we retreated toward the inner doors, covering one another with raised arms.

Injured horses lay in the path of ruin. Most were still alive, but even at a cursory glance it was obvious they couldn't be saved.

No snake bites. But I saw it! *There* was *a viper in here, that's what spooked them so badly. Wasn't it?*

If there had been a snake, it had disappeared in the chaos. No sign of it remained.

Oh, hell. I cradled my burned arm to my chest, hugging it tightly to me. *Am I losing my mind?*

A little less than halfway back down the corridor, we found the stable boy. He lay splayed out in one of the stalls, maybe kicked there, maybe crawled in some last desperate attempt to find shelter. His trampled, beaten body looked almost boneless, like a tattered rag doll tossed carelessly to the ground.

Chapter Twenty-Three

MARA SLAMMED HER fist on the wooden table. "You cannot leave her free any longer!"

Squaring off with Bannon she scowled, her jaw set, her dark eyes sparking with fury. "What will it take for you to *do* something about this witch, Red Bear? Will you let her ruin the rest of our food and poison our water? Open the gates to the jackals and invite them in to feast? She needs to be imprisoned!"

"Executed!" shouted one of the other soldiers, and several others voiced their agreement across the room.

Standing beside Bannon on the opposite side of the table, I struggled to keep my head up in the face of the accusations. It seemed like everyone in Bannon's makeshift war room wanted me beheaded and tossed to the scavengers.

And I couldn't blame them.

Ailsa sat on Bannon's other side, hands clasped together on the table before her. Bruises purpled her knuckles and a raw, red scrape marred her cheek. She hadn't said anything since we'd returned from the stables and told Bannon of the stampede. Rayyan stood next to me, and curled one arm around my shoulder, giving me a squeeze.

I rested my good hand over his, silently thanking my friend. Sweet Rayyan, the only true ally I had anymore.

"It was my *boy* she killed down there!" raged an older, bearded soldier. Tears ran down his ruddy face wracked with woe, and two of the others had to hold him back as he jabbed an accusing finger at me. "She killed *my boy* with her evil arts! You owe me justice! You owe me *blood!*"

I forced myself to look upon him. Not as any sort of answer. Not to stare him down or silence him with my pride. I searched the harrowed lines of his grief and tracked the tears as they ran down.

It is my fault. His loss... the death of his child. It is my fault.

This is the price of my freedom.

"Captain, we will ask you one last time." Mara straightened, snatching a set of shackles from the hands of another soldier and slinging them across the table. "Lock Khan's whore in the dungeons, along with the rest of the serpent worshippers."

Bannon stared at the manacles. I couldn't read his expression. He touched them with two tentative fingers, as if he expected them to burst into a hissing viper any second.

"Ailsa," he said. "You were in the stables with Sadira. Tell me—tell *all* of us—what might have caused the animals to panic."

Ailsa spread out her fingers, flexing and relaxing them, wincing as she did. "I can't think of any reason

Sadira would or could arrange for such a brutal and wasteful cost of life. We'd gone down to retrieve medicine for her, and as anyone can see, she *still* needs something for the burns on her hand."

As though remembering something new, she paused and shot a glance at me. After a second's hesitation, she tapped the side of her head and snapped her fingers.

"You went ahead of me to the wagons, while I spoke with the younger girl. To retrieve the salve."

I nodded. "Yes, I did."

"But then... "

Ailsa's expression faltered. "You were at the other end of the stables when the panic began. Touching the horses and... and speaking to them."

The rumble of the other soldiers rose to a violent pitch. Several shoved their way to the front of the group to shout demands and reach across the table as though to grab me. I took a stumble-step backward and found Bannon's arm supporting me along with Rayyan's.

"Is it true?" he asked me once the angry voices quieted.

"It is, Sir." I bowed my head to him, contrite. "I didn't do anything to push them into a stampede, though. I was only admiring them."

"Lies!" snarled one of the castle inhabitants, a frail older man who'd served as slave to Alaric's family longer than I had been alive. "Why haven't you bound her? She should be answering for herself from the other side of iron bars!"

"I can't say for sure what Sadira did," Ailsa warned, rising from her seat. "She approached the animals, yes, but anyone might have—"

"It was not *anyone*!" a female soldier interrupted. "It was the black magician's personal whore!"

"She's sunk her claws into your father," another accused. "Since the night she bent him to her sadistic practices, he's protected her, and meanwhile she works dark magic on us to avenge her tyrant king!"

"I have *no magic,*" I insisted, though no one seemed to hear me over the din of argument.

Bannon clapped both big hands down on the table and bellowed, "*Shut up,* all of you!"

With a reluctant rumble, the mob quieted down. Dark expressions clouded faces; gimlet glares landed on me, sparking with fury and disgust.

Growling, Bannon drummed his fingers on the wood, a harsh, agitated rhythm. "Sadira. Do you have any explanation for what happened tonight?"

I forced myself to relax my shoulders and lift my chin. When I spoke, though, my voice faltered—I had to clear my throat, and the violent tremble I'd been fighting off for almost an hour threatened to undo me.

"Th-there was—"

Damnit, I will not *sound like a simpering child before these soldiers!*

"A snake." I straightened and took a deep breath. "I caught a glimpse of it just before the horses broke free."

"A *snake?*" Mara crossed her arms over her chest and spat on the floor. "Then tell us, why have we found no snake in the wreckage? Will you have us believe every door on every stall exploded off its hinges because *a snake* slithered out of the hay?"

Wheeling on Mara, I snapped, "No, Lieutenant, I don't expect it to make sense. As I've said many times now—as all of us in this desert know—when these sandstorms rage overhead—"

"*Sandstorm?*" The father of the stable boy lunged over the table, planting his palms flat on its surface to scowl at me through his tears. "You'll not be blaming your evil on some wretched winds! There's no way a little sand and thunder whipped those creatures into a bloody rampage!"

"You don't know Vashtaren sandstorms." Rayyan stepped forward. "They're tainted by the desert's bloody history and the dark powers of the sacred serpent. If the horses rushed the doors to get *out* into the squall, it had surely already driven them insane."

The stable hand's father pinned Rayyan with a bloodshot glare. Before he could retort, though, Ailsa spoke up.

"He's right. Sadira and I had to flank the herd on the courtyard side of the stables and open the outer doors before they wrecked anything more. I watched the poor things, even the mildest old plow horses, stamping and kicking one another."

She grimaced, a slight tinge of green coming over her. "Some were... *eating* the dead."

"I tell you, it's black magic." Mara waved a hand. "Snakes, wooden paddocks bursting open all at once, evil portents in the wind, horses killing and eating one another? *None* of this is coincidence, Captain. There is a sorcerer among us slipping a noose around our necks, and only *one* person in this castle bears the serpent's mark and yet still walks free."

Rayyan rested strong, steady hands on my shoulders. "*Not* Sadira. She is no sorceress. Perhaps Lord Khan's allies in the dungeons have other apprentices. Students who've kept themselves hidden since the downfall of the king and his cult."

"Passing themselves off as refugees?" one of the soldiers challenged. I recognized him: Olson, the man who'd suggested I demonstrate the pleasures of the torture chamber for him and his younger partner.

"You're one of their servants, too, aren't you?" another demanded of Rayyan.

"He is," Mara confirmed before Rayyan could reply. "I remember the captain sent me for you, to have you round up the other consorts and concubines. Your master is among the men still alive in the dungeons, isn't he?"

"Maybe *you're* the one, then." Olson pulled his own set of shackles from his belt and held them up. "Why don't we send them both to the prisons with their patrons, and see if that doesn't end the curse?"

More people shouted their approval, soldiers and former castle servants alike. Even those who had known me and Rayyan, and the other prisoners of the cult, voiced their agreement. Bannon pounded on the table over and over, shouting for order, but this time the argument only grew louder.

I hugged Rayyan close to me. My friend trembled in my embrace.

"I won't let them," I whispered. "They won't take you down there, not you. Not with Bhrune. I promise."

Rayyan managed a stiff nod, all at once very pale. I cupped my friend's face in my hands and leaned close.

"What you told me before," I whispered. "How it makes you happy when the soldiers call you brother? How you can be a whole different person now?"

Rayyan stared at me. "Yes."

"If you wish for me to call you my brother, then that's what I will call you. And I will not let my brother go back to the man who tormented him."

Rayyan smiled—a shaky, anxious smile—and nodded. I embraced him, vowing to myself over and over I would honor my promise.

Even if it meant giving myself up to keep Rayyan safe.

"Sir."

Releasing Rayyan, I turned to Bannon. He stood nearly nose-to-nose with Mara, each one shouting at the other while the group threw louder and louder accusations into the mix. Even Ailsa had started yelling, giving a pair of former slaves a piece of her mind while they glared daggers back at her.

I stepped closer to the Red Bear and said his name. He didn't look my way. I touched his arm and he brushed it off, never breaking eye contact with Mara.

"Barbarian!" I yelled, slapping my good hand on the table. No one paid attention to me. At last, glancing back and forth over the warring parties, I stormed to the table and in one swift, ferocious motion, flipped it over with a noisy clatter.

The argument came to a halt. I planted my fists on my hips, head held high.

"Sir," I repeated.

Bannon, rubbing at the back of his neck with an expression of chagrin, faced me.

"Take me." I held out my wrists before me, inviting him to shackle me as Mara had asked. "I'll go to the dungeon, if it means you and your people, and those who suffered under Alaric, can have some peace."

"No." Bannon cast aside the shackles in his hand. "There's not a shred of evidence you've had anything to do with these misfortunes, and I will not give in to paranoia and rumors."

"He's right." Rayyan touched my arm. "You're not to blame, and you don't need to surrender yourself just to satisfy these outsiders who don't understand."

"If it will put an end to this fighting, allow me to do it." I took Bannon's hands. "Sir, please. I'll have no one accusing Rayyan or any of the other slaves in my place. I don't want that for them."

"She has a good point, Da." Ailsa tapped her chin, gazing at me.

"I don't care what her point is," Bannon growled. "Sadira, think of what happened when you last visited the dungeons, and then you walked among your old tormentors freely while they could only heckle from behind bars. You're asking me to lock you down there in a cell of your own, so they can mock and humiliate you to no end, with no reprieve?"

"That is what I'm asking," I said, resolute, holding my head high and shoulders straight.

He stared at me. In his face I read his outrage, and his fear. Even the great Red Bear of the Highlands had no guidance, no plan of escape from the evil misfortunes befalling us.

I could tell him my true suspicions. One hand came up to toy with my collar. *That these portents* are *my fault. The darkness and evil, they shadow me in the halls. Tragedy and death seem to linger always near me.*

Cursed, the boy in the courtyard had called me. *Cursed,* the barbarians and even the natives now said.

263

What better way to ensure I'd have no life without him?

"Please, my master," I begged in a low tone. "You have given me my freedom, and I chose to will it back to you. I will do whatever you ask of me, but for the sake of everyone trapped in here, imprison me and set their minds at ease."

"If Sadira is down in the prisons, we'll know soon enough if the misfortune continues." Ailsa extended a hand to Mara. "If she's locked up and we see more of these omens, will you—all of you—concede she must be innocent?"

The soldiers and servants exchanged grim looks all around. Five minutes ago, they'd been calling not just for my imprisonment, but for full execution. Could they be convinced of a lighter sentence?

I didn't think so. The flat heat in their eyes made me squirm. Most of them still had murder in mind.

"Bannon?" I asked.

Bannon rubbed at his chin, looking from me to Ailsa, then to Mara, then back at me. He took me by the shoulders, as Rayyan had done, but with a deeper note of comfort.

"You are a very brave girl to do this, my kitten." He pulled me to him to kiss my brow.

"My only desire is to protect you, Sir." I glanced over my shoulder at Rayyan. "And protect those who were victims of the evils done in this castle. If you tell me I am strong enough to endure the sorcerers, then I will be strong enough."

His thumb caressed the inside of my wrists. "If this is your decision, pet... I'll give you the chance to try."

Mara stepped in, bearing the shackles Bannon had thrown aside. "All right then, witch—"

"Can't you be civil?" Bannon snapped. "She's surrendered herself for all our sakes, Mara."

I struggled to keep my expression stoic and obedient as the lieutenant clapped me in irons for the second time. She made no effort to be gentle with my scalded hand—I clamped my teeth down before an anguished shriek escaped. I might concede to their demands, but I *wouldn't* give them the pleasure of seeing me suffer.

Two of the other soldiers flanked her—Olson and Gregor, of course, the same two who'd been there the first time Mara shackled me—and with grim resolve, they guided me through the now silent, staring crowd.

Bannon and Rayyan fell in close behind, the Red Bear practically looming over the guards, as they led me to the dungeons.

Into the pit, with the rest of the snakes.

CHAPTER TWENTY-FOUR

BHRUNE SCOOPED A handful of grit and pebbles from the floor and flung them at me through the bars. "When did the barbarian grow tired of your pleasures, slave?"

Seated on the floor of my musty prison cell, set farthest back from the stairway, and separated from the cultists by two other, empty cells, I took a long, deep breath, and concentrated on quieting my mind. I ignored Bhrune's taunting—the other prisoners had jeered and mocked me when Mara brought me down in chains, but only Bhrune still persisted, almost three hours later, while I tried to meditate.

"Or did he come to despise you, knowing your pretty snatch first belonged to Lord Khan? Could the fierce Red Bear no longer stand to fuck the great sorcerer's whore, who was shared among the worshippers like a plate of fruit?"

I couldn't suppress a twitch of irritation.

"Had his fill of your poison." Bhrune gave a rusty chuckle. "You filthy slut. You know, I always hoped

Lord Khan might will you to me, when he had no more use of you and moved on to some other fresh young thing. I'd have satisfied your masochistic lusts. I'd have found ways to bring you misery like you never imagined."

"Lord Bhrune thinks himself funny," Rikhi spoke up from his cell. His voice, an oily, unctuous tone, made the skin on the back of my neck crawl. "But the king would never have relinquished you. You were much too *essential.*"

I gritted my teeth.

"That is why," Rikhi continued in a slow, musing drawl, "you'll belong to him until the day you die. No matter whose bed you warm... Lord Khan will always be your master."

"And why is that?" I let go of my meditative posture and shot a glower at the old vizier. "Go on, Rikhi, tell me. What made me so different from all the other slaves that I cannot escape him, even after death?"

Rikhi answered only with a nasty grin and said no more.

A ragged groan escaped me as I climbed to my feet and paced back and forth across my cell.

You are very brave, my kitten.

Bannon could barely suppress his fury when they'd brought me down here. After Mara escorted me to the cell—wisely choosing the one farthest away from any other prisoners, probably to avoid any more argument with her captain—he'd stood by with fists clenched at his sides, his visage red with anger. He'd respected my wishes, though, despite the conflicted impatience in his eyes.

He trusts me.

Or, a part of me needled, he didn't trust me at all. Deep down, beneath the confidence we'd started building with one another, perhaps even Bannon suspected what all his people, and many of mine, did.

And... they might be right.

I looked down at my hands. The left one still throbbed, red and raw from the burns. Neither Ailsa nor I had retrieved the burn medicine after the stampede, and the limb had gone untreated. Perhaps I could ask for some bandages when the next guard descended for a check of the prisoners. Now that I was safely behind bars, maybe they'd see their way to at least such a small favor as that.

Am I cursed after all? Is that what Rikhi means? Am I destined to haunt all those I touch with the backlash of Alaric's revenant jealousy?

Maybe it didn't matter. I thought my remaining time would be quite short. Though the lingering threats of execution or starvation had certainly brought the subject to mind, I hadn't yet acknowledged in myself that in truth... I didn't expect to survive this.

"Go on, Dierdre, let me down there."

The voice came from up the stairs, interrupting my thoughts. I glanced toward the dungeon entrance along with the other prisoners, as the mild voice of one of the guards gave a quiet reply too soft to make out. The first speaker didn't bother to keep her voice down.

"I don't care what sort of bastards are down there. Do I look like a little girl? I've got a patient in a cell with a burned hand whose had no proper tending, now *let me down*."

268

Ailsa. I reflexively cradled my burned hand to my chest, filled with hope for the prospect of medicine at last.

A moment later, Bannon's daughter strode down the steps into the prison vault and planted her fists on her hips as she scanned the prisoners. From his cell at the front of the room, Jarl rose with a stiff, weary grumble, and dipped his head in greeting.

"Hello, Jarl." Ailsa crossed to his bars, gripping them as she looked him up and down. "How's your leg?"

"Stiffer than ever. My whole body feels like stone."

"I'll see if we have any willow bark in the supplies for you."

Ailsa turned away from him and made a quick scan of the other cells. Rikhi and Bhrune, and the other former lords of Alaric's court, sneered and spit at her. She ignored them as she passed, making a beeline for my cell.

"I brought the burn medicine." She produced the small tin from a pocket on her belt. "It took me forever to find it again in the stables. I'd have been here sooner but there were so many piles of debris and—"

She didn't have to say *so many dead horses.* I nodded, understanding.

"Hold out your hand. I'm afraid we probably haven't spared you any lasting damage. This salve should have been applied immediately. It should relieve the pain, though, and cool the sting of the blisters."

I did as asked, sliding my shackled hand through the bars. Ailsa dabbed the greasy concoction carefully over my injured fingers and palm, taking extra care on the delicate joints.

"Did you do it?" she asked. "Compel the horses into a rampage?"

"No!"

Perhaps I'd answered too quickly, but a flash of frustration stabbed me in the chest. "I *don't have* magic. I never have and never will! I couldn't even compel those horses to trot across the courtyard in single file."

Ailsa winced. The chagrin on her face satisfied me a little.

"I believe you." Applying the last of the salve, she replaced the lid on the tin and dropped it back into her pocket. Next, she withdrew a length of bandage to begin wrapping the injury. "I'm sorry for causing you more trouble in the meeting. I should have trusted my better judgement and never mentioned what I saw."

"I can't really blame you, I guess." I sighed. "Everyone here thinks I'm no more than Alaric's servant and sex toy."

"Not my father," Ailsa corrected. "And not that friend of yours, the man who stood beside you at the meeting."

I flicked a glance at Bhrune. I silently hoped Ailsa didn't somehow recall Rayyan's name or her—*his*—new identity. Bhrune would find a way to hurt his former slave with the information. I didn't know how he could, but I knew the old vizier would find a way to strike out at his old pet.

That's why I'm down here. So people like Rayyan don't have to relive any more abuse.

270

Ailsa finished wrapping my hand in silence. The medicine went quickly to work, and I breathed a sigh of relief.

"I know it is no comfort," Ailsa said, "but you're safer here. My father doesn't see it. I trust you do?"

"I do."

The castle inhabitants had reached the end of their patience with me. No need for Ailsa to spell it out. Violent outbreaks, spoiled food stores, and rampaging horses weren't the only signs. It had been in the way Bannon's own soldiers nearly declared a revolt that morning. The spitting arguments between him and his trusted lieutenant. The way in which he'd brushed me off, too incensed to listen to reason.

If the madness continued, the Red Bear would have a revolt on his hands, and if his people cast aside his leadership, there'd be nothing between them and their own desperate solution. Executions of the guilty. Rikhi, Bhrune, and the remaining sorcerers... and me.

Safer in the dungeons. Safer among my enemies.
Eye of Akolet. I really am going to die here.

THE ONLY COMFORT in being imprisoned was the silence. Underneath the castle, no howl of wind or blasting sand could reach me. Even my fellow prisoners eventually grew bored taunting and tormenting me, and at long last, I curled up on my pallet of hay and found sleep.

The sound of boots on the stairs woke me. My rest had been so deep and pleasant, I thought it must have been many hours into the night. Sitting up, I stretched and rubbed at my eyes.

The others were awake, too. Their sharp, attentive expressions troubled me.

At the prison entrance, one of the barbarian guards had appeared.

Only doing a round of checks. I yawned and lay back down.

Rikhi and Bhrune seemed to have no wicked taunts this time. As the guard made his rounds, the prisoners remained obediently silent. Maybe he'd been down here before, and knocked some of them around for being mouthy, imparting a valuable lesson. Or maybe they'd grown tired of jabbing at their captors.

I'd just begun to drift away when Jarl's voice caught my attention.

"What do you think you're doing?"

I lifted my head again. The guard stood at the door to my cell, staring in at me.

His eyes were red-rimmed and wild. Tears of blood ran down his cheeks.

Bolting upright, I pressed myself to the wall. My heart gave a fearful leap, beating so fast I thought it would explode.

"Get away!" I snapped.

The guard gave no indication he'd heard. From his belt, he produced a key ring, and flipped through the thin iron keys until he found the one he wanted. He slid it into the lock. There came a click, and the cell door swung open.

If I'd been prepared, I might have made a dash for freedom and managed to knock the man off his feet, but I missed my chance—the guard had already moved into the confines of the cell with me, and closed the door behind him.

"What do you want?" I demanded.

A nasty, hungry grin split the man's face, too wide and ragged to be human. He moved closer in halting, heavy steps, and as he neared me, I caught the low mumble of words coming from deep in his throat.

"You belong to *me,* desert rose... you were meant to die for *me.*"

Terror blazed to life in my chest.

Alaric?

Bright, stinging torment flashed on the side of my face as the guard lifted a hand and struck me. I lunged to one side to duck his next blow, but with my hands shackled and almost no space to move, I couldn't drop into a sweep or roll past him to attack from behind.

His fist hit me in the stomach, doubling me over. A second punch landed on the left side of my face, sending stars exploding across half of my vision. With no other plan, I dropped to the floor and scrambled for the cell bars.

The guard crouched down and seized my ankle, jerking me back across the floor. From the front of the prison, Jarl and the desert boy had started calling for help, bellowing at the top of their lungs, while the sorcerers finally broke their silence to cackle and cheer my attacker on.

The guard crawled on top of me. His red eyes glowed like desert bonfires on far away hills. When he smiled, needle fangs had replaced his canine teeth, and a forked tongue flicked out at me.

"You were meant to *die* for me..."

I shrieked—this time it had *definitely* been Alaric's voice, and despite the wild-eyed insanity in the guard's face, his words sounded perfectly calm and composed. The rotten stink of cinnamon and bergamot fouled his hot, humid breath.

I rolled onto my side and thrust out one long leg in a sharp kick, catching the man in the jaw. A sharp crack, a screech of pain—he fell back, and I kicked again, this time in the chest, knocking him onto his back.

Pulling myself up on the cell bars, I quickly regained my feet and lunged forward before he could rise. I lifted one heel to drive it down at his neck, pinning him.

Hands flew to my calf. Ragged nails dug in, clawing deep furrows all the way down to my ankles. With a strangled cry I twisted my heel as hard as I could, grinding it on his windpipe.

A rough *snap* was my reward as I broke his neck. The guard fell limp beneath me. Blood ran from his mouth.

I wasted no time crouching to retrieve the keys from his belt and unlocking my shackles, casting them to the floor. Looping an arm through the bars I unlocked my cell door too, and darted out into the open corridor, panting.

The sorcerers joined the cries of Jarl and the boy. "She's broken free! The king's witch has killed a guard and broken free! Escape! *Escape!*"

Heart pounding, I raced for the stairs and jogged up them, to the heavy wooden door at the top. When I threw myself at it, though, it didn't budge. Locked—and barred—from the other side.

"No!" I wailed, collapsing against the it. "Please, somebody! Let me out! He's *here, Alaric* is here! You *have* to let me out!"

No one answered. Below me, the prisoners' cries joined mine, and I pounded on the wood as tears streaked down my face.

"Let me out," I squeaked, sliding to the floor. "Please... he's here."

He's here.

CHAPTER TWENTY-FIVE

I WOKE WITH a start at the sound of a key in the lock. Even before the door could open I had leapt to my feet, scrabbling at the wood, throat dry and stinging as I whispered, "Let me out... please, by all that is sacred, let me out..."

There came a neat click, and a sharp, silver panic cut through me when the door still wouldn't budge. It thumped and rattled under my weight, until I remembered it opened inward, and I was in its way.

As soon as I stepped back, the door swung wide, and glorious morning light poured in. I raised my arm to shield my eyes.

"Sadira?"

Bannon's voice. With a dry sob I moved in his direction and his arms wrapped around me. "What happened, Sadi? Where's the guard?"

"Downstairs," I choked. "He came down in the night and—"

He took my bruised face in his hands. I winced.

"By Sherida! Who did this to you? Breathe. Close your eyes, take a deep breath, and try again."

I did. He slid his hands down to my upper arms, holding me firmly, but not tight. I took a breath, as instructed—then took two or three more.

I'm not alone. Sir is here, and I am not alone.

When I opened my eyes, Mara stood to one side of us. She held the key to the door and peered at me, apprehensive. Her gaze shifted over my shoulder, then, to the stairs beyond.

"Captain?" she murmured.

Bannon nodded. "Go down and see."

"It was Alaric," I told him as Mara disappeared into the dungeon. "The guard came to my cell, but he was Alaric, in spirit. The stigmata of conjuration was upon him, and he spoke to me as Alaric did."

Bannon released my arms, and, fear subsiding, I straightened, folding my hands before me. He touched my cheek, careful as he brushed two fingers over swollen skin.

Mara reappeared, a scowl on her face.

"Captain. Come down. Bring *her* with you."

I spun, startled by the note of accusation. Without a word, Bannon took me gently by the elbow, and we followed Mara down the steps.

The smell hit us first. Emerging from the passageway into the main dungeon, I staggered to a stop. Bannon balked, but Mara said nothing, standing aside with her halberd to let us take in the sight. It reeked of sour, metallic blood and offal. The unpleasant buzz of flies cut through the silence, and the temperature had to be more than ten degrees colder than it had been at the top of the stairs.

How had I not smelled it before?

Every cell hung open. The prisoners lay splayed across the dirt floor, throats slashed, splattered in gore. A few lay split from guts to groin, insides spilling out. Bhrune, the most savage of them, hung from his ankles like a side of meat in a meat cellar; the shackles which had bound my wrists now circled his ankles, the chain looped over a torch sconce. He'd been cut right down the middle.

"I..." I took a step back, staring from cell to cell, thoughts racing. "I don't understand... how..."

The guard—whose neck I'd broken—now leaned slumped in a sitting position at the farthest wall, his own throat gaping open and his forearms gashed to the wrists.

That's not how he died, though! I know *what I did to him!*

Even Jarl and the young Vash boy had been murdered. I shivered, and my stomach filled with dread.

Mara's dark expression told me everything I needed to know. Who else could be blamed but the sole survivor of this apparent massacre? The black magician's most loyal servant, and the woman who'd admitted such deep familiarity with his darkest rituals?

This was the scene of a blood sacrifice. An *enormous* working, of the foulest arts. And only one suspect for the crime.

"Sir." Mara moved to block the passage behind us, holding her halberd before her as a barrier. "It's black magic. You see for yourself. The witch must be killed."

"I did not *do* this," I protested in a tiny voice. There seemed to be no point in denial, though.

"Sadira... "

Bannon let go of my arm and crossed to the dead guard. The man's axe—the only weapon in the room—lay across the man's splayed legs, and Bannon picked it up. More gore smeared the blade. He looked from it to me, and my heart sank.

"Tell me the truth," he said. "What happened in this dungeon last night?"

I couldn't meet his gaze. I stared down at the floor, fighting my body's urge to tremble.

"The guard came in and opened my cell," I whispered. "He closed himself in with me and tried to grab me. His eyes were red and bloodied, like Jarl's and the boy's, when they, too, were enthralled. Then..."

You belong to me, desert rose.

"He was possessed, Sir. He spoke to me as my former master did. He used my master's nickname for me, a name I would expect none of your people to know or use."

Mara snorted. "Don't you see she is *lying*, Red Bear!"

"You ask me to make a terrible choice, Sadi." Bannon stared at the weapon in his hands. "Can I believe this tale of insanity? Put my people, and the people we have fought to save from your king's hands, at risk?"

"Sir..."

My heart ached. Bannon, too?

How can I blame him? How, when even I believe this terrible fortune is my fault?

All of it. The fits of madness, the sandstorm, the slowly spreading chaos. I'd thought Alaric's poison had made me a beast inside, a twisted creature hungry for violence and subjugation. No. He'd not made me a simple beast. I was a gorgon, hideous and deadly to all those around me.

A living curse.

Bannon pointed the axe at me.

"She stands trial," he told Mara. "Whatever else we have endured, we are not monsters, like our enemy was. Lock her in one of the upstairs rooms, alone. When I've seen to this—"

As though the words sickened him, he paused, and glanced once more at the murder around us.

"—this *travesty,* we will prepare for her prosecution."

I shut my eyes. I had no tears.

The point of Mara's halberd pricked my back, and I held out my hands to be chained once more. She pushed me toward the stairs, and I silently let the lieutenant to escort me to my doom.

MARA CHOSE AN old seamstress's workroom as my new prison. Once, it had contained a loom and spinning wheel, and stores of linens for mending. Bannon's people had cleared it of all its supplies, though, and now it stood empty but for four old wooden benches and a washtub, and the empty chain for hanging a lantern.

Mara lowered this chain to hitch my shackles to it, then hoisted it back up until I had to stand on my toes to keep my balance. I'd expected Bannon's lieutenant to be full of perverse pleasure, but Mara worked with a perfunctory air, avoiding eye contact, and touching me as little as possible.

When she finished, she backed toward the exit, examining her work.

"You know," she said. "I actually hoped I was wrong about you. You are a good soldier. You and I... we're more similar than I want to admit. You might have been through great tribulation, but I'd started to believe you had a warrior's heart, underneath."

I didn't say anything. There seemed to be no point.

Mara snorted, as though my silence further proved my guilt.

"But you really were *too* twisted by his perversions." The lieutenant shook her head. "Whatever warrior you might have been... he ruined you."

She left, shutting and locking the door behind her. I hung alone in the small room, and gave a deep, weary sigh.

Mara had left me one torch.

Just like that first night. Here I wait, trussed up in the dark. Until the Red Bear appears to decide my fate.

My limbs throbbed and my chest grew tight, strained from the arduous position in which Mara had left me. Yet the discomfort came to me like an old friend—the hard and harmonious blending of tension and endurance. My stomach muscles ached from the blow the guard had given me the night before, but I'd known worse. If Mara had considered how used to bondage I really was, maybe she'd have lifted me higher, and left me hanging up like a fish on a hook.

Ah, well. At least they don't know how to truly torture me.

Hours passed. I'd fallen into something like a dozy meditation when the click of the lock pulled me back to attention. Bannon slid open the chamber door and stepped in. He carried a second torch and set it in a sconce, never taking his eyes off me. I returned his gaze, impassive.

After a long beat, he slid the door closed behind him. We stood face to face in the little room, as though shut into a quiet pocket of time all our own.

Bannon frowned, his attention shifting up to the chain which held me.

"Mara..." he growled, glancing back and forth, searching the walls. Spying the hook which managed the suspension, he crossed to it and unlooped an extra length of the chain, giving me some slack and lowering me until I rested flat on my feet, though my arms remained upraised. Maybe he remembered how I'd been able to vault obstacles and disable my opponent, even with my hands bound.

"It is not so bad," I whispered. "You've seen such discipline in our book before."

"They don't know I've come." He swept me into an embrace. "Not yet, at least. They believe I've gone to the archives above to search for your secrets. I had to see you myself—had to hear the truth from your lips—without them goading me into judgement."

I blinked, and my heart gave a hopeful flutter. "I thought you'd made your decision."

"No." The corner of his mouth twitched uneasily. "Not yet."

"I swear to you, those prisoners did not die by my hand." I glanced toward the door. How long before Mara or one of the others discovered Bannon hadn't made it to the library after all? After a pause, I added, "The guard, yes. I had to kill him. I don't know what he'd have done—what he'd have been compelled to do—if I hadn't."

"You really believe *Khan* somehow possessed him?"

"I know of no other way he could have known what Alaric has only spoken to me in my dreams."

Bannon stared into my eyes. He raised a hand to stroke my bruised cheek—not as careful this time, and I flinched at the unexpected sting. Then, before I knew it, he'd leaned in to kiss me, a soft and urgent kiss, full of emotion.

"You believe me," I breathed as our lips parted. Tears burned under my lashes and my voice cracked. "Eye of Akolet, my barbarian... you believe me."

"You're shaking." His hands slid down to my hips, firm. "It's going to be all right, Sadira."

"I don't see how. I may have your trust, but you can't protect my life over the lives of everyone else in this castle. By now, even Rayyan must suspect me of carrying on Alaric's bidding."

"How could a dead man wreak such havoc?" Bannon asked. "You saw him at all hours. You said so yourself. Did you ever suspect he had any sort of magic to defy death itself?"

"No," I whispered. "He attempted the summoning of spirits. To speak to those beyond the veil. Conjuration and séance. I never imagined he'd devise a spell of vengeance from beyond the grave."

"Is that what this is?"

"I think so. A death curse on his enemies. A manifestation of some sort, probably through a powerful talisman."

Bannon's eyebrows went up. "Talisman? If we could find such a thing and destroy it, will it break the spell?"

"Perhaps." I bowed my head. "But I think he only ever prepared one which could be used for a conjuring such as this."

"What?"

Looking up, I met his eyes with a somber, apologetic expression. Bannon stared back at me. His face fell, as he seemed to understand.

His thumb traced one tattoo winding over the contour of my hip, and the faintly raised lines of a scar following it in deliberate design.

"Ink, scars, brands..." His brow furrowed. "These aren't just decoration or his marks of ownership. He made *you* his talisman. A living, breathing talisman."

"A dark fetish," I murmured. "Do you see now, Bannon? Mara and your guards are right. You must put me to death if you wish to save anyone at all."

His rough hands tightened on my waist, jerking me a step closer to him. "I refuse to accept that. He can't have you. Not anymore."

The heat in his voice, possessive and fierce, kindled a spark inside me. Not hope—I could have no hope, with Alaric's indelible claim on me, even beyond death—but something liberating, something galvanizing, nonetheless.

Bannon seized my head and kissed me again. Heat bloomed in my chest and I pushed myself closer, offering myself up to him. His fingers tangled in my hair—his tongue found mine. There was no gentleness in him now.

His heartbeat raced beneath his skin, matching pace with mine. Who knew how long we had left? As our lips parted I breathed his name, helpless in his arms and so desperate for this, our last, passionate embrace.

Bannon seized the fabric of my bodice and pulled it open, freeing my breasts, and then shoved my breeches down my legs and off. Sliding his hands under my buttocks he lifted me, and I wrapped my legs around his waist. Now his kisses found my stiffened nipples, and when he ran his tongue over them, I uttered a soft gasp.

"You must be quiet, kitten." He tilted his face up to mine but gave one breast a heavy squeeze. "As quiet as you can be, or someone will hear."

I nodded and rolled my head back between my upraised arms. The strain in them ached all the way down to my chest, a delicious counterpoint to the sweet flicker and glow of pleasure from his hot hands and his mouth on my skin.

He dropped a hand down to my ass and gave it a slap, making me arch to him.

"Oh, Sir!" I whispered. He gave my bottom another slap, this time sliding his other hand down to the opposite side. He grasped my flesh, greedy, possessive.

"Please, Sir..."

"He can't have you anymore, Sadira," Bannon repeated between tasting and tonguing my breasts, my neck, my earlobe. "You're not his. You never will be again."

"Bannon—"

Still holding me up one-handed, he shifted enough to unbuckle his belt and release his cock from his trews. Firm, hot, slick with the first beads of pre-ejaculate, he slid into me with a lustful ease, and I tightened my legs around him. My shackles jangled as I thrust to meet his motions, and we moved together like a regal, primal creature, our bodies alight with shared desire glowing just beneath the skin.

Bannon grabbed my hips and guided my rhythm. "Kiss me, kitten."

I obeyed. His thrusts intensified.

"You're like sweet, wet silk," he rumbled. "So beautiful. You're so beautiful, Sadira, every inch of you—"

"Thank you, Sir—"

He came in a frantic, forceful rush. Grasping my buttocks, he clutched me to him and thrust to the very hilt. I threw my head back, barely containing the cry that rose inside of me as he filled me, his throbbing cock pouring hot seed into me. My toes curled—my breasts flushed with bright, tingling joy. Soon it overwhelmed me, and a rush of ecstasy raced through my body. Up and up it sped, and my body tightened as I choked on a silent shout of bliss.

Bannon kissed my lips, my cheeks, my eyelids. "Good girl. My sweet, beautiful girl."

"Is this how a barbarian loves his woman?" I asked with a laugh.

"Yes," he assured me. He held me tight and stroked my hair. "I love you, kitten. I love you, and I will never, ever let *him* have you."

He finished with a long, warm kiss on my mouth. When we parted, he took a key from his belt, and reached up to unlock my shackles. I settled into his grasp, and he caressed my cheek.

"Get dressed," he whispered, letting me down. "We're going."

"Where?" I stooped to retrieve my breeches and closed my bodice once more.

"To the ritual chamber of Akolet," he told me. "We're going to find a way to break his spell for good."

CHAPTER TWENTY-SIX

HOW DID HE expect to break any sort of spell when neither of us possessed any hint of magic?

I followed Bannon through the halls on silent feet, keeping an ear out for approaching voices or the sound of guards' boots upon the stone. Bannon held his torch aloft and searched ahead, but so far, we'd avoided crossing paths with any of the castle inhabitants.

Worry about magic when it is time to do so, I chided myself. *For now, you are only borrowing trouble, and you have enough of it already.*

We reached an intersection of corridors, and together we checked in either direction to see the coast was clear. I directed him down the next passage with a silent motion.

I hadn't entered the ritual chamber in months. A wide, windowless vault beyond Alaric's throne room, the site of the cult's darkest rituals and sacrifices. Not every ceremony required a flesh offering like myself, to give my body over to their wills—in the last days of the war, I'd been called on less and less. Alaric, however, had continued to visit his holy sanctuary every night. He'd even closed it off to the other sorcerers, and on those nights, his madness seemed to fester and seethe in his mind. We could hear him talking to himself, wild and excited, and he emerged with eyes full of rapt anticipation.

Bannon reached out one arm, blocking me from going farther. "Duck into that room."

I did as asked and found myself in a servant's cupboard. I crouched behind an empty bathing tub propped on a crate of astringent-smelling soap and held my breath. Bannon put out his torch, then flattened himself to the wall immediately inside the door.

Two low, muttering voices came into earshot. Not guards: I recognized one of the castle stewards, and whoever his companion might be, they sounded too young to have come with Bannon's people.

I couldn't make out their conversation, but it seemed to be something simple and inconsequential. No urgency. So, Mara hadn't yet discovered Bannon's deception, or if she had, the news hadn't spread beyond the soldiers.

The men's footsteps moved past the doorway and on down the hall. I pressed my hand over my chest. My heart thudded.

"I think they're gone." Bannon peeked around the doorway before extending his hand to help me up. We were both checking the direction in which the two men had disappeared, when I ran headfirst into a skinny, armored figure and took them tumbling to the ground.

The other person gave a startled cry, but I quickly covered their mouth with my hand. Wide, bright brown eyes stared up at me in the flickering light of the torches.

"Rayyan!" I whispered. "Oh, dear heart, forgive me. You can't make a sound, not a single sound, or we're done for."

Rayyan blinked up at me, brows furrowed. I had knocked the sword from his grip when we fell, and Bannon snatched it up. The soldier's gaze darted between us with an angry glint of betrayal.

"He'll summon Mara," Bannon hissed. "We should bind him and throw him in the storeroom."

"Please, Rayyan," I begged. "You've been the only person I could trust, for years. I love you, I truly do, and I hope you will say you love me, too. And trust me. I am not Alaric's witch, no matter what they say of me, no matter what happened in the dungeons last night. Please tell me you believe me."

Carefully, slowly, I removed my hand from Rayyan's mouth. Rayyan searched me, wary.

"It's true what Mara said? The sorcerers—all of them—are dead?"

"Yes." I said. "Bhrune, too. All of them."

Rayyan brought a hand up in a swift motion, and I thought my new brother meant to slap me and raised my own arm in defense. Rayyan only grabbed my hand and squeezed it with fierce affection, a dark, grim smile on his face.

"Go," he told me. "Do what you must. I will tell Mara you've headed for the cellars to seek escape through the drainage shafts."

Ferocious love blazed in my chest. I bent down to kiss Rayyan on both cheeks. "Thank you, dear heart. Thank you for everything."

I climbed to my feet and helped Rayyan to his. He embraced me once, then tipped a nod down the hallway.

"Mara has the soldiers patrolling in pairs. I only came this way alone because the guard posted with me had to relieve herself and feared having a man too close by while she was vulnerable. So far all the attackers have been men assaulting women."

Bannon handed the sword back to him. "It's a sorry thing to count on for our opportunity, but I'll take it."

"We're going to the serpent's shrine," I told Rayyan. "You know the way. What sort of patrols are there near the throne room?"

"Two, keeping watch over the east and west halls. Mara's probably in the antechamber, though, unless she's gone to search for the captain."

"Will you go ahead of us and find her?" Bannon asked. "Steer her to the cellars. We'll slip past the guard patrols in the corridors."

"The throne room is open to those corridors," I pointed out. "Once we're past the antechamber, we'll be out in the open trying to cross the great hall without being seen from the colonnade."

"Not if you cross *above* the throne room."

Bannon and I traded a quick glance with each other before both looking back at Rayyan.

"The galleries run along either side of the throne room on the second floor," Rayyan reminded me. "They are closed off now—no one is patrolling them.

If you can break the lock to get through the western gallery, and escape out the windows at the far end—"

"We could break *into* the throne room above the colonnade and reach the head dais and the throne." I tapped my bottom lip. The sculpted frieze above the dais would hide us from sight until the very last few feet. "It... *could* work. But we'd have to go out into the sandstorm and crawl along on the outside of the castle—"

"We can do it," Bannon assured me. "Grab a few linens from the storeroom. I'll be damned if this howling squall is going to trap me inside this nightmare any longer."

"Once you're down to the dais, you should be able to make it to the inner chamber without being seen," Rayyan assured us. "The guards are only patrolling the halls. They don't like crossing the throne room itself, and the colonnade only runs partway up the length of it. You'll be past them, as long as you don't draw any attention."

A significant caveat. I glanced at Bannon. "How are you at climbing?"

He flashed me a wide grin and punched his fist into his other palm. "When I was a boy, they called me *Red Squirrel,* instead of *Red Bear.* What about you?"

"My strengths lie elsewhere," I admitted. "But the way of snake and scorpion requires agility and flexibility. I think I can manage."

"Hurry, then." Rayyan ducked into the storeroom and grabbed the sheets as Bannon advised. "The soldier paired with me will be along any minute. I'll draw as many people away from the throne room as I can."

His sweet, brown eyes met mine. "Whatever you intend to do in Akolet's sacred ceremony chamber, my sister, make it count."

I embraced him again. "I love you, dear heart. Please be careful."

"You, too." He gave my shoulder a squeeze. "With any luck, we will meet once more in safety."

The slaves of Alaric's kingdom had never been lucky. Our world comprised of torment and obedience.

I suppose if Bannon expects me to discover some long-hidden magical talent Alaric could never unleash, I resolved as we parted ways with Rayyan, *braving the sandstorm outside to walk along the window ledges isn't much more to ask.*

SINCE BANNON HAD played along with Mara's call to lock me up and slate me for trial, the lieutenant and the other soldiers hadn't demanded he surrender his weapons—or his keys. When he and I reached the entrance to the western gallery, the way was blocked by chains. He whipped the keys from his belt and set to work, while I kept watch over the stairs leading up from below.

Voices came and went with more frequency now, but rarely in any sense of urgency. If Rayyan had deceived Mara as promised, I would have expected to hear the woman's barked orders ringing back and forth through the stone passages. No such tirade yet.

Bannon struggled to pop the lock, but finally it clicked free. We flinched, then stared at one another, then exchanged incongruous looks of nervous amusement.

A scuffle of boots ran past the end of the stairs below. Backing away, I let Bannon sweep me into the gallery.

With windows shuttered, Alaric's grand arcade of colored glass and collected desert artwork stood in total darkness. I didn't mind; the statues Alaric favored and the lurid portraiture discomfited me, even in the most placid circumstances. Tonight, the sandstorm yowled and clattered at the windows, threatening the thick panes of ruby red, violent oranges, and deepest black glass. Though the casements were built with sliding stone panels to protect the dramatic pieces, I doubted anyone had ever planned for a tempest like this. Who knew if Alaric's prized depictions of the desert's meanest tortures would survive this hungry, unending squall?

"Why is the blasted light so dim?" Bannon growled, shaking the torch in his hand. He'd claimed a new one from the brackets in the hallways below, but though it had crackled and burned with steady light, now it seemed it could barely illuminate two feet in front of us. We moved together through Alaric's private collection of torment and affliction, hands locked together, listening and watching the darkness as though some ugly, ancient horror would materialize inches in front of us, slavering and infected.

And why is it so cold? I silently added. I'd never been so cold in my life—I didn't think it would have been possible, *anywhere* in the Ruined Sands, to be so cold, unless it was the heart of a grave.

Outside, the wind gusted into a yowl, racing along the side of the castle, thumping the protective panels over the windows. An icy chill ran down the back of my neck like a single, skeletal finger. I pressed Bannon forward.

"Come on. Nothing in this hall but tasteless, ugly statues and paintings of bloody tortures. The longer we hesitate, the more chance Mara has to find us."

Bannon nodded, and held the torch higher. It did little good. We pressed forward, moving on silent feet, and straining to hear over the voice of the wind for any other voices—human voices—approaching our position.

"*Fuck,*" Bannon spat. "This torch is *useless.*"

"Put it out, then. It's an open corridor down the middle. There's nothing to crash into or maneuver around if we keep moving straight ahead."

Something in my heart warned me not to douse the torch—if we did, surely we *would* find one of the statues had moved of its own accord to bar our path—but with jaw set, I slid my hand to Bannon's wrist and guided it down, until together we shook out the flame. I slipped in front of him then, taking him by the hand to guide him through pitch darkness.

No statues. No unexpected monsters bursting forth unseen. I felt my way forward until I came at last to the thing I'd been searching for: the rough, woven length of a tapestry I knew to be hung at the very end of the hall. The map of the dynasty which had ended with Alaric.

"To the left, now," I whispered. Another gale outside rattled the windows at just that moment, guiding my hands until I found the edge of the panel we would need to release. I searched for the struts keeping the panel in place and slid them free, then, with a grunt, pulled the panel back.

Eerie, red-ochre light spilled in as I opened the shutter and revealed the window. The stained glass depicted an image of a giant serpent strangling blasphemers in its coils and swallowing them with great, grotesque, distended jaws. The wind gusted, and the glass rattled like bones; tiny, discordant screeches and squeals ticked across the surface.

The sand. I raised my hand to touch the window, then dropped it to my side. *The sand is cutting and scraping the glass right in front of us.*

"All right," Bannon whispered, drawing his axe. "Through this window, up onto the eastern side of the throne room, and into the nave."

Right into the serpent's jaws.

We hastily wrapped our sheets around our faces in makeshift balaclavas. I crouched down just by the edge of the sill, while Bannon waited for another long, loud wail of the storm. When it came, he raised one booted foot and kicked.

The glass shattered, and immediately flew inward as the tempest screamed, sending scorching sand and crackling lightning into the gallery. Leaping to my feet, I pushed Bannon to one side, catching the clean slash of a bright red fragment right through the linen of my hood and across my cheek.

Blood spilled down my face and rough grit blasted me, making me blind. Bannon's hand seized my wrist and pulled me to him.

He tilted my face up and carefully probed the skin around the cut. "Did it get your eye?"

"No." I fixed the edge of the balaclava. "We need to be quick. I don't think these sheets will serve us very long."

He nodded, knocked the last few slivers of glass out of the way, then climbed out into the storm.

I had never felt such heat in the air before. As I crawled out onto the stone ledge after Bannon, the wind seemed full of fire. Silent lightning flashed, raising the hairs on my arms, and rattling my senses.

Bannon moved slowly, clinging to the rough granite like a spider as he sidled, step by step, toward the landing ahead. It wasn't a great distance from the outside end of the gallery to the outer wall of the throne room, but with the driving winds, it might as well have been miles.

I moved on my hands and knees, shrunk down against the snatching, whipping gales. The sand made it nearly impossible to see—Bannon had become a vague figure already, and every noiseless flare of light made the world into a blank, white void, filling me with panic until I made out his silhouette in the red glare that followed.

An awful, heart-stopping moment came when I *couldn't* find him. The ledge ahead seemed completely empty, and I snapped my gaze down into the whirling vortex of the storm, certain he'd lost his grip and fallen, screams lost in the gale. A second later, though, a hand appeared before me, reaching out to guide me on, and I moved forward, chest aching with relief.

The shape of the man awaiting me wasn't Bannon, though. Squinting in the wind, I recognized the familiar lean frame, the haughty set of shoulders, just as the hand seized me and pulled me onto the landing.

Alaric.

CHAPTER TWENTY-SEVEN

"*No!*" I SCREAMED and struggled in the cold, pale arms embracing me. The hot, spicy scent of him, that *horrible* mix of cinnamon and bergamot, made me want to retch. His hissing, nasty voice filled my ears.

"You're mine now... *kitten.*"

I broke free of his grip and wheeled backward. My heel struck the edge of the stone and the wide, yawning emptiness of open air stole over me like the world turned upside down.

"Sadira!"

A strong arm wrapped around me and yanked me back onto the landing. The storm winds pushed me into the broad, tawny shape of the Red Bear, and together we crashed into the stone wall of the castle with grunts of pain.

"What happened?" Bannon rubbed the side of his head, peering at me out of one eye. "Why did you pull away from me like that?"

"You?" I sputtered. "It was Alaric! Alaric was here, he grabbed me through the storm! I *heard* him—"

We were alone on the landing.

I groaned and buried my head in my hands. "I can't stand this! I'm not even sure what's real anymore and what I'm imagining."

"Get inside," he commanded. "We're almost there, and then it will be over."

"You can't promise that. We don't know what we'll find in the serpent's shrine, or if any of it will make a difference."

Bannon rose to his feet. His voice hardened as he helped me up.

"Sadira. You've trusted me with your safety and now your life. Don't pick now as the moment you doubt me."

I forced myself to relax. "Yes, Sir. Forgive me."

"Good girl." He gestured ahead. "There's another window. Let's get it open."

Moving the inner protective panel proved much more difficult from the outside. Bannon took a knife from his belt and pried at the stone until he managed to get purchase and levered it back on its traces far enough for me to push it the rest of the way. Another firm kick shattered an image of thirteen figures—the thirteen sorcerers of Akolet—and we crawled into the throne room, atop the colonnade.

"Hurry," Bannon urged me, and I scrambled to an alcove formed by the edge of the serpent frieze. If any of the guards still patrolled below, the sudden crash and wail of the storm would bring them running. Bannon darted into the space beside me.

While we waited for sounds of voices, I rested my head on Bannon's shoulder. In the shadows, his hand found my arm and gave me a reassuring squeeze.

"Almost there," he promised. "Whatever you think you saw out there, put it out of your mind. We're almost at the end."

I took a long, deep breath, basking in his warm, welcome scent and the comfort of his nearness.

Long moments passed. The sounds of the storm made it difficult to hear anything else, but at last Bannon crept from the shelter of the alcove to search the dark room below.

"I think it's clear."

I followed him out. We climbed the last few feet to a circular column and slid down to the floor.

Again, we crouched, silently waiting for any sign of Mara's soldiers. The throne room appeared abandoned.

"She's probably figured out you're free," Bannon murmured.

I nodded. "This way to the shrine."

The entrance to Alaric's ceremonial chambers lay directly behind the throne: a set of double doors flanked by more sculpted snakes. Bannon's people had closed it off after ensuring none of Alaric's loyalists hid within, and no one had entered it since. I didn't have to ask why. The chamber practically hummed with an otherworldly—and evil—magical glow, a presence one felt more than heard, a feeling like strange, cold mists brushing along the skin.

We pulled open the heavy doors and stepped into darkness.

"Leave it open just a moment," I said, and as Bannon kept watch I crossed to the center of the room, where a shallow pit was sunk into the floor. The remains of the last ritual fire lay at the bottom. I seized a pair of wooden logs from the beside the pit and heaved them in, then found the box of long, thin matches stored within the altar.

Once we had the light of the fire to see by, Bannon pulled the chamber doors shut. Silence filled the room.

"*Oh,*" I groaned, looking over the shrine with a leaden feeling in my heart. Old, ruinous emotions overtook me.

The horrors I witnessed here. The pleasures. They clashed like waves of water and whorls of fire. I never felt more... more lost... more afraid...

A sob hitched in my throat. I sank to my knees and covered my face, and Bannon rushed to my side.

"Is it too much?" he whispered. "Can you face it?"

"What if I can't?" I asked. "Will you let me leave?"

"I don't want to." Bannon rested a hand on my shoulder. "I believe you are strong enough, Sadira. I trust in your spirit. But you know what to say, if you need to stop."

What then, though? I let my hands slide into my lap. *The curse goes on? Mara kills us both? Or will my barbarian try to escape with me into the storm?*

"I am poison, through and through." I stared at the room before me, not Bannon, as I spoke. "I'll never relinquish my *deviant* desires. My love of pain, and pleasure."

My hand found his. "And... even more so... the passion you have brought to it. The affection—and trust—that was never there before. I hated Alaric, and I hated the person he made me in this room. I hated the slave who crawled for him even when he left her

301

bleeding and broken. The whore who let him trade her to others. Alaric overpowered me when I had no power to resist. He used me. He never *cared* for me."

Tears pricked at my eyes. I bowed my head.

"*She* is who I see in this room. Not a slave of pleasure. A *true* slave. A victim... and a *willing* victim. I *hate* it."

"And we are here to free you from it," Bannon promised. "Come on. Let's find Khan's secrets and how to end this black magic for good."

He rose, but I stopped him, holding on to his hand.

"I mean it when I say I am poison," I said. "Whatever comes of this night, my barbarian, I will still—always—be who I am. A hungry, twisted beast."

"You're no beast." He clasped his other hand around mine, holding it tight. "You are a fearsome creature, wild and strong. And such wild beauty begs to be tempered, and purified, and forged anew through fire. You told me once you would not deign to relinquish yourself to just any man. Only one who could master you."

He bent forward and kissed me, guiding my hand to the tattoo on his chest.

"I, too, am named for a beast. They call us so because we will not be tamed. Except by one worthy of our power."

What power? I wanted to ask him, for in almost thirty years Alaric's most rigorous tests had never revealed any in me. At the same time, though, Bannon had managed to still my riotous emotions, and calm my heart. I concentrated on the slow, strong beat of his under my fingers.

"All right," I said at last. "Thank you, Sir."

He caressed my cheek. "Ready now?"

"Yes. I think I am."

We scanned the room together. I pointed to a shelf of books set upon one wall.

"You should begin there, I think. I'll look over the ritual implements and see if I can guess what sort of spell he cast."

Bannon dipped his head in a nod and moved to peruse the shelf. I approached the altar, setting my hands flat on its surface, and inspected the last things Alaric had arranged there.

The Order's holy text, the book of Akolet's Reign, lay open before me. A creeping surprise came over me as my fingers brushed over manic scrawls across the pages—nearly illegible writing, stains, and spots of ink, written *over* the sacred teachings.

"He defaced it?" I muttered, mostly to myself. Flipping the pages, I found more of Alaric's writing, mostly unreadable, sometimes broken by a few clear sentences here and there that only seemed madder than the rest.

"Wait!" I flipped back a page, comparing one strange, looping scribble to another. "This looks familiar."

Dae Caedon. Dae Catori.

"Dae Catori..." I touched my fingers to my lips. "Dae Catori. I said that, didn't I? But I don't know this language, I don't know what it means."

I turned ahead several more pages and found a messy black tangle of lines. A picture of some sort. A flower? A whirlwind?

Abandoning the book, I searched the artifacts Alaric had laid out on the tabernacle. Most were the same tokens used in most rituals: sticks of incense and sachets of dried herbs, scattered teeth and fingerbones, the skull of a cobra set in the very center. Lying before the cobra skull, though, was some sort of metal charm. The original shape was impossible to determine, as it had been warped and bent, parts of it flattened as though by a hammer. The shattered white pieces of some kind of gem glittered up at me—once, the stone had been the centerpiece.

What was it? Why did he destroy it?

Without even realizing it, I'd brought my hand up to fiddle with the ring of my collar again. As I studied the broken talisman, my fingers traveled along the embossed leather to the back of my neck, and I touched the bronze buckle stamped with Alaric's own sigil.

Without warning, another hand seized the collar and yanked me away from the altar. I stumbled backward as Bannon swung me around and pushed me into one of the pillars flanking the shrine. His arm came up, pressing into my throat, and I choked.

"Bar... barbarian..." I wriggled under Bannon's stony grip. "What are you doing?"

"It occurs to me," he snarled. "I've been exceptionally forgiving of your past transgressions. I thought I could see past the whore you were. Standing here, though, in this place... I can *feel* what they did to you. Black magic and blasphemy... I was wrong. There's no escaping your sins."

I tried to speak but couldn't breathe. I pried at his bicep, struggling for some give, and my nails dug into his arm.

"Mara is right. They are all right. You belong to *him* and will never wash clean that stain."

"*Atala!*" I managed to gasp. "Bannon—Sir—*Atala!*"

"You want me to stop?"

He released me and I braced myself on the pillar before I could fall to the floor. Then he grabbed me by the arm and threw me down.

"*Beg.*"

No... his voice...

"*Atala...*" I squeaked. The room washed out in shades of cloudy gray, as dizziness made me swoon.

"No, Sadira."

That voice!

"No. This time I don't think I'm going to stop."

I blinked and gulped in another desperate breath. Bannon came down on me, straddling my chest, looping a finger through the ring in my collar and forcing me to look straight into his face.

An icy grasp closed on my heart at the sight of blood running in tracks from his wild, red-rimmed eyes.

CHAPTER TWENTY-EIGHT

THE REEK OF Alaric's familiar incense rolled over me as Bannon held me pinned to the floor, boring into me with his maddened, crimson glare. With it came the stench of decay, the cold, rotten smell of the grave.

In a matter of seconds—less than the time it had taken him to drag me away from the altar and throw me to the floor—the roots of Bannon's rich, brick-red hair had gone a pale, silvery-white, and his hands, which I had so adored and admired, seemed to have thinned and turned dry, delicate. Yet when I struggled under his grip, he held me with an unyielding strength.

"At *last*," came Alaric's hollow, sinister voice out of Bannon's mouth. "I can't tell you, *kitten,* how infuriating it's been to have to crawl my way back to power. I didn't count on you surrendering yourself so readily to my murderer. A poor oversight on my part... I should have known you wouldn't have the willpower to resist."

"What have you done?" I seized Bannon's forearm in both hands, trying to wrench his fingers off my collar. "*How* are you still haunting me?"

"If you'd just kept your legs together, my power over this place would have remained even greater. Instead you betrayed me the first chance you had. It's made my rebirth so much more difficult. And thanks to you, so many more people are dead as a result."

I gave up on tearing free from his grasp, and instead lifted one leg and drove my heel down on the stone, pushing us into a roll and carrying it through until I straddled him.

"Let me go—"

Laughter—*Alaric's* laughter—poured out from Bannon's mouth, and his hands moved from my collar to close in around my entire neck.

"What do you think you're going to do, slave? You have no power! I've always been stronger than you. I made *sure* of it."

"You ruled over me through fear." I fought for purchase to bring up my knee. Beneath me, Bannon's face contorted into a ghastly grin. It seemed too big and too wide, and his skin had slowly begun to blanch and grow pale.

"I *took* your power," he sneered. "As a Master does."

In a surge of strength, I got my knee up and thrust it forward, deflecting his right arm and breaking his grip. As he rebounded, I lunged to my feet and sprang back, out of his reach.

"Try and take it now," I snarled.

"Has my little she-cat grown claws?" The man who seemed part Bannon, part Alaric rose in a smooth, otherworldly motion, coming up as though pulled on puppet strings. He spread his hands to either side. "Come now, Sadira. You've carried me with you all your life. *You* kept me here when this brute struck my head from my body. *You* fed me with your own spirit until I found a vessel suitable to take as my own."

Pausing, he looked down over Bannon's muscular form. "And I must say, I quite like this one."

"*You* possessed the men." I backed away from him, mentally scanning my surroundings for a weapon or a vantage point to launch a strike. "Not some malicious spirit conjured by your sorcerers... *you*. A craven, sadistic ghost."

"All for you." He waved a finger at me. "Of course, it took time to gather enough strength again to take over a worthy host. At first the only vessels I could dominate were small, petty things. A child. A cripple. Skittish horses."

He took a step toward me, raising his arms as if he meant to reach out and catch me when I ran. "The guard in the prison would have been acceptable. If you hadn't killed him."

My foot struck the edge of the altar. Bannon—Alaric—gave a husky chortle.

"Nowhere left to go, pet..."

He sprung at me. I fell back onto my elbows on the altar, lifting both feet and planting them square on Bannon's broad chest, pushing him and the possessing spirit of Alaric into a backward tumble. With a loud grunt, he fell on the edge of the firepit and his right hand came down in a pile of glowing ash.

The bellow of agony was purely Bannon's, with no hint of Alaric's voice. On impulse I started toward him, reaching out, but caught myself before I came within his reach. Tears stung my eyes as my barbarian pitched to one side to smother the burns under his own body, but I dared not get any closer.

Instead, I ducked to the side and ran for the door, putting the firepit between us. Without warning, though, moving with a speed no natural human could have managed, Bannon rose and blocked me, snatching my wrists as I collided with his chest.

He's cold as stone... cold as a corpse! Oh, Sir...

"*That* will mean discipline, Sadira," Alaric snarled through Bannon's scowl. Even his burned hand felt like ice on my skin, cold enough to bite into me and sear me. "And you won't like what I have in mind. When we're done, you won't be able to walk for a week."

"How do you propose to reclaim me, or any of your power?" I shouted. "You're surrounded by Bannon's people and the people you oppressed. Do you think they'll just let you walk out of here with the body of their leader?"

"Who's to know?"

I pushed him and he pushed back, refusing to budge. "I have all this savage's thoughts and memories at my disposal. Once I've handled you, I'll take his life as my own. They'll question a few things, of course." He ran a hand through Bannon's changing hair, as if he understood exactly how he'd begun to alter Bannon's appearance. "The lieutenant will pose a problem, but I'll deal with her as he should have— *execution.* Execution for her and anyone else who defies *their captain's* will!"

I hooked a foot behind his ankle to try and trip him, but Alaric evaded the trick and used my momentum to twist me off balance. He flipped me onto the floor again, this time on my stomach, and pinned me with a knee on my back.

"And even if they don't obey, I still have you. You, and all the power you give me."

"You said yourself I have no power," I choked out. Every move he'd made seemed to be aimed at stealing my breath; he wanted to strangle me into unconsciousness.

"Nothing is yours, remember?" he sneered. "You belong to me. Your body, your loyalty, and any scrap of magic you manage to conjure for me. You and the savage worked it out. With everything I did to you, I crafted you into my talisman. My *phylactery,* tying me to this world. We are connected in ways you can never imagine, and never escape. You are only an extension of me, now. As long as *you* live, you will carry me wherever you go."

"No," I growled through gritted teeth. Slipping my hands under my body I tried to push up from the floor, straining under his weight to draw in a fresh breath of air. Alaric leaned forward, putting more pressure on me.

There must be something here... something I can use...

I groped blindly across the floor. At last my fingers found rough burlap, and I thought immediately of the bag of sparkling sand the sorcerers threw in the fire for invocation. As the edges of my vision began to cloud, I managed to pull the bag until it toppled over, and I closed my fist on a handful of fine grains.

I flung the sand in a clumsy backward motion, hoping to hit him straight in the face. He gagged and fell into a violent coughing fit—I'd probably missed his eyes but from the sound of it I'd managed to get a good deal in his mouth.

I rolled away the instant his weight came off my back. Snatching up the bag of sand, I threw it into the fire, and a burst of red sparks exploded into the air. Alaric choked and doubled over, and as a thick, dark fog filled the room I scurried across it to the opposite corner.

I must find something to break whatever bond he forged between us. Seizing the books Bannon had been searching moments before, I frantically flipped through the pages, searching for Alaric's notes. *Any kind of journal about it. About me. There's got to be something!*

"You're wrong," I taunted Alaric as I scanned an entry full of symbols and patterns that looked like my tattoos. If I could keep him talking, make him search for me through the clouds of smoke, I might buy time enough to find the secrets I needed.

"Bannon claimed me, Alaric. He strode right into your master chambers and fucked your woman on your bed. The laws of your own people therefore accord him all your possessions and your authority. Whatever was yours belongs to him now. *I* belong to him."

"It doesn't matter if a hundred foreign warlords have their way with you."

He sounded close. I scooped up the books and backed away, staying low to the ground, searching for a hiding place.

"My mark is different. My mark is indelible. You can run all the way across the world from me, and we will be bound together still. Surrender, Sadira. You lost before this began. You've been lost since the beginning."

His mark.

My fingers flew to my collar. *Of course.*

I'd worn his collar all my life. I'd carried *him* with me every hour of every day, even when I trained, even when I slept. He'd cursed the *collar,* not me! But no slave would remove her collar without permission.

At least, not me. When the others had been freed, they'd cast off the symbols of their imprisonment first thing. Only I kept mine. Because *Master's pet wore a collar.*

My master had changed—I'd given Bannon my literal leash—but the *collar* was still the one Alaric had put on me.

I'd hesitated too long in one place. Alaric's footstep struck stone only inches away and I sprung to the side, but he'd found me. Getting down on all fours, he crawled toward me, one hand shooting forward and closing around my ankle.

I didn't bother to try and strike him. I grabbed the leather of my slave collar with both hands and tugged, grinding my teeth and digging deep for the strength to snap it. Alaric's eyes—yes, Alaric's eyes, now, his virulent green serpent's eyes, still ringed with crimson and streaks of blood—went wide, and in that instant, I had my answer.

His harsh laugh made me wince. "Look at you! Such a smart girl. It won't do you any good, though, my darling. I've taken your precious barbarian, after all. What do you think will happen to him if you destroy my phylactery? None of the other hosts I abandoned have fared very well, have they?"

"I think Bannon would prefer to be free of you," I snapped. "Just like I prefer!"

"He might prefer it, but he won't survive it."

Alaric dragged me to him, climbing over my body and pressing his arm down on my throat once more.

"You can't remove that collar. I made sure of it when I locked it with no key. Even if you could, you *kill* Bannon Sha'kurukh. When my spirit leaves this body, you'll find nothing left but a cold corpse. He is mine now, just like you, and without me, he'll be nothing but bones."

His other hand came up in a horrible, affectionate gesture, stroking my hair.

"Poor Sadira. You really have become so confused without me to guide you. You are nothing without me. You've always been nothing without me. It's only your good fortune you never developed any magical talent. If you had, I'd have had to kill you as Akolet commanded me. I *saved* you from him, and his master, and I made you useful despite your unremarkable, defective soul."

I spat in his face, making him snarl. As he lifted his hand to wipe it away, I grabbed for Bannon's belt, and the blade he kept sheathed there. Before Alaric could intercept me, I snatched the knife free and brought it up to my own throat, sliding it between the collar and my flesh.

"*Stop!*" Alaric grabbed my chin, forcing me to look him in the eye. "If you destroy it, your barbarian dies!"

"You've stolen his mind and mean to steal his life," I shot. "If all that is left of him is you, then Bannon is already dead. And *I* will never kneel to you again!"

With a sure, scything stroke, I sliced through the embossed black leather. The point of the knife cut a fine, stinging line along the bottom of my jaw and blood ran down my neck.

The collar slid free.

Alaric howled, arching backward in Bannon's body, hands flying to his head. The sound of the storm echoed up from within him, a baleful and inhuman scream, and with it the voices of the dead. He contorted in ugly distress, thrashing back and forth until there seemed to be more than one of him, ghostly figures straining to be free of their flesh prison.

A flash of light, an ugly, poisonous green, washed over the form of my barbarian, and in a final, dying wail, it shot upward into the darkness and disappeared. Bannon collapsed on top of me, cold to the touch.

"Bannon!"

I rolled over, laying him out on the floor. "Bannon, please! Let him have lied, let Alaric have lied like the snake he is, *please* wake up!"

A scrape of stone interrupted me. Light poured into the chamber from the throne room. I raised my arm to shield my eyes, and then Rayyan dropped to his knees beside me and took me by the shoulders.

"Are you all right? Sadira, speak to me!"

"We heard the sound." Mara's voice, somewhere above me. "Like a banshee! As though someone set a demon loose in the castle!"

The lieutenant towered in the entryway, faintly visible through the last of the thinning smoke, Ailsa beside her.

Before I could explain, Mara caught sight of Bannon's lifeless form. She leveled her halberd at me, poised to strike. "She's slain him!"

"He is not dead!" I protested, though I didn't know and only prayed it was so. Mara lunged anyway, and I threw Rayyan out of the way, putting my hands up in defense.

The lieutenant stumbled, dropping her weapon, as a violent quake rumbled through the earth beneath our feet, shaking the castle all around us.

CHAPTER TWENTY-NINE

I GRABBED BANNON'S arm and struggled to pull him up. "Somebody help me with him!"

Rayyan came to me, sliding an arm under Bannon's other side and lifting. A sharp crack sounded behind us, and I shot a glance over my shoulder—a jagged black split had appeared in one of the pillars beside the altar, and dust and stone chips rained down.

"Out!" I commanded the others. Despite the roaring tremors, Rayyan and I managed to hoist Bannon between us, and moved as quickly as we could for the door.

Mara reached for her halberd, only to snatch her hand back with a cry when a fragment of stone came crashing down from overhead, landing square on the weapon and snapping it at the shaft. Ailsa hurried to the lieutenant and helped her up, rushing her from the sacred shrine just as the altar at the front of the room toppled over, and the pillars flanking it cracked apart, falling to the floor.

The four of us dashed into the throne room, making it halfway across before an enormous crash erupted from the direction we'd come. I spun around.

The frieze above the throne—the serpent Akolet, with the face of Alaric and his long-gone ancestor, had shattered across the middle and come thundering down upon the dais, destroying the throne and the entrance to the shrine beyond.

While I stared in disbelief, the trembling earth grew still.

The throne room hung in stunned silence. Several of the pillars of the colonnade now bore serious cracks, some broken entirely, with rough stone chunks split away from their sides. All the glass in the high windows had shattered to pieces, and sharp shards of it littered the floor. A section of the western wing had caved in, and light streamed in from the bright, midday sun.

Sun. The storm has stopped. It's over.

Relief flooded my chest as, beside me, Bannon stirred.

"Da!"

Ailsa swept in, wrapping her arms around her father in what first seemed like a desperate embrace. All business, though, she guided me and Rayyan in laying him out upon the floor, then began questioning him.

"Can you see me clearly? Can you speak to me, Da?"

"Yes, Ailsa, I can," Bannon replied in a weak, weary tone. "I'm all right, I think... except for this blasted hand..."

Ailsa switched her attention to the deep burns across his palm. The salve appeared from somewhere among the pockets on her belt, and she set to applying it.

"Sadira?" Bannon croaked. "Where is Sadira?"

"Here, Sir." I scooted closer to him on my knees and took his other hand in mine, pressing it to my cheek. "Do you know what's happened?"

"I do." He coughed, then swallowed as though he'd had a lump in his throat. "The black magician... *possessed* me. I think it happened when we went out into the storm... something didn't feel right, and then you... you saw him..."

"I think perhaps he waited *in* the storm," I told him. "Maybe he was the storm. A final outpouring of vengeance."

As Ailsa wrapped his injured hand in clean, white bandages, Bannon sat up. He pressed his good hand to his temple with a low groan.

"In the shrine, he spoke to me. He... started to wind his way into my thoughts. I didn't even realize it was happening until—"

"Until he had you," I finished for him. "It's all right now, Sir. He's gone."

Bannon blinked at me. His brow furrowed, and he shook his head.

"No, Sadira. He isn't."

Before I could respond, another rumbling, rolling earthquake shuddered to life. Mara turned her head, seemingly drawn by some sound, and moved to help Ailsa up. Bannon and I rose together, while Rayyan took a few careful steps toward the hall beyond.

"Shouting," he said. "From the yard."

Bannon took a shaky step forward. "Let's go then—"

A rain of stones came falling from above. We looked up just in time to leap aside from a boulder-sized section of the ceiling as it hit the ground, sending rubble and splinters of debris everywhere. Bannon grabbed me by the arm and pulled Ailsa to his side, hurrying out with us. Mara and Rayyan sprinted behind.

We ran through the entry hall and out the great iron doors, into the bright white light of day. Already guards were gathering, glancing back and forth for instruction, and Bannon let me and his daughter go, striding forward.

"You four," he ordered, gesturing at a group of his soldiers. "Evacuate everyone. Get as many as you can out here into the open. The rest of you, to the walls. We need eyes and weapons at the ready."

They did as they were told, and for once no one shot any nasty glances at me or questioned my presence.

"Mara, get yourself a weapon, and one for Sadira, too."

"Don't worry about me," I told him.

"Your fighting skills are exemplary, but I fear your former king has something much worse in store for us than a brawler can handle." Bannon waved Ailsa to a corner of the courtyard as he spoke, and she obeyed without a word, shouting to her assistant healers as she moved. "Can you handle a spear, Sadi?"

A fresh tremor shuddered through the yard, throwing scattered guards and castle refugees off their feet. I caught Bannon's arm to steady myself before shaking my head.

319

"You forget I'm trained with another weapon. Give me three minutes—I'll be back and ready to fight."

He threw a glance at the castle. "Be careful. I'm afraid the whole thing might come down any minute."

I ran for one of the side entrances, the doorway closest to the western stairwell. I ducked out of the way of oncoming refugees as they fled for the courtyard, then took the stairs three at a time to the top. Another quake came just as I burst through the doors of the master bedchambers, and I braced myself in the doorjamb until it stopped.

The chamber appeared undisturbed, besides the table displaying Alaric's favorite toys having toppled over, scattering crops and candles and leather restraints across the floor. I moved to the personal altar, flinging open the doors to a compartment below the tabernacle.

Here gleamed Alaric's magnificent swords. Curved blades like crescent moons—his khopeshes. I'd had a pair just like them, but the barbarians had stolen them from me when they'd taken me captive, and I never discovered what had become of them. Alaric's were superior blades, forged of shining steel and studded with jet up the hilts. Why he'd left them behind on that last day of the war, the day he'd come to battle bearing nothing, covered in asps, I'd never know. I'd discovered them, stored here as though no war had ever occurred, during my long days stuck inside waiting for Bannon to arrive.

I'd had weapons all along, and the guards never suspected. How ridiculous of them to think throwing books and plates was the worst I could do.

Outside, a fresh howl rose. Not the wail of the sandstorm this time, but something wild and weird and primal—the sound of the Ruined Sands and all its dead, screaming in outrage.

I crossed to the window. Outside the walls, the desert seemed to be moving. The dunes vibrated, seeming to move toward a central point as though drawn by gravity. The dead men and the debris of the city were carried along with them, and where they met, a spiral of motion had begun. A cyclone sweeping up the remains of destruction.

I tightened my grip on the khopeshes and headed back for the courtyard.

Bannon waited by the gate, now bearing his broad axe and great wooden shield. As I joined him, he shouted orders to the guards on the wall, who passed out bows and arrows along the line. The howl beyond the walls had grown louder, joined by the yips and yowls of desert dogs and the ugly caws of buzzards. It didn't surprise me, though, to see no wildlife at all when the gates were opened.

"He wants you and me," Bannon told me as I took my place beside him. "I could sense much from him when he invaded my mind, but I think this is the last resort he has, without his phylactery. Whatever comes out of that wind, expect it to be bad."

"I am ready, Sir."

Mara appeared beside us, with Rayyan and three others armed with spears. Bannon gave his lieutenant a nod of approval, then raised his axe.

"This time we kill the black magician for good."

As if in answer to his challenge, the scream of the cyclone became a low, monstrous roar. Something moved from within—an enormous form rose, a

321

shadow easily twenty feet tall, a writhing mass of limbs. The sands slowed and died away, and in their place loomed a golem of bone and sinew, stone and flesh. A seven-headed serpent, arched as though to strike, whipping a deadly scythe of a tail across the dunes behind it.

The seven heads each opened their skeletal jaws and let out a series of venomous, hissing screeches. Bannon, the soldiers, and I all flinched. A cold trickle of blood ran from the cup of my ear.

Bannon signaled the charge, and I followed, first of the soldiers into the fray.

Two of the serpent's heads dove for me at once. Three made a lunge for Bannon. I managed a rolling dodge and leapt back to my feet, khopeshes raised, and my gaze met my captain's across the field of melee.

We didn't need words to communicate what we'd both just seen: the seven heads did not attack as one.

We dashed in opposite directions, hoping to divide the monster's attention, while Mara and the others moved in for the kill. The golem fell for our ploy at first, but soon appeared to catch on: two of its heads remained high above the battle, watching, seeming to guide the others with careful observance. Still, it couldn't catch all of us at once.

Bannon ducked back from another strike, then pushed forward in a parry, cleaving his axe deep into the base of one of the necks. The creature screeched, and all seven heads turned toward Bannon as though on reflex. I seized the moment and raised one kopesh, sickle-like, over the joint of another neck on my side of the monster. Bringing it down like a cleaver, I hacked into the patchwork mess of bone and hide.

Mara collided with me from the side, shoving me out of the way as the massive tail came crashing down. I shot a startled expression at the lieutenant, but Mara had already resumed her attack without a word.

The monster wove and struck at the soldiers. Six of the seven heads had engaged now, and the hollow, wretched hisses escaping them seemed to reverberate all the way down my spine. I scowled, glaring up at the seventh head, to find it staring back at me.

It has eyes. The others are all empty skulls, but that one has eyes.

Not really eyes, but flickering, green-gold balls of flame. They burned in the sockets of the skull, full of an alien intelligence.

As we stared at one another, it caught me by surprise: one of its other heads struck me, sinking fangs deep into my thigh.

"A-ah!" I screamed as it pulled me off my feet. I swung one sword at its neck, slashing into a net of corpse-flesh, but it didn't let go, raising me high over the field.

A volley of arrows cut through the air under me, half a dozen bolts striking home in the serpent's throat. A seventh arrow flew high, burying itself halfway in the bony plate of the giant skull, right between the empty eye sockets. This time the creature gave a screech, jaws opening wide, and I dropped from its grip. Twisting as I fell, I thrust out my khopeshes and hooked the crescent ends into the side of a massive vertebra, arresting my descent and clinging to one of the beast's seven necks.

This is the one. The one with the eyes.

323

I scanned the field below me; I hung fifteen, maybe twenty yards over the others. Bannon, driving off one of the heads with powerful strokes of his axe, had seen me fall—between attacks he shot a glance in my direction, and moved toward me as the serpent continued to lunge at him.

A horrendous throbbing sound caught my attention. The khopeshes thrummed and vibrated in my hands, and a putrid rush of heat shot up at me from below. Frowning, I glanced down.

Where the creature's seven heads joined its body, a hard, smooth breastplate spread across its front. From my vantage, though, I caught flashes of light and movement behind the plate. Some sort of gruesome heart?

"Captain!" I called out.

Bannon took one furious strike at the head attacking him, and it recoiled. In the space between strikes, my barbarian looked up at me. I released my hold on one sword to point at the breastplate.

"Crack it open! I think the thing's heart is hidden underneath!"

Without waiting for his response, I grabbed my sword and worked my way downward, climbing over the bones and sinew using my curved blades to grapple. I had just enough time to see Bannon rid himself of the serpent head and make his way to the base of the breastplate before I dropped into the gap. I caught myself with the hooks of my khopeshes and wedged myself between the skeletal substructure and the plate.

The bone creaked as I pushed and pried. On the other side of the plate, a muffled grunt and cry of attack told me Bannon had joined the attack, working his axe around the edge of the bone.

The monster screamed, as though it had suddenly realized what we intended. Too late, though: I gave a cry of triumph as the breastplate cracked under the pressure, and a flat, thick segment of it gave way, exposing the chamber beneath.

Not a heart. An *eye*. Enormous, reddened, rolling in alarm. It oriented on me, full of deep, ugly hate, and the monster gave up a keening wail.

Over my shoulder, Bannon shouted in surprise, and a shuddering crash shook the monster. I glanced up to see one of the heads attacking its own body, fighting to get at me. A look behind me revealed a second head doing the same, and a third set of fangs closed over the remaining edge of the breastplate, prying it free.

It's willing to tear itself apart to protect this eye.

Alaric's eye. Virulent. Poisonous. Insane.

And at the same time, *not* Alaric's. It belonged to something bigger, something far more powerful. Something *feeding* on the last of Alaric's power, the desperate madness of this hideous golem, like a parasite.

I raised my khopesh, and with a ferocious cry, I plunged it into the glistening pupil. The eye burst in a spray of gore, and the golem swung into a violent paroxysm.

Bannon's strong arm swooped in around my waist and pulled me free of the inner carapace.

"Hold on tight," he warned me, and I obeyed, clinging to him.

Bannon sprung into the air. We hit the sand together, tucking into a roll, until momentum brought us to a stop several feet away.

The monster thrashed, sweeping the dunes into messy chaos with its tail. It began falling apart, pieces of dead flesh and chunks of bone dropping from it like shedding skin. The foul smell of death and decay burned off it in dark tendrils, making me want to retch, until piece by piece, it disintegrated into smoldering, blackened heaps of ash.

Bannon still held me tightly in his arms. As we watched the last of Alaric's power dissolve away, he pulled me close and planted a kiss on my brow.

"It's over, kitten. My good girl... you have put an end to Alaric Khan and his serpent god, at last."

Epilogue

THE SOUND OF approaching footsteps drew me out of my reverie in the golden noonday sun. I sat on the rim of the courtyard fountain, face upturned to the warm, clear sky, and waited for my barbarian to take a seat beside me. I didn't want him to speak. The moment he did, it would mean our time together had come to an end.

As though he, too, understood this, Bannon remained silent for several moments. I drew in a slow, deep breath of the sweet summer air, and leaned my head upon his shoulder. Bannon looped his arm around my waist and drew me closer to him, kissing the crown of my head.

"The regent has arrived," he finally said.

The younger brother of Bannon's King Rhode had never been found after his caravan met the foul black magic of Alaric's storm. Word had been sent, and when it reached Bannon's homeland perhaps the king would send another to take lordship of this desert stronghold. For now, a lesser noble—a second cousin, or maybe she was a niece—had come from the Sanraethi outpost at the river delta. She would hold Vashtaren until Rhode decided its worth and made his next move.

I doubted the king would bother to keep this devastated capital. The earthquakes had leveled the last of the city to the ground, and as I'd suspected, there were no people left. Dead or fled, the citizens of Vashtaren had disappeared, leaving only the castle refugees and the invaders who'd come to free us.

The castle itself lay mostly in ruin. The throne room had collapsed, taking with it the serpent's shrine and the galleries above, as well as a hive of rooms on the second story, where some of the former slaves had made their temporary residences. By good fortune, no one had been in those rooms when they fell.

The kitchens were partially intact, but the boilers had been destroyed. It didn't matter, though, because Alaric's grand bathing chambers had been cracked right down the center, and half of it now lay in the eastern bailey. I could admire the intricate sculpture of the fountain from where I sat, in fact. It lost some of its elegance, lying on its side in a heap of rubble.

The master bedchambers had been spared, as well as the pleasure chamber. Neither Bannon nor I felt any urge to remain there, though, in the aftermath of the quakes.

What bittersweet regret. I twined my fingers with Bannon's. *I wouldn't have wanted to sleep in that bed anymore... but I could have shown my Master so much more of my world before he must leave it.*

"Have you decided what you will do, now you are truly free?" Bannon asked.

"No." I scooped up a glistening white flower that had fallen into the fountain. "Perhaps I'll find residence in one of the cities to the south. Go far enough, and you'll find plenty of them where Alaric and his ancestors are only a vague, half-forgotten history. Places where maybe no one will recognize who I am, or what these tattoos mean."

He reached over and took the flower, spinning it slowly between his fingers as he admired the glossy round petals, slightly gold along the edges, and down near the heart of the bloom.

"Sadira. There is much you don't know. So much Khan kept from you... but could not keep from me when he invaded my mind."

Straightening, I peered at him. "I don't understand, Sir."

He tucked the flower behind my ear. "Khan told you he had access to my thoughts while he possessed me. I could also find his. The truth about your abduction... his obsession with finding magic in you. Making you bear him a child—"

I pivoted to meet him face to face. Too many thoughts came at once: I wanted to be angry, and yet a wild curiosity demanded to know more. A vague sense of disbelief warred with a fearful note of violation. I'd thought all Alaric's actions stemmed from his desire to dominate, just as I bore the lusts of a hungry submissive.

And Bannon *discovers these truths before me? What other secrets did he uncover?*

"You're saying these things were connected?"

Bannon nodded. "I've been piecing together the fragments in my mind. I think I have the truth, now."

329

I want to know. No, I don't want to know. Why does it feel like something far heavier and wider and deeper than I am prepared to accept?

I leaned closer to him, my heart picking up pace.

"He stole from you, Sadi," Bannon whispered, caressing my cheek. "More than you could guess. More than even he knew, I think."

"What do you mean?" I asked.

Bannon pulled me into his lap. He kissed me, then pressed his thumb lightly to my lip. "Are you ready to hear? All of it?"

"I won't know that until you tell me."

He gave a soft chuckle. Then, his eyes found mine, and he brushed back a strand of my hair.

"It started before Alaric Khan even ascended the throne. He served his father Alistair as a warlord, and Alistair sent him across the sea. To find you. Not to bring you back as a slave. Alaric was meant to murder you."

My hand flew to the place where my collar had been, but of course, there was no ring to touch or worry anymore.

"Alaric was never told why." Bannon took a firm hold of my searching fingers, arresting their nervous movement. "And while he and his raiders searched for you, the elder king was slain."

Despite the warmth of the day, I shivered.

"The younger Lord Khan returned successful— and brought you back with him, despite his orders— but he returned to a country divided by civil war. He did as I was made to do: killed those among his father's retainers who questioned him. Took his father's royal possessions. Claimed the women of his father's harem. He didn't go unchallenged—the

330

former king had plenty of illegitimate heirs, and plenty of noblemen and even the sorcerers who would have preferred one of the bastards on the throne instead of Alaric. Amid his struggle for power, he didn't bother to finish off the little girl he'd been meant to kill."

How old would I have been? Four? Five? A heavy, uncomfortable feeling weighed on my chest and head. I wanted to cry.

But why? I don't remember any of this. None of it matters now, does it?

It did, though. Because it was my story, and Alaric—my master no more—had kept it from me. Not only kept it. *Stolen* it.

"So instead, he made you a slave." Bannon slid a hand behind me to cradle my neck. "But he put his mark on you. No, not the ones you are thinking of. This one here."

He stroked his thumb across the back of my neck. "Hidden under your slave collar your whole life. From the very beginning, he intended for you to be his. I suppose you didn't even know it was there."

My hand followed his. My fingers brushed the spot he had, and a tiny, electric jolt shot down my spine.

From the very beginning.

"What is it?" I asked.

"What else?" Bannon brushed my hand away from the mark and pulled me into his sheltering embrace. "A snake, coiling itself in a knot. My people have a similar symbol—the lemniscate knot. It is meant to represent infinity."

I closed my eyes. "Because he meant to hold me forever."

331

"I don't know exactly where he traveled in order to find you," Bannon said. "But I know it was across the ocean, and it took him well over a year before his search paid out."

He tilted my face up to his. "Sadira... come back to my homeland with me. I don't know all the secrets of Alaric's plans for you, but I know there was a *reason* it had to be you. Your people are out there, and if there is anyone left who might know why the black magician and his Order wanted you, it is them. If you come, we will track them down together. We'll find out the truth."

I glanced aside at the ruined castle. Yes... soon, it would surely be abandoned.

Everything I ever knew is just like these piles of rubble. What would become of me if I stayed? Over time, I'd become only a relic of a violent, evil age.

Of course, leaving Vashtaren would not protect me. I'd carry my darkness—my beautiful, beastly love—wherever I went. Even if no strange perfume of bergamot followed me, even if no phantom vipers slithered at my feet, and nobody ever developed those horrible bloodshot eyes, I'd be a symbol of violence and depravity.

Except... in his bed.

Bannon tempered my flame. He could master the beast, and the beast liked it. There was more, though. More than the violence, more than the pain.

He is kind. I... I trust him.

"If I go with you," I said, "will you still care for me as hard as you fuck me?"

"As long as you wish it. And when you no longer wish it, you need only say the word, my kitten, and it will end."

332

Somehow, despite the fresh anxiety tugging at me, urging me to flee these new riddles and mysteries Alaric had left behind, I managed a smile.

"And if I don't want it to end?"

Bannon kissed me, a long, warm, wonderful kiss.

"Then we go as far as we dare," he whispered. "Together."

Walk away, a fearful, wounded voice told me. *Whatever once was, you are safe from it now. Stay where you know your footing. Say 'atala' and end it before you are taken too far.*

I caressed Bannon's cheek, and my hand slid down to the place over his heart, where the ursine tattoo covered old battle scars.

"You think I have some destiny, some great truth, across the sea?" I asked.

"I think, if you trust me, we can find out."

The End
***

Seek out the truth.
Travel across the sea in Book Two:
Beauty's Secret

ABOUT THE AUTHOR

When she isn't visiting the worlds of immortals, demons, dragons and goblins, Brantwijn fills her time with artistic endeavors: sketching, painting, and working on graphic design. She can't handle coffee unless there's enough cream and sugar to make it a milkshake, but try and sweeten her tea and she will never forgive you. She moonlights as a futon for six lazy cats, loves tabletop roleplaying games, and can spend hours penciling naughty, sexy illustrations in her secret notebooks.

Brantwijn is the author of *The Chronicles of the Four Courts, Shifter's Dawn,* and *The Dark Roads* series, as well as many short stories and novellas. Follow her on

Facebook, Twitter, or visit her website at www.brantwijn.com.

Join Brantwijn's newsletter for a free book! Get updates and special offers from Brantwijn and other indie authors.

https://www.brantwijn.com/newsletter.

THANK YOU FOR READING

Please help indie authors and their books be seen!
Take a moment to leave your honest review at your
regular book purchase site,
and share with friends.

The author thanks you kindly.

#WriteOn
#IndieBooksBeSeen

Made in the USA
Middletown, DE
22 May 2021